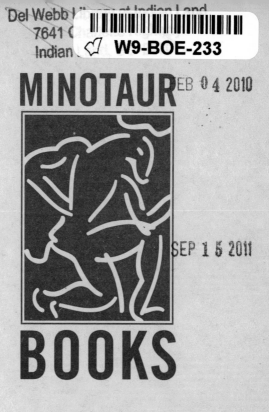

MINOTAUR

BOOKS

GET A CLUE!

Be the first to hear the latest mystery book news...

With the Minotaur monthly newsletter, you'll learn about the hottest new Minotaur books, receive advance excerpts from newly published works, read exclusive original material from featured mystery writers, and be able to enter to win free books!

Sign up on the Minotaur Web site at:
www.minotaurbooks.com

Praise for
PUSHING UP DAISIES

"If you like gardens and like reading mysteries, this is the book for you—a clever mystery full of garden lore, fast-paced and engaging, with a heroine who isn't afraid to get down in the dirt."
—*Seattle Post-Intelligencer*

"A charming debut." —*Library Journal*

"Quirky, original, and captivating . . . marks the debut of a sure-to-please series."
—Carolyn Hart, Agatha, Anthony, and Macavity Award-winning author of the Death on Demand series

"A mix of sophisticated comedy, romance, and murder."
—*Connecticut Post*

"[A] funny and entertaining first installment. May there be many more." —*Kingston Observer*

"Think Diane Mott Davidson's caterer extraordinaire Goldy Schulz or Earlene Fowler's quilting aficionado Benni Harper. Harris plots out a good story."
—*Omaha World-Herald*

"An appealing main character . . . Recommend[ed] to fans of Veronica Heley's series starring avid gardener Ellie Quicke." —*Booklist*

"Paula Holliday is a sleuth to watch. With an intriguing mix of gardening savvy, sassy wit, and smart plotting, Rosemary Harris has crafted a clever mystery."
—Susan Wittig Albert, author of the China Bayles herbal mysteries

"Paula Holliday knows her andromedas and her viburnum. Her creator, Rosemary Harris, knows her pacing and suspense. Fast-paced and full of garden lore, *Pushing Up Daisies* is a great read. If rosemary is for remembrance, Rosemary Harris is an author to remember."
—Barbara D'Amato,
author of *Death of a Thousand Cuts*

"A very enjoyable read and great tips for gardeners as well."
—M. C. Beaton,
author of the Agatha Raisin series

"Get ready to meet a smart, engaging heroine who isn't afraid to get her hands dirty—literally."
—Brian Freeman, author of *Stalked*

"I just love it—intriguing mystery, great characters, and very funny."
—Alison Gaylin, author of *Trashed*

PUSHING UP DAISIES

A DIRTY BUSINESS MYSTERY

ROSEMARY HARRIS

St. Martin's Paperbacks

This is a work of fiction. All of the characters, organizations and events portrayed in this novel are either products of the author's imagination or are used fictitiously.

PUSHING UP DAISIES

Copyright © 2008 by Rosemary Harris.
Excerpt from *The Big Dirt Nap* copyright © 2009 by Rosemary Harris.

For information address St. Martin's Press, 175 Fifth Avenue, New York, NY 10010.

Library of Congress Catalog Card Number: 2007040329

ISBN: 0-312-94372-5
EAN: 978-0-312-94372-1

Printed in the United States of America

St. Martin's Press hardcover edition / February 2008
St. Martin's Paperbacks edition / February 2009

St. Martin's Paperbacks are published by St. Martin's Press, 175 Fifth Avenue, New York, NY 10010.

10 9 8 7 6 5 4 3 2 1

For Paula V. Simari

ACKNOWLEDGMENTS

Special thanks to Kathy Schneider, Betty Prashker, and Michele Tempesta for getting me off to a good start. To Deborah Schneider for making it happen. To Marcia Markland, Diana Szu, Martha Schwartz, Maggie Goodman, Jonathan Bennett, and the talented people at St. Martin's for making it better. To Andy Martin for making it fun. And to Bruce Harris for keeping me relatively sane during the process.

In the garden,
beauty is a by-product.
The real business is sex and death.

—Samuel Llewellyn

CHAPTER 1

My first guess was heirloom silver, or maybe the family jewels, buried and forgotten years ago by some light-fingered servant or paranoid ancestor. I was wrong.

The metal crate was heavy, about two feet wide and three feet long with a small handle at one end. Crouching down at the edge of the flower bed, I dragged it out of the hole and used my trowel to pry it open. I was hoping for a reward or at the very least an interesting story to tell. That time I was right.

Inside was another, smaller container, ornately carved and cushioned by paper, padding, and disintegrating excelsior. I opened the smaller box and took out a tattered bundle wrapped in many layers of thin material. Given the weight of the box, the bundle was lighter than I expected—as if the fabric surrounded nothing more than a handful of feathers. That's when the butterflies first entered my stomach.

Picking at the rotting fabric with gloved fingers, I exposed a slim chain with a tiny medal. Above it, leathery and doll-like, was a shrunken head.

I fell back on my butt, flinging the bundle into the air, then I watched it land and roll over until it stopped facedown in the decomposing leaves behind a stone wall. I looked around, half hoping there was a witness but just as happy there was no one to see me act like such a chicken.

I got up and tiptoed over to where the bundle rested. I couldn't bring myself to touch it but wanted to get the tiny face out of the dirt, so I nudged it with my toe. It didn't move. I did it a second time, but pushed too hard and the bundle rolled again, this time picking up speed on the sloping lawn that would take it into Long Island Sound if I didn't act fast. I wasn't much of a football fan but instinctively knew what I had to do. I tackled it. I scooped up the body and ran up the hill, back to the garden, as if I were heading for the end zone. When I got there, I shook off my hoodie, made a circle on the ground with it, and nestled the tiny body inside, so it wouldn't roll over again. Then, on unsteady feet, I walked a few steps and puked, over by the Album Elegans rhododendrons.

But I should start at the beginning. Six hours earlier, I'd been minding my own business, lingering over burned cinnamon toast at the Paradise Diner. The coffee was better at Dunkin' Donuts, and the food was better almost anywhere, but the Paradise was my third place—that place you go to that isn't work or home.

Chalky turquoise and hot pink, with Christmas lights on twelve months a year, the Paradise is a little bit of the Caribbean inexplicably transplanted to southeastern Connecticut, courtesy of the proprietor, Wanda "Babe" Chinnery.

Detractors claim Babe stays in business by dealing pot on the side, and there *is* a suspicious patch of ground in the back surrounded by a hodgepodge of lattice, but I don't believe it's anything more sinister than your garden-variety suburban debris, and probably a lot less toxic.

Though only the boldest of the soccer moms ventured in, the Paradise is a magnet for every male in town between the ages of twelve and eighty. That's also due to Babe. Babe is every young boy's fantasy bad girl and every older guy's shoulda-woulda-coulda. They come in to see what color her hair is this week or what sexy, tattoo-revealing getup she'll be wearing. And if none of them can really have her, at least they can dream, for the price of bad coffee and artery-clogging donuts.

Twenty years ago, Babe and the late Pete Chinnery bought the Paradise. She'd been a backup singer and he was a roadie for a fair-to-middling metal band that'd had one big hit and toured on it for years. They socked away the money they'd made hawking rock 'n' roll memorabilia, and when they decided to settle down, they moved back to Babe's hometown and bought the Paradise. Less than a year later, Pete and another member of the Son Also Rises Christian Bikers Club were killed in a freak accident on Route 7 when some crazy antiquer hit the brakes for a tag sale and sent the two men flying. To hear Babe tell it, there was more leather at Pete's funeral than at an S & M convention.

Now the Paradise staff was just Babe, a revolving part-time waitress—this one named Chloe—and the cook, affectionately referred to as Pete number two. Babe claims she hired him only because it would be easy to remember his name, and from some of the food I'd sampled there, she might have been telling the truth. Despite our glaring differences, Babe and I had hit it off immediately.

"Top you off, Paula?" she asked.

I threw caution to the winds and held out my cup for more.

"You seen the *Bulletin* this morning?"

"I didn't know they bothered to publish that thing once March Madness was over."

"*The New York Times* isn't the only newspaper in the country, wiseass."

Springfield, Connecticut, is a bedroom community, one of New York City's many moons, more famous for the planet it orbits than for anything in the town itself. Springfield has a healthy mix of low, middle, and upper-middle classes, and we're within spitting distance of the blue bloods in Greenwich and Bedford.

The Springfield Bulletin is our local paper, and unless it was college basketball season, when the UConn Huskies ruled, it took all of five minutes to read. Example? Now that the Huskies hadn't made it to the Sweet Sixteen, a recent feature was **THE WONDERFUL WORLD OF WALNUTS.** I was saving it for some really lonely night by the fire.

Babe slid the paper across the counter to me. The entire front page covered the death of someone named Dorothy Peacock, last member of one of the oldest, most prestigious families in Springfield. We had a Peacock Lane, a Peacock Road, a Peacock band shell, and undoubtedly lots more a relative newcomer like me hadn't heard about.

"I didn't know there *were* any actual Peacocks."

"I guess there aren't. Anymore. Not exactly the crowd I ran with," Babe said, "but I always thought their house was cool"—pointing to the paper. "Weird, but cool. They even gave tours of Halcyon's garden."

"Their house had a name?"

"Sure, doesn't yours?" she said, grinning.

"Yeah. Right now it's Chez Citibank." I pushed my cup and plate to the side and spread out the skimpy paper. "Ever meet her?"

"Dorothy? No. A pal of mine did. I saw her a few times though, from a distance. Looked like quite a character."

"Oh, yeah, not like us," I said, returning to the article.

In one deft move, she cleared the plates and wiped down the silver-and-gold Formica counter, then consolidated the ketchup bottles in that precarious upside-down way they must teach in diner school. She used a balled-up napkin to erase a few words from the blackboard behind the counter, changing the breakfast specials into the lunch specials.

"Have you ever considered adding some heart-healthy options to that menu?" I asked gently. "It might help business."

"You gotta be kidding. I should take business advice from you? Just don't eat the fries," she snorted, dismissing my health concerns and substituting the word *French* for *home*.

I realized she was right and went back to the paper. The *Bulletin* carried a basic bio of Dorothy and her late sister, Renata. There was no mention of survivors. Archival photos of Halcyon and the garden were provided by the Springfield Historical Society. I'm something of a regular there, too, as well as at the diner. Not that I'm such a history buff, but designing on a dime is easier when you frequent the local thrift shops. And the Historical Society had a great one.

"I bet those old girls at SHS could even help you get the job," Babe said. "The Doublemint twins?"

"Who says I need another client? I'd have to leave all this," I said, barely looking up from the paper. But her arrow had hit the mark; my dance card was hardly full, as my almost daily presence here confirmed. Did I mention I'm a gardener? Zone 6. I've got my own small landscaping business, emphasis on small. I'm also a master gardener and periodically volunteer with local landscaping programs as part of the classes—and to drum up new business.

"Since we're in advice-giving mode, why don't you volunteer at Halcyon—that'd be a real community service. That place has been an eyesore for years. And it'll move you into the high-rent district."

Not a place I'd been visiting recently. The year before, a global media conglomerate swallowed up the boutique production company I worked for. My once-promising career as a documentary filmmaker had degenerated into endless speculations about Who Killed Diana. Or worse. Who killed some poor bastard no one had ever heard of.

That had been the catalyst for this new chapter in my life. I took the moral high ground—and my severance package—loaded up the car, and made an offer on the bungalow I'd been taking as a summer rental. Then I hung out my shingle—PH FACTOR, GARDEN SOLUTIONS. PH is me, Paula Holliday. PH is also the measure of how sweet or how sour your soil is. The name was supposed to be clever, but so far, few people got it. And few people called.

Every time the wolf seemed to be at the door, Babe chatted me up to one of her customers, so I had a handful of clients, which kept the bank happy; but working on the Peacock garden could definitely jump-start things for me.

"I'm not a licensed landscape architect. This may be out of my league."

"And you think all the women around here who call themselves *decorators* have some kind of sheepskin? Can't hurt to ask. Besides," she said, "I need to clean that spot where you've been sitting for the last two hours."

"I have a mother, you know."

"She just called. She thinks you should go, too."

I guess I *had* been hanging out at the Paradise a lot. Newly single, I dragged my feet going back to my empty house. It was one thing to be a regular, quite another to be a fixture. Babe waved away my halfhearted attempt to pay.

"Forget it. We're still working off the plantings you did out in the parking lot. Get outta here. And good luck," she called after me, betting I'd take her advice.

Outside, I inspected the beds I'd put in last fall. Not bad, and they'd look even better in a month or two. The diner's Las Vegas–style neon marquee was now surrounded by a tasteful assortment of foliage plants to harmonize with the tropical paint job. Very tiki bar. On the marquee was Babe's thought for the week. This week's WAS A CLEAR CONSCIENCE IS USUALLY THE SIGN OF A BAD MEMORY. Babe, in a nutshell.

I climbed into my Jeep, mulling over her suggestion. Why not? The girls at SHS may know something, and, if not, I'd treat myself to the vintage ceramic lamp I'd been eyeing the last few times I'd been in.

The Springfield Historical Society is located in a formidable brick building, early nineteenth century, with impressive white pillars and a great expanse of front lawn sloping down to the street. They'd approve of that tasteful description. Unfortunately, the owner of the property next door is one of those cheerful retired fellows who think even minor holidays need to be celebrated with a display of lights, hundreds of ornaments, and larger-than-life inflatables, so now the Historical Society is known countywide as the building near Holiday Harry's.

I made a right at the giant bunny (Easter was coming), parked near the bicycle rack in the SHS lot, and picked my way down the stairs to the shop, sidestepping boxes of recent donations. That's where I was, poking through the castoffs, when I overheard the news of an even bigger donation. Halcyon and all Dorothy Peacock's property had been left to the Historical Society.

"Well, there really wasn't anyone else to leave it to, was there, Bernice?"

I cleared my throat to announce myself.

"Hello, Paula. I almost didn't see you over there." In theatrical fashion, Inez Robertson covered the mouthpiece of the old rotary phone and pantomimed that she'd be off soon.

Inez and her friend Bernice were known locally as the Doublemint twins. They were lifelong friends who sported identical upswept hairstyles (Inez's jet-black and Bernice's Sunkist orange) straight out of the sixties, although it's probably unfair to blame an entire decade for their molded, shellacked heads. In addition to being the well-coiffed guardians of Springfield's best junk, with the slightest encouragement they were good for a little local dirt.

"Paula, you should have seen that garden." Without missing a beat, she hung up the phone and continued, with me, the conversation she'd been having with her friend. "Once a year, the sisters opened it to the public. All the local children were invited for games, and there were Shetland ponies that took us from one end of the garden to the other. Then there was a race through the maze and all sorts of treats and exotic candies. It was a wonderful tradition," Inez added wistfully. "What a shame Dorothy couldn't keep it up." She patted her immovable hair for punctuation. "Their brother helped, of course."

"The paper didn't mention a brother."

"I'm sure of it." She tapped her chin, mentally flipping through years of town history. She slammed her powdery hand on the counter in triumph. "*William* was their younger brother. He disappeared years ago. Went to Alaska or someplace. No one ever heard from him again. At least not as far as I know."

"Well, whoever's handling the estate will have to look for him," I said, wondering when I could tactfully get around to the real reason for my visit.

"Now I remember. Margery tried to find him once, years ago, for some Historical Society function. Richard was just as happy she didn't succeed. Probably jealous, the old fool."

Richard was Richard Stapley, the Historical Society's president; Margery was his wife. And now the house had been left in their care.

"William *was* a handsome boy," Inez droned on, oblivious to my mounting impatience. "Quite a heart-breaker, too. He might have gone to Hollywood."

Yeah, maybe he was James Dean, I thought meanly but didn't say. I picked her brain some more about the Peacocks and local history, then when I couldn't stand it any longer, I popped the big question. "Any idea what will become of the garden?"

I was not the first to ask.

"Well," she said heavily, grateful for a new line of gossip. "People have been traipsing in and out since yesterday. I've seen three landscapers' trucks this morning," she said, unnecessarily puttering with the dusty costume jewelry in her display case. "I just hope it isn't that awful Mr. Chiaramonte. I don't know what Richard sees in him. He was here again this morning." She wrinkled her nose as if there were any doubt what she thought of him.

Great. Competition already. And from landscapers established enough to have a fleet of vehicles with their names plastered on the sides.

"Of course, it's Richard's decision. After all, he *is* the president," she added, stretching out the verb and hinting that there was a story there, too; but time was short and I didn't take the bait. She peered out of the thrift shop's high casement window and into the parking lot, where she had a tire-level view of any visitors. "I don't see his car, but it's such a lovely day, perhaps he rode his bicycle."

"I noticed a silver Specialized when I parked," I said.

"That's his. Go on, dear. He'll need lots of help," she said. "And you *are* one of our best customers. I held this for you." From behind the counter she pulled out the lamp. It was one of those aggressively ugly lamps from the fifties that optimistic sellers on eBay refer to as Eames era, an amorphous green and gold affair almost three feet tall from base to finial with a ring of small sputniklike balls shooting out of the top. Frighteningly enough, I already owned the perfect lampshade for it.

"I'm not exactly dressed for an interview," I said, as she painstakingly wrapped the lamp in copies of the *Bulletin* so old I wouldn't have been surprised to see NIXON RESIGNS on one of them. Suddenly I felt amateurish and grubby in my baggy jeans, sweatshirt, and ever-present Knicks hat.

"Don't be silly," she said, finishing up. "You're a gardener—he won't mind. And Richard's a newcomer, too, you know. From Boston."

I took the lumpy package, said good-bye, and made my way up the stairs. To the right was the exit to the parking lot, and to the left was the long corridor to Richard's office, the hallway filled with vintage photographs from Springfield's past. I caught my reflection in the glass of one of them and made a feeble attempt to fix my hair. What the hell—all Stapley could do was say no, and whatever he decided, it wouldn't be based on my having hat hair. Outside his office, I took a deep breath and tried to exude an air of competence. I knocked.

Richard Stapley was in his seventies, a little over six feet tall with thick white hair and a closely cropped beard. His dark eyes were framed by thin wire-rimmed glasses, and he wore the womb-to-tomb WASP uniform of light blue Brooks Brothers shirt, khaki pants, and Top-Siders.

"Have a seat," he said in a way that was outwardly friendly but still made me feel like I was there to take dictation.

The bicycle had undoubtedly kept his weight down, but he still looked like he was no stranger to good food, good wine, and good cigars, as evidenced by the decanter, humidor, and crystal bonbon dishes on his credenza. Just under the portrait of Winston Churchill.

"One of my heroes," he explained, when he saw me staring. "Do you play?"

Was he hitting on me? Maybe I didn't look as bad as I thought I did. "Excuse me?"

"Do you play golf? Those look like golf clubs in your package."

Inez had wrapped my lamp in so many layers of newspaper that it did indeed look like a set of golf clubs.

"No." I laughed, finally at ease.

Stapley settled into his tufted leather chair and got right to my point. "I expect you're here about Halcyon. I've gotten very popular with the gardening community since poor Dorothy passed. She was a fine woman," he said, clipping off the end of a fresh cigar and rolling it between his fingers. I hoped he wasn't going to light up, but I was hardly in a position to protest.

I spoke too fast, babbling incoherently about why I was the right man for the job, even though I wasn't sure what the job was. Stapley nodded sagely, occasionally smiling at one of my obscure gardening references, which I couldn't believe he actually got. *(Ah, yes, what would Vita Sackville-West do?)*

I was not optimistic, but less than hour later, he was giving me a hearty, politician's handshake and wishing me well on the job. Somehow I'd managed to convince him I could handle the restoration of Halcyon's garden. And he'd managed to convince me to do it for next to nothing.

"Here's a copy of our Halcyon file," he said, handing me a bulging manila folder. "Helen Cox at the library should be able to help you dig up a bit more. And the Society will hold a small event, just some wine and cheese, to raise funds for any new plants you may need. Give me a wish list and we'll see how much we can pry out of some of these old tightwads around here." I was on cloud nine.

He led me out to the front steps of the building to say good-bye. From the corner of my eye I saw his eyes narrow at his neighbor's joyously tasteless holiday display.

"You won't be sorry, Mr. Stapley."

"I have every confidence in you."

I needed to celebrate. There might have been no one at home to party with, but Babe would fill in nicely. Things were quiet at the diner, just a handful of stragglers and some teenage boys working up the courage to flirt with Babe.

"You again?" Babe said, looking up from her book. She switched a wooden coffee stirrer from one side of her wide mouth to the other. "You got nerve, after trashing my menu. What's with the cat-who-ate-the-canary grin?"

"I got it."

"You didn't get it here."

"The job. I got the job." I looked at her suspiciously. "Why aren't you more surprised?"

"Why should I be?"

"I don't know. I was. I'm not a native, and although I *am* incredibly talented, it's not as if I have a lot of experience."

"Stapley's not a native either—he's only been here thirty years or so."

"You guys are tough. Look, I'm not sure I want anyone else to know about it yet, okay? There may be a few noses out of joint that I got the gig instead of one of the established nurseries."

"I won't say boo, but you should consider not walking around saying 'I got it! I got it!' if you don't want people to know."

I smiled and spun around on one of the duct-taped counter stools, promptly banging my foot into a nearby seat and the man on it.

"Try not to wreck the place," Babe said. "The *Bon Appétit* photographer is coming later."

I mumbled an apology, and continued. "It was almost as if he was expecting me. I talked nonstop. I was sure I wasn't going to get the job, so I figured I had nothing to lose. I wowed him," I said, moving from surprise to swagger in a nanosecond. "Some of your voodoo charm must be rubbing off on me."

Babe gave me a lopsided smile. "Stick with me, kid."

I banged my hand on the counter, this time sloshing my neighbor's coffee. "I am so sorry. I'm not usually such a jerk. I just got a bit of good news."

"So I gathered," he said. "Don't worry. Mum's the word."

"My name's Paula Holliday. Can I buy you another coffee?"

"Gerald Fraser. That's okay. Nature's way of telling me I've had enough. I'll take a rain check, though. Congrats on the job." He folded his paper, got up slowly, and made his way to the door. Sitting down, he looked fit and ready to spring, so I was surprised to see him move so stiffly out to the parking lot.

"Who's that?" I asked, after he was gone.

"Like he said, Gerry Fraser," Babe said. "Nice guy. Ex-cop. Comes in a few days a week. Walks over from Sunnyview."

Despite the creaky moves, Fraser hadn't looked more than fifty, fifty-five tops. "A little young to be in a nursing home, isn't he?"

"Injured on the job. Some sort of mandatory retirement."

"Looks okay to me."

"Now you're a doctor?"

"No, I'm a landscaping professional, dammit. And I'm celebrating! Give me a very large iced coffee, no sugar, skim milk, and don't be stingy, baby."

She used the chewed-up coffee stirrer as a bookmark, and started making my iced coffee with the dregs of this morning's pot. I leaned over the counter on my elbows and motioned toward her book. "Whatcha reading?"

"Biography of Jim Morrison. I was just a child, of course, but he and I shared a beautiful moment once. The man was a god, if you get my drift." She raised her voice just a bit, so the booth full of raging hormones could hear her. It had its intended effect.

"So, uh, when do you start on that thing we're not supposed to know about?" she asked in a more natural voice.

"ASAP. I'm going over there now to get started. I've got research to do, and I want to make some sketches and collect soil samples first. In fact, better make that iced coffee to go."

Stapley's file included directions to the Peacock house. I hadn't been to that part of town before—three-acre zoning kept out the riffraff like me, but Halcyon wasn't hard to find. As Babe had mentioned, it was weird, not your basic New England saltbox. There were turrets, spires, domes, and loads of tiny windows—a drunken collaboration between Nathaniel Hawthorne and Antonio Gaudii Cornet.

Back in the day, Halcyon had been snidely referred to as "Peacock's Temple." More recently, it'd been dubbed the Addams family house by local kids. They'd dare each other to egg it on Mischief Night, the night before Halloween, and I wouldn't have been surprised if more than a few of them had done the nasty in the Peacock's hidden, overgrown gardens. Apparently, Dorothy had been a good sport about both kinds of intrusions.

The iron gate was open, and one door was off its hinges. I rolled up the weedy gravel driveway and parked in a partially cleared spot on the right side of the house. I grabbed my backpack and took a quick inventory—plant identifier, camera, notepad, Stapley's file, trusty Felco nippers, Ziploc Baggies, labels, trowel, gloves.

Years of broken branches, leaves, and general garden debris littered the front garden. There was old storm damage, and one enormous rhododendron had rotted out from the center, splayed open like a blooming onion, but the good bones were evident. New growth struggled against the weight of the dying branches.

Although still comfortable financially, the Peacock sisters inexplicably hadn't engaged a landscaping service in years; and each year, Dorothy and Renata did less and less themselves. Stapley seemed to think the last time the lawn had been mowed Jimmy Carter was president. It looked it. Against the odds, scattered bulbs were coming out, peeking through the layers of leaf clutter. Another hopeful sign.

The early spring day was brilliant and chilly. It could have been fall, and I was as nervous as if it were the first day of school. "Get ahold of yourself. There's nothing here but a bunch of half-dead shrubs," I said out loud.

"I beg to differ" came a cool voice from behind a large arborvitae in serious need of pruning.

I must have jumped a foot. "Hi. I didn't think anyone else was here."

"Clearly. I used to live near here. I stop back sometimes, to see what's become of the old place." She looked around. "It's hard to believe all the Peacocks are finally gone. Flown the coop, so to speak." So much for respect for the dead.

Halcyon's other visitor was a striking woman—of a certain age—with short auburn hair brushed off her face, the way you can wear it when you have luminous skin and perfect bone structure. Her arms were folded across her chest, holding a large clutch purse, and a woolen shawl was perfectly, effortlessly tossed over her shoulders in that irritating way that some women can pull off and I cannot, but hope to by the time I'm fifty.

"You've got your work cut out for you. In their prime, these gardens were lovely. So were we all, I suppose." She lost herself in her thoughts for a moment, then recovered.

"You must have seen them in pictures, right? You couldn't have seen them yourself."

"Of course I did, flatterer. Dorothy Peacock was one of my teachers, and an old"—she waited for the right word to come, "—an old *beau* of mine used to cut their grass. Not recently, as you can probably tell." She nodded at the overgrown meadow behind me.

"Really? I'd be very grateful for any advice or information you could give me." I whipped out one of my cards and handed it to her, still searching for a pen and paper to get her info. "E-mail is always the easiest way to reach me. Now, if I can just get your coordinates, phone number, maybe an e-mail address . . ."

I jogged back to my car for a pen. By the time I'd finished rooting around in my backpack, she'd silently wandered off.

"Thanks a lot," I muttered to the late March air.

Well, it wasn't the Pine Barrens. She was around here somewhere; I'd catch up with her later. I wondered how she knew I was here to work on the garden. Guess I wasn't dressed for anything else, although in this getup, I might have been a burglar.

Whoever she was, she was right about one thing: I had to get cracking. I got out my pad and Richard's file. At some point I'd make a detailed map of the garden, but for now a rough sketch would do.

The magnificent elm in the photos was gone. Dutch elm disease, I was guessing. Sometime in the 1930s a boatload of beetles stowed away in a shipment of veneer bound for the United States. The beetles carried a fungus, and the rest, as they say, is history. By the sixties, over fifty million elm trees in the United States were dead.

The pines were in good shape. Removal of a few broken branches was really all they needed. The rest of the shrubs in the front garden—rhododendrons, azaleas, andromedas, viburnum, forsythia—and the lawn were wildly overgrown but nothing that couldn't be pruned into submission or fertilized back to life over time. Very few things in the garden were stone-cold dead. Plants have this incredible will to live and if there's even a glimmer of life in something, I always think I can coax it back to good health.

Oriental bittersweet and euonymus burning bush, the Connecticut equivalents of kudzu, were running rampant. I had a love-hate relationship with the burning bush, but the bittersweet would have to go. Labor intensive but not impossible. I was counting on Hugo Jurado's help. Hugo was my own part-time gardener. Going from a fat regular income to a slim irregular one had forced me to make some economies, but I'd sooner give up food than give up Hugo. He was from Temixco, a small town about two hours south of Mexico City. A tireless worker, Hugo juggled three jobs and sent almost every penny back home to his silver-haired mother. He'd probably *own* the town, or be its mayor, in a couple of years.

Although a complete restoration of the garden would take numerous growing seasons, I knew Hugo and I could make a dramatic improvement in as little as sixty days. Things were looking up. I started designing new business cards in my head and thinking of an easier, less obscure name for my soon-to-be-successful company.

The Peacocks' wraparound porch had been filled with containers and window boxes. I couldn't tell from the faded black-and-white photos what kind of flowers they'd held, but if I stuck with the classics—sweet alyssum, petunias, nasturtiums—I'd be fine.

Like a happy puppy, I lumbered around to the back of the house. It was like slamming into a brick wall.

Whatever confidence I'd had a few moments before totally vanished. The back garden was a disaster area. And so much of it. A large herringbone brick terrace, cracked and choked with weeds, held about a dozen moldy planters. Guarded by two moss-covered stone dogs, a short flight of stairs led down to an allée about ten feet wide and a hundred feet long, lined with dead or dying boxwoods. The path looked like pea gravel, but upon closer inspection I saw it was crushed oyster shells, much of it ground to dust. At either end was a garden, each approximately one thousand square feet.

The first was walled, with a central raised bed. According to the file, the other had been an herb garden; only the rampant mint betrayed its former use. Beyond them, there was an overgrown privet maze; half a dozen spindly hemlocks barely screened out the neighbors.

On the far side of the allée was a freestanding stone wall covered by espaliered pear trees. Behind the wall stood a row of cypresses, at least two dead, separating the garden from a lawn that sloped down to a rickety floating dock. Broken statuary, a falling-down greenhouse, a tiny shed, and a musty-looking cottage completed the picture. Only the gnomes were missing.

I retraced my steps and sat down on the brick terrace, somewhat shell-shocked. I checked the pictures again. It had been impossible to appreciate the size of the job from the photos I had. On paper it looked like a few manageable beds, in person—Monticello. No wonder those old ladies hadn't kept up with the landscaping. What was I thinking when I said I could do this? What was that idiot Stapley thinking when he gave *me* the job?

Tears were welling up, but I willed myself not to cry. My attack of self-pity didn't last long; it couldn't. Otherwise it was back to sucking up secondhand smoke at film and TV markets and feigning interest in yet another documentary on the Kennedys or World War Two, and I definitely didn't want that.

I walked to the walled garden on the left side of the property. The walls were about eight feet high with arches and openings in the style of an Italian *giardino segreto,* or secret garden. In the corners were medium-sized understory trees and shrubs, including a fifteen-foot leatherleaf viburnum, bursting with health, and an evergreen magnolia covered with fat golden buds. Overhead, the dogwoods were still beautiful and looked vigorous, unusual since they don't have a very long life span. In a month or so, they'd explode, some pink, some creamy white. Underneath were hostas and peonies, their pointed, reddish crowns just starting to break through the crusty top layer of soil.

I shuffled through the papers in the file. The walled garden had been Renata Peacock's contribution. It was a white garden. Moonflowers, clematis, bleeding hearts, nicotiana, spirea—anything white that would catch the waning light and shimmer in the evening. A few crumbling columns and stone benches lined the walls of the garden room, which were covered with wisteria, Virginia creeper, and a thick mat of English ivy. I sat on one of the cool stone benches, imagining the property sixty or seventy years ago, beautiful and as serene as its name would suggest, a place where well-heeled young ladies sat with their tea and cakes, oblivious to the world outside the boundaries of their cozy retreat.

There'd be no shame in going back to Richard Stapley to tell him the job was too big for me. I could do that, or I could simply dig in and see how far I got.

I'd get Hugo and anyone else I could shanghai into working with me. Tools would be a problem, but I knew where I could borrow some heavy-duty equipment. It would require some hair flicking, a skimpy tank top, and industrial-strength lip gloss, but I'd make the sacrifice. And the Historical Society would have to hold more than a "small event"; I'd need at least a hundred plants, probably more. I added to my already voluminous notes and lists.

Making a quick sketch, I named all the different garden areas. Then I labeled the Baggies I'd brought. Call me crazy, but I love taking soil samples. All you do is dig up some soil, ship it to your local extension university, and for five bucks they analyze the soil's texture and structure; make fertilizer recommendations; and, most important, determine the pH factor—something no serious gardener would consider proceeding without.

Okay, where to start? The center of the white garden was as good a place as any. I reached into my backpack, like a doctor going into his medical bag, and got out my favorite trowel and my thinnest goatskin gloves. I regretted not bringing a tiny airplane bottle of booze to have a little groundbreaking ceremony.

With my first stab, I hit something. When you garden in Connecticut, this is not an unusual occurrence. We grow rocks here. But this didn't sound like a rock. I plunged my trowel into the soil again, this time scraping a surface that was definitely metal. Ten minutes later, I had unearthed a box. Eleven minutes later, a small body. Stone-cold dead.

CHAPTER 2

Until that moment my involvement with the local constabulary had been minimal. Three years of summers and eight months of full-time residence had netted only a few brushes with the law—once when my neighbor had an unusually rowdy party and another time when my flag was stolen. (What kind of lowlife steals a flag?)

Uniformed cops, Officers Guzman and Smythe, responded first. I told them I was alone but knew they wouldn't just take my word for it. I stayed put until they'd made some calls and done a preliminary search. Then they returned to get a statement from me. More cars arrived while we spoke, including one bearing the state seal. People hopped out and sprang into action as if they did this sort of thing every day in our little town. I watched, fascinated.

I didn't have much to tell, but I still had to repeat it all when Sergeant Michael O'Malley arrived about twenty minutes later from the local town center, where he'd been speaking and handing out bicycle safety helmets to kids.

O'Malley was five foot eight or nine and had black hair with the kind of pale skin that made him look like he always needed a shave. If there were two kinds of cops—the rock-hard not-an-ounce-of-fat-on-their-bodies kind and the other—he was one of the others. Not exactly fat but soft; this guy looked like he knew his way to the donut shop. With the whisper of an accent, O'Malley grilled me, repeating and expanding on the same questions asked by the uniformed cops.

"Paula Holliday, two ells. No, I didn't go in; I didn't need to. Besides, I don't have the keys."

"What made you start digging there?" he asked.

"Nothing in particular. Path of least resistance— maybe there were fewer roots and leaves there."

He nodded gravely. I repeated my answers in an impatient, slightly singsong fashion, shifting my weight and hugging my arms tightly over my chest to keep warm.

"Is that your sweatshirt?" he asked, standing over the flower bed.

"Yes. It—it was rolling over."

He picked up the sweatshirt, shook out the imaginary cooties, and draped it around my shoulders. I was taken aback by the intimate gesture.

"Why didn't you just put it back in the box?"

"I don't know. It didn't seem right."

He nodded again and scribbled more notes. "I see you, uh, mulched the rhododendrons," he added, referring to the breakfast I'd left in the flower bed.

That shook me out of my stupor. "Haven't taken that sensitivity training yet, have you, Sheriff Taylor?" I said, snottily suggesting that Springfield was Mayberry and he was out of his league.

"You'd do well to take this a little more seriously," he said, straightening up and taking his own advice. "Did you see anyone else?"

"No. Oh, wait. There *was* another woman here. Well, briefly anyway. I almost forgot about her. The other guys didn't ask."

"Yeah, well, that's why I get the big bucks," he said in an obvious attempt to reestablish some connection.

"I see. You can joke, but I can't."

"Point taken. Did you know her?"

"No. She said she used to live near here. We talked a bit, then she disappeared."

He looked at me as if I'd said the dog ate my homework. "All right, she probably didn't really disappear, but when I came back—I was looking for a pen and paper to get her phone number—she'd taken off. I figured I'd bump into her later somewhere around the grounds, but I didn't."

Another blank look from O'Malley. Maybe he thought I'd hit her on the head with a weed whacker and tossed her onto the compost pile. I described the woman and our brief conversation. After that, O'Malley loosened up and so did I. We chatted politely while he took more notes and dozens of pictures with both a Polaroid and a digital camera. Stupidly, I thought it was casual conversation, then I realized he was getting background info on me, to see if I was the kind of psycho who might have buried a baby here.

"Who knew quiet little Springfield was such a hotbed of criminal activity?" I mumbled. "I assumed the worst crime ever committed here was some soccer mom running a red light."

"Unfortunately, we have everything they have in the big city, just a bit less of it," O'Malley replied. I couldn't tell if he was sorry or proud. "If you remember anything else, give us a call," he said, handing me one of his cards, "or stop by the substation on Haviland Road. If I'm not there, ask for Officer Guzman. She'll be working with me."

Renata's white garden was cordoned off with yellow tape. Other people kept arriving. One of them, a cheery blonde about my age, had three cameras slung around her neck, and she rattled off a running commentary as she videotaped the entire area. She might have been at Disneyland.

I was pushed farther and farther to the edge of the property. I made a few feeble protests to no one in particular about needing to get back to work, and finally someone barked, "So do we, lady. Check back with Mom in a few days, okay? You're sort of in the way here."

"Mom?"

"Sergeant O'Malley. Nickname."

Just as I was climbing back into my car, Richard Stapley arrived, gliding in on his bike.

"Good Lord, is it true?" he asked, swinging his left leg gracefully over the seat, dismounting, and resting his bike against an oak tree. Tall and patrician, he was just as ready to take command of this situation as he had of me a few hours earlier.

"I'm afraid so, Mr. Stapley."

"Please, call me Richard. What did the police say?"

"Not much they can say at this point, except that I seem to have stumbled upon a very old corpse."

"Good grief," he said, bending down and fussing with his bicycle clips. "What was it?"

"A baby."

He shook out his pant cuffs and recreased his pants with a quick thumb and forefinger on each leg. "I knew those girls were strange, but I never imagined anything like this." He straightened up, resuming his military bearing. "Mike O'Malley called me; I'd better go talk to him."

I was getting tired of being dismissed, so I decided to return the favor. "I have had a long day. All I want to do now is head home. The police will let me know when I can come back, but I'm sure it'll be at least a few days. That's okay. It'll give me a chance to do some research."

"That's the spirit. Go home and try to relax. We'll take care of everything here."

On the way home, I slowed down as I drove by the police substation. The two-story strip mall was diagonally across the road from the Paradise Diner and was home to a handful of local businesses—Shep's Wines and Liquors, Penny's Nails—and sandwiched in between the Martial Arts Family Center and the Dunkin' Donuts was the substation. I'd been kidding about the donuts. Now I wondered if O'Malley got the belly from the donut shop or the liquor store.

Suddenly I was anxious to get home. I picked up speed. The same manicured lawns and tidy flower beds I'd passed in the morning whizzed by, but instead of critiquing the plant selections, now I wondered what long-buried secrets they, too, might be hiding.

CHAPTER 3

Eagle Road is a dead end. Turning into my driveway, I thought, *Not many secrets here—single woman, thirties, no kids, no cats.* Obsessive devotion to mini pine bark nuggets. The mailbox reads HOLLIDAY AND MAZ-ZARA, although that second name should have been razored off months ago.

My house was built about thirty-five years ago. The perky real estate agent I rented—then ultimately bought—it through said it had once been owned by a basketball player. Must have been a college player, because it was small, not the humongous estates even the benchwarmers have nowadays. It might have been true, though. When my ex and I first started spending summers up here, we saw a few of my beloved New York Knicks having breakfast at the Paradise. Perky real estate agent aside, that may have closed the sale.

Anyway, the player got cut by the team and the bank foreclosed, so I was able to pick the house up for a song—just about all I had.

I pulled into the garage and hopped out for a quick stroll around my garden before it got too dark. My own little controllable environment. That's a laugh. All you can do is deal with the weather, the soil, the sun, the bugs, the bacteria, the fungi, and then resign yourself to the fact that the deer will eat most of it anyway. I didn't kid myself that I controlled the garden. But at least there were no dead bodies here—or none that I knew of.

Outside the garden, control was no easier. Chris Mazzara had moved out months ago. The body had stuck around, but, to paraphrase B. B. King, the thrill had gone. Now the only thing left was the name on the mailbox, which I hadn't had the heart to remove, since that made the departure more final.

I ended my short garden inspection, picking off a few dead leaves in the process, then went inside.

"Anna?" I yelled. No answer.

Anna Peña is my cleaning lady. The cushy days of double income no kids were gone and I couldn't afford her anymore, but Anna didn't seem to want to leave. And it was anyone's guess when she'd show up. I suspected she came to watch English lessons on cable, which she didn't get at home, but she never said. There was only the inconclusive evidence of the laundry being done and the TV being on channel 106. Far be it from me to discourage her.

Anna was a hardworking single mom and she'd decided that polishing her English and being my "assistant" would land her a job at the country's biggest tequila distributor, based in neighboring Greenwich. So sometimes she came by to answer the phone and do a little filing to practice. "I don't want to clean houses forever. I have ambition," she'd told me.

To that same end, she'd recently embarked on a cut-rate makeover including the permanent tattooing of her eyebrows, eyelids, and lips; so it was also possible she was just lying low until all the swelling went down.

My voice echoed through the empty house. I dropped

my backpack in the entrance and hauled myself up the open staircase. Tonight the climb felt longer than usual, but it was worth it. Upstairs was the living room, kitchen, bedroom, and a small deck. Downstairs was the entrance, office, and—for want of a better name—the TV room. It also housed all my workout equipment: rowing machine, free weights, Fat Boy punching bag, and any new gizmo guaranteed to flatten my stomach.

Eight hours before, I thought I'd be celebrating with a bit of bubbly, but I was going to need something stronger now. I made myself a very large, very dirty martini: lots of vodka, lots of olive juice, three olives, and "just say the word *vermouth*," as an old friend once instructed. I opened the slider out to the deck, took my glass, and headed out to the old teak chaise I'd found at a yard sale.

I kicked off my shoes, put my feet up on the railing, and took a long pull on the drink. If the martini was a vacation in a glass, as that same friend once told me, my deck was a freaking sabbatical. No noise (usually), lots of sky, and a chance to contemplate my latest gardening project.

The land adjacent to mine was a bird sanctuary, but subscribing to the Japanese concept of borrowed scenery, I enjoyed pretending I was mistress of all I surveyed. And usually I was, except for the occasional birder who strayed off the trail. What more could a woman want? I drained the martini and went back inside for another. Second drink in one hand, door handle in the other—the phone rang. I prayed it wasn't Richard Stapley or, worse, my mother. With no lunch, and having left my breakfast in the bushes, the large economy-sized drink I'd just polished off had gone straight to my head. I wasn't sure I could compose an intelligent sentence.

"Hello?" I said, working hard to sound sober.

"Ms. Holliday?"

"Speaking." *Just barely,* I thought.

"It's Mike O'Malley. I wanted to see how you were doing."

"Great, once I get all the cadavers out of that place." I hadn't meant to sound that flip; it was the vodka talking.

"I'm glad you got your sense of humor back. It's understandable, of course, but you seemed a bit stunned this afternoon. I almost suggested you go to Springfield Hospital."

I *had* been surprisingly calm that afternoon; O'Malley probably thought I was in shock.

I'd seen plenty of dead people before. My large Italian-Irish family generated boisterous wakes, watered by beer, wine, and anisette for the ladies in black dresses. Ancient relatives, the deceased generally looked better dead than they did when they were alive thanks to the talented folks at Torregrossa's Funeral Home in Brooklyn. ("That's the dress she wore to Donna's wedding, periwinkle blue. It was always a good color for her.")

The vodka kept me babbling. "I'd also like to thank whoever took such good care to keep the blowflies and the earthworms at bay." That last graphic description rang in my ears. "God, that must have sounded terrible. I don't know where that came from. Black humor—just my way of dealing with things."

"I find it useful myself sometimes." He finally sensed this wasn't a good time to talk. "I just called to let you know we'll be at the house for the next couple of days. Someone will give you a heads-up when you can go back. Glad to hear you're okay."

I replaced the phone in the cradle, missing the contacts the first two times. That's when I noticed the red light and the flashing number 17. The first three messages were all from the same person, Jonathan Chappell, a reporter from the *Springfield Bulletin*. I didn't bother playing the rest.

The sun was about to go down and I knew that would mean a drop in the temperature, so I pulled on an old black cardigan, big as a blanket and at least ten years old. I popped a Van Morrison CD in the player, cranked it up a bit, and padded back to the deck just in time to see the sun setting through the trees.

Most homes up here have a lot of house on a small piece of land—McMansions; mine is just the opposite. Tiny house, more land than most. Only the one noisy neighbor and a family I've never even seen on the other side. The far end of the property bordered wetlands and the bird sanctuary. A seasonal stream there, heavy from all the spring rains, was lined with rows and rows of swamp cabbage, ferns, and jack-in-the-pulpits. The birds were having a field day drinking and hunkering down for the night. Just like me.

CHAPTER 4

The cold woke me, and the sky was so clear, it seemed as if Orion's belt was dangling over my head. I briefly considered dragging my telescope outside, then the memory of the day's events shook any fanciful notions of stargazing out of my head.

Inside the house, last Sunday's dutifully purchased but unread *New York Times* made excellent kindling. I started a fire and went to clean myself up. A hot shower and fresh clothes made me feel almost normal again, normal enough to be hungry. Back in the kitchen, I checked out the dismal contents of my fridge: yogurt, wilting veggies, water, and every condiment known to man. I was always so virtuous when I went food shopping, but once home, hanging on the refrigerator door, I invariably craved high-fat food of no nutritional value. Since I never had any in the house, I opted for my patented Greek yogurt with flaxseed, honey, and raisins sundae; if I was feeling really reckless, I might throw in a handful of wonderful walnuts. Why not go to hell in a handbasket?

I settled in on the floor in front of the fireplace with the Halcyon file, my laptop and garden books spread out around me.

Oddly enough, finding the body hadn't scared me. Everything pointed to its being evidence of someone's old secret, as opposed to someone's new crime. Perversely I even found myself thinking it would add to Halcyon's mythology and make it even more of a local attraction once the gardens were restored. I got to work.

Renata Peacock's birthday, June 18, would be an appropriate date for an opening. And there was a certain symmetry to it. Richard's file revealed that was the date the sisters used to do their noblesse oblige thing and invite the locals. Problem was, it was only two and a half months away. Tomorrow I'd get in touch with Hugo and maybe rope some of my city friends into pulling weeds and mulching in exchange for a pleasant weekend in the country. I pored over the stacks of garden books and old pictures, adding to my bulging folders of notes and shopping lists.

I didn't doubt Richard Stapley's ability to raise funds. He was handsome, in a rugged, old-fashioned, Mount Rushmore way; I could see the blue-rinse crowd getting weak in the knees and handing over checks after just a few flattering words from him. I also saw that every once in a while I'd have to remind him I was a grown-up—not some kid he'd brought in to mow the lawn.

I'd need everything within a month, preferably by Easter if the shrubs were going to get established early in the season. Despite the inevitable consequences, I would throw myself at Guido Chiaramonte for the loan of a chipper, chain saw, some leaf blowers, and whatever other equipment I didn't own.

Guido was a local nursery owner, in his eighties and notorious for hitting on women of all ages, shapes, and sizes. Women on walkers did not escape his advances.

One of my early Springfield fantasies had been to buy Guido's place when he retired or went back to Sicily, but the old reprobate had shown no signs of doing either. I once took him up on his offer to teach me about the nursery business, and I was met with amorous overtures that were half-amusing, half-revolting. Now I was planning to flash a little cleavage and bat my eyelashes at the old letch. For *tools*. I was shameless.

I made a timeline for the Halcyon job and refined my sketch of the garden, eventually getting around to the white garden and the spot where I'd found the body. Unconsciously, I'd been avoiding it, but I would have to go back there—mentally and physically.

Not tonight though. My legs were stiff from sitting on the floor, and my neck ached from scrunching down to inspect old photos with a magnifying glass. I gave myself a good stretch, packed up my notes, and went downstairs for some mindless entertainment.

Mindless was right. The former programming exec inside me couldn't help but criticize. Five shows devoted to moving your furniture and cleaning your closets? No wonder cable television kept resurrecting classics. That was my first job in the business, screening vintage sitcoms for TVLand. Uncle Miltie must be turning over in his grave. And the shopping channels were growing like ground cover. Who really needs another peridot pendant? I sure didn't, but the disembodied hand dangling the necklace lured me the same way the tarnished chain had that morning. I shook off the urge.

I passed on the plastic surgery shows in favor of something called *Island Survival*. Very realistic. Someone should produce *Manhattan Survival*. It's an island. The winner would have to score a good table at a trendy new restaurant, pick up a model, get a hair appointment with this month's stylist-to-the-stars, and get a cabbie to take him to one of the outer boroughs—all the really useful survival skills.

A couple of hours later, all but brain-dead, I was glued to one of the grisly true-crime programs I might have been producing had I stayed in New York. "John claimed his wife went shopping and never returned, but he really killed her, put her in a metal drum, and left her in the basement for thirty years until *we* found her."

That was the direction the new owners of my old company wanted me to take. I'd cranked out a few episodes, but my heart was never in it. It was too hard to take. And there was always one cop who still had all the facts at his fingertips, as if the crime had just happened yesterday—his own Lindbergh baby.

There were lots of those cases. Too many. And just as many on the other side. The Jane Does who turned up and remained unclaimed. I started to wonder what my little baby's name was. Wait a minute. *My little baby?* Who said that? I didn't have a baby—get a grip.

But I did have a baby. At least I did for the twenty minutes or so it took the cops to find me in the Peacocks' garden, crouched down, the taste of vomit fresh in my mouth and my eyes locked on the partially unwrapped body of a dead baby.

A noise upstairs shook me down to my Polarfleece socks. I put the TV on mute and strained to hear what it was. Between the acorns and the bird feeders, my place is one giant salad bar for critters, so I don't usually get too spooked by the odd noise in the middle of the night. I grew up in New York, so not much scared me, except when things were *too* quiet.

Heart pounding, I tiptoed upstairs to investigate. I still held the remote in a white-knuckled death grip. It'd make a dandy weapon if the intruder was a munchkin.

Outside my kitchen window, the blackness held all

sorts of bogeymen. I imagined shadowy figures with outstretched arms in the weeping hemlock but, happily, saw nothing. Behind me, another log in the dying fire collapsed, repeating the sound that first startled me. I hadn't realized I'd been holding my breath, until it came out in a whoosh. What an idiot. Sheepishly, I went back down the stairs, but not before setting the security alarm. The previous owner had had it installed, probably to safeguard his collection of bling. I didn't have anything worth stealing, so hardly ever used the alarm, but it wouldn't hurt to have advance notice if an ax murderer was coming up the stairs.

My usual antidote to stressful situations is sports, but at this hour only ESPN Classic sports was broadcasting. I recognized the vintage Knicks game where Willis Reed limps out of the locker room, plays for three minutes, but so inspires the team that it carries them to victory. The clip is shown ad nauseam at Madison Square Garden, usually when all hope is lost. Not exactly a surprise ending but just what the doctor ordered. So I fell asleep again, not dreaming of dead babies and bodies stuffed in fifty-gallon drums but of Earl "the Pearl" Monroe and Walt "Clyde" Frazier. And the scariest thing in my dream was Clyde's postgame outfit.

CHAPTER 5

Like everyone else in Springfield, Babe Chinnery had heard about the body. She'd left me a voice mail message the next afternoon, so I checked in at the Paradise at around 5 P.M. before heading to the library, where I planned to spend my downtime researching the Peacock garden. I'd barely walked through the door when she rushed over and hugged me, showing a maternal side I hadn't known existed.

"How the hell are you?" she whispered, steering me to a booth. She sat down with me. This was about as common as Rick having a drink with someone in *Casablanca*.

"You okay?"

I nodded.

"Really?"

"Really. I just didn't expect to walk into a local ghost story my first day on the job. I thought they were kidding when they called that place the Addams family house."

She motioned for Chloe to bring us some coffee. "I found a stiff once. Backup singer. OD'd right before a show. Pretty unprofessional, if you ask me."

The midriff-baring waitress came over with two

cups and a plate of Pete's homemade donuts, which I suspected could also be used to border flower beds.

"Why does every sixteen-year-old kid think we want to see her belly?" I asked. Then I remembered who I was talking to. I sipped the coffee and broke off a chunk of the donut. Babe wasn't moving until I told her everything.

"It was so old," I whispered, donut in midair, "it looked more like a museum piece than a body. Like a toy papoose you'd see in a Thanksgiving pageant." That crack finally convinced her I was all right.

"I heard you hurled in the flower bed. Is that what you call adding organic matter?"

"What, is that in today's *Bulletin*?" I angrily popped the hunk of donut into my mouth. Stress eating.

"O'Malley stopped by this morning. Don't be mad. He was worried about you."

"Mr. Sensitivity. If he's so worried, he can finish up fast and let me back onto the property. I'm losing time. I don't work, I don't eat."

"You don't eat anyway. Get an advance. Tell Stapley you need to order things. Don't you need stuff?"

"I don't even know what I need yet." Mysteriously, the entire donut on my plate had disappeared. "Not until I hit the books. Any idea how late the library's open?" I asked.

"Beats me. I get all my books from Kathy's Book Nook; us little guys have to stick together."

After a minute or so, someone said, "The main branch is open until nine P.M. tonight."

I turned to a lean Hispanic guy reading at the counter. At first glance, you might mistake him for any one of the dozens of guys who stand around downtown Springfield at six or seven in the morning. They wait for contractors or landscapers to give them the nod like the

rotten union boss does in *On the Waterfront*. I'd met a
lot of the Manual laborers at the nurseries; most of them
looked sad, slump-shouldered in their cheap T-shirts
from places they'd never been and weren't likely to go.
Not this one.

"There is a book club meeting tonight from seven to
nine."

"Thanks. I wonder what they're discussing."

He held up a copy of *Lolita*. "I am almost finished.
Lots of work at the beginning of the season."

"I know, I'm a gardener, too. Paula Holliday."

"Felix Ontivares."

"Nice to meet you."

He nodded in my direction, then he peeled a few
dollars from his wallet, paid, and left.

"Just another conquest," I said, shaking my head as
the door flapped closed behind him.

"Don't take it personally. Most of the nursery guys
are quiet, but it's a language thing. Felix doesn't have
that problem. He's new, only been around a couple of
weeks. Guido says he's a good worker, too. And you
know Guido—he doesn't like any of the immigrant guys.
Only the women," she added with a smirk.

"Babe, is there anything else I should know about
the Peacocks? You kind of suggested Stapley didn't tell
me everything."

"Nothing I can tell you. You think I'd have sent you
there if I thought you'd find a stiff? There were so many
rumors about the old girls, I didn't think he had the
time to tell you everything." She changed the subject.
"Are you okay for cash? What's he paying you, anyway?"

I looked down, groaning inwardly. "Well, it's such a
great opportunity, I thought . . ."

"That cheap bastard. Look, the library's open for

hours. Stay here for a while. I'll tell you about the time I met the Lizard King. Chloe," she yelled, "we're gonna need some more coffee. And a couple more donuts."

As an old Doors fan, I couldn't refuse.

The Ferguson Library is a large white clapboard building in the center of town, the kind of place that's either the library or the funeral home in a small New England town like Springfield. I hadn't been there before, and Mrs. Cox, the librarian, did everything but ask for a tissue sample before issuing my temporary library card. After the presentation was made, she kept me under surveillance.

The Historical Society's Web site was still under construction and the *Bulletin*'s wasn't much better, but it did yield a number of useful links and more pictures of the garden. The lion's share of the info was still on microfiche, the seventies' version of index cards. Mrs. Cox directed me to a file cabinet that looked like it was waiting for a tomb raider to open it.

Dorothy Peacock was ninety-three or ninety-seven years old when she died, depending on which piece of local folklore you chose to believe. She followed the colorfully named Renata, who had passed away four years ago. The two had lived alone for many years, any other Peacocks having died or dispersed years before.

Halcyon had been built in 1830 by Dorothy's great-great-great-grandfather Owen for his bride, Olivia, on a lush piece of property right on the water as befitting the former sea captain.

Although the captain was wealthy, and another of Dorothy's ancestors had made a tidy sum in the railroad business, the original three-hundred-acre homestead had been whittled down to the current seven acres through a combination of greed, bad investments, and the inevitable wastrel descendant or two. Dorothy's father recovered from the stock market crash, but his untimely death left the Peacocks' real estate assets in a holding pattern, and he was never able to fulfill his dream of buying back the acreage other family members had sold off. And Dorothy had other interests.

I was wandering in turn-of-the-century Springfield when my cell phone jolted me back to the present. Mrs. Cox scoured the room for the perpetrator. Not wanting to incur her wrath or disturb the book club crowd, which was just gathering, I ducked outside and fished the phone out of my bag with the same mixture of annoyance and surprise I always registered when it rang these days.

It was Lucy Cavanaugh, childhood friend and former colleague, currently orchestrating a seven-figure children's television deal (international and DVD rights included). I could hear furious keyboard clicking in the background; at 7 P.M. she was probably still in her office.

"Bravo for actually having the phone on. Listen, I just had drinks with the programming director at the Garden Channel. They have a fat budget, and they're looking for producers. They need you, and you can do both of the things you love: TV and gardening. It's perfect. What's that stuff you're always going on about— mulch? You can produce the definitive history of mulch. Every other history from guns to candy canes has been done, why not mulch?"

"Is mulch in the air today?" I asked incredulously.

Then I told her what had happened, and the keyboard clicking finally stopped. "Jeez. Are you all right?"

"I'm fine. I'm like one of those utility workers who accidentally uncovers ancient burial grounds. The cops'll do their thing, and eventually I'll get back to work."

"Oh, yeah. I don't know—is it inappropriate to congratulate you on the job, I mean, under the circumstances?"

"Inappropriate? Okay, who are you and what have you done with the real Lucy? It's cool. Thanks."

"In that case, were any of the cops cute?"

Same old Lucy; priorities in order: work, men.

"One of them was sort of cute, if a little tubby."

"I'm not prejudiced. In fact, I'm tired of guys who are cuter than I am," she said, keyboard clicking resumed.

I delivered my pitch. "Come up next weekend. You can check out the men in uniform yourself. We'll have a spa weekend, you can detox from the party circuit. We can work out," I said sneakily. I could get a good eight hours of gardening out of her if I told her it burned fat.

"Sure. We'll have a little mystery party—rent a few Hitchcock movies, play Clue."

"Sounds like a plan," I said, pleased with myself for signing on my first unsuspecting volunteer.

"Good. Look, I'm off to a screening. Pick me up at the train station a week from Friday; I'll get the six oh four. Call if you—I don't know—if you need anything or find another body."

"Thanks, I will."

Okay, my best friend is off to quaff champagne, flirt ferociously, and make financially lucrative deals at a film screening, and I'm pulling weeds at a haunted house. What's wrong with this picture?

Back inside the library, I collected my things and tidied the table where I'd been working. This earned me an approving smile from Helen Cox. Her thin lips had been set in a straight line since the moment I'd gotten here, reserving judgment until she was sure I was a responsible library user. I whispered "Good night" to her, and that really sent my stock soaring. On my way out, Felix Ontivares strode in. He nodded but kept going.

I might not have stopped at the substation at all if it hadn't been next to the Dunkin' Donuts. I felt momentarily disloyal to Babe, then the moment passed.

"Great One, skim milk, no sugar, please."

I heard a voice behind me. "This late in the day, a coffee that size will have you up all night alphabetizing your seed packets." It was Officer Smythe. He had the body of a serious weight trainer, so I was a little surprised to see him there, licking powdered sugar off his fingers.

"You caught me," I said. "I'm a sucker for Dunkin' Donuts coffee. I thought I'd stop next door to see when I can get back to work."

He shrugged. "Mom's not in. Talk to Guzman." He picked up his bag of Munchkins and pushed the door open with his tiny, rock-hard butt. "Later. Gotta go mind the speed trap."

It didn't hurt for a single woman living on her own to have a good relationship with the local police. Maybe next time weirdo neighbor acts up, I'd impress him by being on a first-name basis with the Man. I took my supersized cup and went next door to the Haviland substation.

"Hi. Are you Officer Guzman?" I asked the first guy I saw.

"No, I'm much better looking."

"I'm Guzman," came a voice from the back of the office near the watercooler. "Pay no attention to him—he's a lonely man. What can I do for you?" she said.

I closed the door behind me. I'd forgotten Guzman was the name of the female cop. She was my height but more muscular, with dark hair pulled into a stubby

ponytail, held on the sides by half a dozen metal clips.
I told her why I was there.

"No, Mikey would have called. He's good that
way—if he says he's gonna call, he does."

She must have seen how disappointed I was, and
added, "Sit tight, you'll be back digging in the dirt before you know it. Off the record," she whispered, "I
think you'll be hearing from him soon."

Very soon, in fact, because just then O'Malley
walked in.

Guzman shrugged with a little smile. "I saw him
through the window."

"Hello, Plant Lady. I hope that's decaf," he said,
eyeing my extralarge coffee.

"Is that my official nickname?"

"Oh, no, just trying it on for size. It needs tweaking."

I knew it wasn't my business, but I asked how the
case was going.

"Not going too far, truth be told. Have a seat."

While he got out the files, I checked out his cubicle.
The bulletin board was layered with yellowed WANTED
posters for missing persons and for information regarding a cop shot close to twenty years ago.

"I guess there's not much crime here. Those flyers
look pretty old."

"Or it could mean that we catch most of the bad
guys, and those are just a few that got away."

Touché.

There were perfectly edged stacks of papers lined
up against the far edge of the desk. A couple of pictures
of kids (his?), a few postcards from national parks, and
a wooden plaque inscribed WORLD'S BEST MOM. A pencil cup had the quote MEASURE TWICE, CALL A #*%!
CARPENTER. Anal, I thought.

"Okay," he said, "the corpse, as you know, had been

a corpse for some time, tucked away quite lovingly, until the new gardener came along."

"How come it didn't decompose? Just working in the garden or hiking I've seen animals . . ."

"Any number of things can cause a body to mummify, but it doesn't usually happen by accident in Connecticut's acid soil. Most probably someone intentionally treated either the body or the material it was wrapped in. It's also possible the body was moved from some drier, more airtight resting place. That was suggested by the outer box, and the absence of seedlings and rocks that unconsciously led you to dig in that particular spot."

All right, maybe he wasn't just a suburban donut hound.

"So whose baby was it?"

O'Malley shrugged. "That we don't know. We may never know. The two obvious candidates, those being the dead sisters, aren't talking."

"What about DNA testing? Can't you do tests to figure out who the baby is?"

"That's the problem with law enforcement nowadays," he said, looking around to his colleagues for confirmation. "Too much television. Everyone's an expert."

I felt a sermon coming.

"Here's the CliffsNotes version," he continued. "We can take a sample from the corpse, but we have nothing to match it to without exhuming the bodies of the two dead women. To go through the legal hassle and considerable expense just to confirm that some woman had an illegitimate child forty or fifty years ago . . . who seems to have died of natural causes anyway . . . what purpose would it serve?"

"What about finding the father?"

"You want us to take DNA samples from all the

geezers in the area? And what if Dad was a traveling salesman or a sailor on leave? That little tidbit of information may never be known, but odds are very good that the mother was one of the Peacock sisters."

"I guess you're right. I just thought with all the stuff you hear about DNA testing, you know, it would be easy."

"It's a wee bit more complicated than it sounds. Without a reference sample you can't prove much more than that it was a human child, a boy, by the way." I was a little ashamed that I hadn't asked. "There are half a million DNA samples sitting in labs waiting to be analyzed. And thousands of people currently in prison hoping to have convictions overturned because of them. And these are mostly rape and murder cases, mind you. So don't judge us too harshly just because some dead lady's indiscretion of fifty years ago doesn't rank high on anybody's to-do list. If there's no real payoff, it's hard to justify. We can't exactly drop the sample off at our local drugstore like vacation pictures."

"Okay, Sergeant, can I help you with that soapbox? You're right—too many reruns of *Law and Order*."

"No, *you're* right. We should be able to do this, but it all boils down to money and priorities. The medical examiner's office just doesn't think it's worth it, given the circumstances. There will be an autopsy, but that will, most likely, just give us the cause of death. If that's suspicious . . . well, I'm getting ahead of myself."

He paused for effect. "I can tell you that the baby wasn't one of the Romanovs."

"You guys must be a riot at your Christmas party."

I shook my head and tried not to laugh.

"Does this mean I can go back to the house soon?"

"Yes, ma'am. Someone will be there tomorrow to

clean up our mess; you can start making your own in a day or two."

"Thanks." I got up to leave. "So, they have Cliffs-Notes in Ireland, too?"

"Indoor plumbing, but no CliffsNotes. That's why we moved," he teased. "Dad and I came here from Ireland twenty-five years ago after my mother died." He held the door for me.

"You know, Sergeant, even if the baby did die of natural causes, someone did move it. And recently. Isn't that a crime?"

"I said *maybe* someone moved it. Let us deal with that, Ms. Holliday."

As soon as he closed the door behind me, I could hear the conversation inside start up again, but I was damned if I was going to turn around to see if they were talking about me. I jogged back to my car, then drove home, faintly pissed off but not sure why.

CHAPTER 6

The next morning, the *Bulletin*'s front page was plastered with updates on the Peacock story. Almost everyone at the Paradise Diner had a copy. And a theory. Most of the articles were written by Jon Chappell, the intrepid reporter who'd been bird-dogging me since I'd found the body; twelve phone calls that first night alone. He'd tapered off to two or three a day, but every time I played messages there he was, hounding me, hoping for his Nancy Grace breakthrough story.

"More coffee, honey?" Babe asked. "You look like you could use it."

"I didn't sleep much last night."

"Well, it's understandable, given recent events. I mean, it looks like the Knicks aren't even going to make the play-offs this year. I know a few other people losing sleep these days, too." Babe motioned to a tall, quiet guy I recognized as one of the Knicks' assistant coaches. Even he was reading the *Bulletin* this morning and not the sports section.

"Anything else, Herb?"

"Got a center?" he muttered.

In the corner, I saw the guy whose coffee I'd spilled

the other day. I saluted him with my mug. "I still owe you one."

"So you do," he said, getting up and joining us at the counter.

"It's Gerald, right?"

He nodded, then motioned to the newspaper. The lead article repeated what O'Malley had told me the day before. The body found at Halcyon had "almost certainly" been the child of one of the two dead sisters. What the paper suggested, but didn't say outright, was that there wasn't likely to be any further investigation—though the writer was clearly disappointed. With no tangible evidence of a crime, what was there to pursue?

"*You* were first on the scene," he said. "You buy it?"

"Sure. Why not?"

"Just asking. Dead women, dead baby, dead case. Awfully neat and tidy, don't you think? Most crime is messier. Most crimes are never solved."

I shrugged.

"Sorry. Old habits, as they say. Used to be my line of work."

"Babe mentioned. It was here in Springfield, right?"

"I got out of it. Mostly this," he slapped his bad leg. "But I couldn't stand it when the bad guys won."

"Did that happen often in a town like this?" I asked.

"Not often. There was . . . There was one case . . . missing girl. Gnawed at me for years."

"Pretty girl? Long, dark hair?" I asked.

He squinted at me. "How'd you know?"

"I saw an old poster in the police station. What do you do now?" I asked, relieving him of an unwanted memory.

"A little carpentry, a little painting."

"Handyman?"

"Handyman?" Babe said, coming back to us in between customers. "This guy is an artist. Have you seen the bar at Café Gennelli's? Gerry hand-carved the bar *and* created the sculpture outside. I'm saving up for one."

"Just working down my bar bill; it was easier than washing dishes," he said modestly.

I hadn't been to Gennelli's but recognized it as a downtown restaurant popular with the designer martini crowd, not a place I would have thought appealed to a guy like him. He saw what I was thinking.

"My friend's kid owns it. I was just helping him out; the clientele's a little underripe for my taste. By the way, forget what I said about that other thing. I've just got too much time on my hands. Aside from the corpse, how's the new job going?"

I gave him the brief, polite answer I'd been conditioned to give most people, but when he asked a few intelligent gardening questions, we launched into a lengthier discussion on bamboo, something he had wrestled with at his last house. I was for, he was vehemently against.

"Well, don't try to plant any on the Peacock property. Dick Stapley will never let you. If he can't control it, he doesn't like it. Besides, they never had it at Halcyon."

"We could plant some here," Babe said. "I'd like that . . . maybe put a hammock outside. . . . I could get a hula girl tattoo." She swiveled her hips in a way that drew ahs from the customers at the counter.

"I'm gonna run," Gerald said. "Thanks for the coffee, kiddo. Next time's on me."

As he left, he crossed paths with Mike O'Malley. They acknowledged each other with the universal male grunt "ay" instead of "hello."

Babe held up the paper. "Nice bit of detecting. Take you guys long to figure that one out?"

"You cut me to the quick. Here we are, making the streets safe for you and yours, and all we get is grief and the occasional stale-donut joke." Mike held his hand to his heart and faked a pained expression. Then he leaned over the counter and whispered something in Babe's ear. She howled.

"Two large coffees to go and a couple of those fine greasy donuts. Extra trans-fatty acids on mine, please."

From the kitchen, Pete yelled, "I made those myself this morning. No partially hydrogenated anything, just pure unadulterated fat."

Yum.

O'Malley paid little attention to me and left soon after. The rest of the early morning crowd drifted out, too, and Babe came back to me.

"What was so funny?" I asked.

"Mike told me you thought he should be looking for the baby's father. He said he couldn't imagine trying to get the old coots in this town to jerk off in Dixie cups. He thought the effort might kill some of them."

"They don't even have to do that anymore. I saw this on TV the other night, they can just use a cotton swab—"

"Honey, honey, it was a joke."

"All right, he has a sense of humor and knows what trans-fatty acids are. That's promising. What's the deal with him?"

"Why—you interested?"

"Please. I'm a gardener, remember? I dig. Never mind. I'm more interested in that guy Felix who was here the other day."

"He's a honey, isn't he?"

"I'm wondering if he'd work on the garden with me. I could use another pair of hands."

"On your budget? Don't count on it. But leave a note for him, and I'll put it on the bulletin board. I'll make sure he sees it next time he's in."

We returned to our postmortem of the Knicks and their abysmal season, eliciting a few more grunts from the tall guy in the back and prompting him to leave.

"Hey, think lottery," Babe called after him, as he stooped to walk out the door.

A voice came from the back of the diner. "I could use some service here."

"Sure, honey. I almost didn't see you back there behind that newspaper," Babe said. She picked up a menu and headed to the far corner of the diner. "What can I get you?"

I overheard the man ask what I was having.

"Paula? Egg-white omelet, no fries, skim milk in the coffee."

"Yes, well, that doesn't really work for me. Two eggs, scrambled well, on a bagel, hash browns, bacon on the side. And coffee with real milk, please."

"You got it."

I fished out a business card and scribbled a few words on the back of it for Felix Ontivares. Then I wedged the card in the upper-right-hand corner of the Paradise bulletin board on top of the signs for handymen, gently used furniture, and a new miracle weight-loss program that promised to "melt 10 lbs. in 2 days."

"Yeah, right," I mumbled.

"What's that?" Babe asked.

"Oh, nothing. You just can't believe everything you read."

From behind his newspaper, I thought I heard Babe's last customer grunt in assent.

CHAPTER 7

A few days later I got a call that the yellow crime scene tape was down, so I hustled over to the Peacock house to start work. When I arrived, I was surprised to see two cars already in the driveway. The first I recognized as Hugo Jurado's old junker. An Olds 88, it either had a custom paint job or all the rust spots had finally connected to give it an eerie, radioactive glow. The other was a baby-blue Caddy, the type favored by Floridian retirees who wear those flattering plaid pants and white belts. I knew who owned that one, too.

I walked around to the back of the house and saw Hugo and Felix Ontivares standing together, talking. They walked toward me.

"*Buenos días, amigos. ¿Qué tal?*" I asked, brandishing my high school Spanish. "Something tells me you talked to Babe."

"Yes. We couldn't find your card, so I just brought my cousin Felix to meet you. It may be at odd times because of other jobs, but we can each work fifteen or twenty hours a week until the job is done," Hugo said.

"That's wonderful. I wondered if you two knew each other. There's a ton of work to do here. If Felix is as good as you are, you won't need a lot of supervision either, so you two can be here even if I'm not."

I felt obliged to deliver the bad news sooner rather than later. "You do know I can't pay you much," I said to Felix.

"Babe told us. I can use the experience, though. And Hugo said you were a decent person to work for. We can do it."

I couldn't believe my good luck. "Once the business gets going, things will be different. I'll need full-time help and for three seasons, not just spring and summer." I mumbled some more stuff that I hoped sounded attractive, but I'd already made the sale.

We walked around the property, discussing the work. Hugo and I quickly fell into our shorthand way of speaking, half English and half Spanish, and I breathed a sigh of relief, thinking I might actually be able to tackle the Halcyon job.

Because of the body, I hadn't gotten beyond the planning stage. Our first week would be all cleanup; the area near the herb cottage would be our base of operations. Behind it, out of sight, we'd build a frame for our compost piles. All the dead plants and garden debris, unless diseased, would be recycled. Downed branches and those I planned to prune would be chipped and used as mulch. When Hugo said he could have the frame built by the end of the day, I had to restrain myself from doing a little fist pump.

"It's quite a coincidence you two are cousins."

"Well, we're not exactly cousins—that's just a figure of speech, like *paesani* in Italian. We come from the same town in Mexico, and our fathers know each other," Felix explained.

Hugo smiled and remained silent, but I thought I caught a flicker of surprise in his expression.

"I don't mean to be nosy. It's really none of my business."

"No, no, it's quite all right," Felix said. "You'd be surprised how many people wouldn't even ask. Or don't really listen when you tell them."

Clearly he was pleased that I did, but he didn't volunteer any more information, so I didn't press.

When we reached the white garden, we all fell silent. Hugo crossed himself. I didn't have any bright ideas for the space. I knew I wanted to memorialize the child that had rested there, but not to the extent that it turned into one of those morbid roadside shrines that sometimes mark fatal traffic accidents.

Just then, Guido Chiaramonte came out of the hemlocks.

"Every good garden has a toad," I muttered.

Guido strode toward us like some padrone coming to inspect the peons. Happy to avoid him, Hugo volunteered to start on the compost frame, and before I had time to say anything, he and Felix were gone.

"Mr. Chiaramonte, how are you?"

"I'm good, I'm good. My men are doing some work next door at Mrs. Fifield's. I came here earlier to see how my competition is doing."

"I'm hardly competition," I said, shaking my head. "Is that *Congressman* Fifield's home?"

"His mother's. Dina Fifield. She's a lady friend of mine," he said, making sure I didn't miss the implication.

Guido pointed to my helpers. "Are those muchachos working for you?"

"They're helping me, but it's not an exclusive arrangement. Hugo is a friend."

"If you need anything, you should let me know. I'm always happy to help my lady friends. I see your girl

Anna waiting for the bus. Sometimes I try to give her a lift." He cackled. "So far she says no, but one day she'll say yes."

Not if she's smart, I thought. "That's very kind of you, Mr. C. As a matter of fact, there is something you can do for me." *Just one little old, teensy-weensy thing.* "We won't have much of a budget for equipment. None, in fact. The Historical Society, and I personally would be very grateful for anything you'd care to donate or lend. I'm sure they'd publicly acknowledge your generosity." I added that last bit because philanthropy was not one of Guido's strong suits. He'd need every incentive to part with the smallest dibble free of charge.

"I should be angry with you. You were a *cattiva*—a bad girl—for underbidding me on this job. But if it wasn't you, I suppose it would have been someone else. Getting money out of Stapley is like trying to get into Anna's pants. Difficult but not impossible."

I still needed him, so I said nothing.

"And I couldn't have asked for a prettier bad girl to be so close by. Come and see me," Guido said. "I'm sure we can work something out."

"Would this afternoon be possible?" I suggested. "If you're not too busy?" *Fiddle-de-dee. And I promise to eat barbecue with you at Twelve Oaks!* I didn't have much experience batting my eyelashes—I probably looked like my contact lenses were bothering me—but Guido bought the Scarlett O'Hara routine. And he promised me everything but a backhoe. He'd be pissed when Felix and Hugo picked up the tools instead of me, but I'd think of some excuse.

He hitched up his pants and stood a little straighter, like some 1980s lounge lizard who had just scored big. He bent down to kiss my hand, and it was a good thing I had five inches on him, otherwise he'd have seen me roll my eyes. Then he flashed a gold-toothed smile, his version of courtliness. It took all my willpower to suppress a snort. Guido waved his hand dismissively at Felix and Hugo, then swaggered out to his Caddy, no doubt planning this afternoon's seduction scene.

Felix and Hugo were speaking back and forth in rapid-fire Spanish; I couldn't understand much. Something about trees, money, and Guido. When I heard his name, I broke in.

"I worked for Chiaramonte last season," Hugo explained. "There's a small matter of some unpaid salary."

"That's terrible. I have a few slow payers, too. Would you like me to speak with him, Hugo?"

"No, *gracias*. I will handle it. *Perdóname,*" Hugo said. "A Mr. Chappell from the *Bulletin* was here earlier. We told him you weren't here."

"Good. I'm never here for Mr. Chappell, okay? I'm already as famous as I want to be."

We spent the rest of the day planning, deciding what to rip out and what was salvageable. Then I sent them off, with my apologies, to Chiaramonte's, where Guido would probably be waiting in a satin smoking jacket with a bottle of Asti Spumante on ice and Dean Martin on the CD player. I almost wanted to see it. Almost.

CHAPTER 8

If most of the following days were spent in the garden, most of my evenings were spent either online or at the Ferguson Library ferreting out snippets of information from a variety of sources on the specific plants at Halcyon. With the help of my new best friend, Mrs. Cox, I'd just about wrung everything out of the library and the newspaper archives. She'd even contributed some useful firsthand info, like the fact that Dorothy Peacock was severely allergic to roses and didn't grow them.

Exhausted, I'd fallen into bed fully clothed the night before, so it was no surprise I was up like a shot at 4 A.M. the next morning, raring to go. It was far too early to leave for Halcyon, and, as dedicated as she was, I didn't see Mrs. Cox opening the library for me at this hour, so I took my coffee and oatmeal downstairs and turned on the computer.

If I'd had any special gift in my last career, it had been finding things. Obscure documentaries, forgotten films, foreign gems. My biggest coup had been finding a reclusive film producer hiding out in a yurt in New Mexico. He was living an ascetic lifestyle while holding the rights to his seventies' cult classics which were now, unbeknownst to him, worth two million dollars to

an interested party. He still has the yurt, but now it's
sitting next to his Taliesin-style home in Scottsdale,
Arizona.

All of my once state-of-the-art equipment was now
available smaller, cheaper, and faster, but for my pur-
poses the old setup would do. People searches had
changed, too, since I left the old job; it was a helluva
lot easier than it used to be. Disturbingly easy. People
you hated in high school could find you in minutes.
How disturbing was that?

I silently apologized to the woman whose privacy
I was about to invade, but this was business. Meeting
Dorothy Peacock, even electronically, would help me
restore her garden. At least, that was how I rationalized
poking around in her past.

"You look lovely today. You've got some letters." It
was Hugh Grant with my wake-up call. I didn't need
another mortgage, cheap prescription drugs, or the
dozen press releases from companies I no longer cared
about. And I wasn't interested in the few e-mails I suspected were from my stalker, Jon Chappell. Delete all.
If anything's important, they'll send it again; otherwise
it was relegated to Spam Heaven.

I googled Dorothy. No, not a school in British Co-
lumbia, not a porcelain doll named Dorothy from the
Peacock company, no, no—. I scrolled down through
the obviously incorrect matches.

"Hello, I think we have a winner."

The New England Women's Hall of Fame. Who
knew? *Dorothy Charlotte Peacock, b.1911(?)–d.2008.*
And they keep current.

A small picture loaded: Dorothy, in her twenties or
thirties. She looked lovely, head thrown back a bit, like
the lady in the moon, even had the necklace. Dark hair,
dark lipstick. Then the copy appeared.

Dorothy Charlotte Peacock was born on December 6, 1911(?) in Springfield, CT, to Walter and Sarah Peacock. Attended Miss Porter's School in Farmington, CT, where she studied Latin, French, German, algebra, trigonometry, geometry, chemistry, history, geography, music, and natural philosophy. In 1928, she entered Wellesley College. Upon her graduation, she embarked on a Grand Tour of Europe, eventually settling in Italy to study art history at Florence's Villa Merced. In 1933, she was joined by her younger sister, Renata (née Rose).

The sisters were forced to return from Florence in 1934 when their parents were tragically killed in a fire aboard the cruise liner *Morro Castle*. Dorothy became principal heir to the family fortune and the guardian of Renata and younger brother, William, age five.

After her return, Dorothy emerged as a significant patron of many of New England's rising artists of the time, hosting salons, exhibiting their works, and sponsoring numerous study trips abroad. At times, her home, Halcyon, was used as an art studio, and Dorothy herself gave drawing lessons to William and other talented local children.

In addition to Miss Peacock's cultural pursuits, she was a vocal and generous supporter of various feminist and community organizations—among them the Maternal Health Center, Connecticut's first birth control clinic, and the Farmington Lodge Society, founded by Miss Sarah Porter, of Miss Porter's School fame, which brought "tired and overworked" girls to Farmington for their summer vacations.

Although their home was unscathed, the hurricane of 1938 destroyed the famous Peacock gar-

dens and toppled the giant "Olivia" elm that had
graced its entrance. The two sisters spent many
years redesigning the gardens, introducing an Italian influence, which reflected on their happy days
in that country. With the help of landscape designer and herbalist Beatrix Shippington, the garden regained its place as one of Connecticut's most
notable.

In the years that followed, Dorothy's activities
were severely curtailed by the declining health of
her sister, to whom she was devoted. Together they
made numerous trips to specialists all over the
country, but Renata's health was poor for the rest
of her life.

Despite the fact that Dorothy Peacock was a
renowned beauty, she never married, remaining her
sister's constant companion until Renata's death in
1997. There are no known survivors.

Well heeled, well-educated, and with quite the bohemian
lifestyle for a single woman in the 1930s. And my
friend at the Historical Society was right: there was a
brother. But all that glamour, travel, Wellesley, the Villa
whatsit, and then she stays tethered to Halcyon for
much of the next fifty years. Trips to medical specialists
were no substitute for spending the season on the Italian
Riviera.

The Miss Porter's Web site didn't give me much except its endless athletic schedule and a recipe for an
icebox cake that Jackie Kennedy supposedly liked.
Wellesley's was a bit more promising—friends' names,
clubs, and the mildly interesting factoid that Dorothy
was the hoop-rolling winner of her senior class; that's
something to put on the old résumé. Back then, it was
supposed to mean she'd be the first of her graduating

class to marry. Guess again. I made a note of the friends'
names but doubted any of them were still alive.

I keyed in William Peacock's name, entered a search,
and went upstairs to refuel while the computer chugged
away. When I returned, the screen was full of William
Peacocks. Apparently, this name was right up there in
popularity with John Smith and Bob Potter. Assuming
Inez at the thrift shop was right again, and he was on
the West Coast, Google found no fewer than thirty who
were about the right age. Eighteen in California, six in
Oregon, two in Washington, two in Texas, and two in
Alaska.

It was also possible that *my* William Peacock was
deceased or had somehow eluded the Internet gods and
was not accessible to just anyone with a computer and
a nosy disposition. I printed out the names and addresses
and made a note to run the list by Margery Stapley at
SHS before bothering to contact any of the Mr. Peacocks.

Beatrix Shippington, the landscape architect who ad-
vised her friends, had hundreds of references. Most
were for her gardens but many linked her to her famous
clients, including an acid-tongued New York playwright
reputed to be her lover.

I was bleary-eyed from too long at the computer,
and while this background information was interesting,
it wasn't helping me decide what to plant in Halcyon's
many empty beds. I hit print again, and went upstairs to
dress.

I had one other client to see before returning to
Halcyon, a real estate chain whose seasonal planters
I looked after. Three offices, six planters. This early in
the year I had to go with annuals—boring but reliable.
And the company paid its bills on time. That would take
two hours, tops. On my way out, I grabbed all the pages

that had printed out and stuffed them in my backpack. Just as I was signing off, I heard Hugh again, but didn't bother to check my mailbox. I had pansies to plant, and Hugh would still be there when I got home.

CHAPTER 9

After two more days of hard labor digging up dead shrubs, I was looking forward to the weekend. I packed it in, said good-bye to the guys, and left for the train station. In a sea of sweaty, gray commuters, it was not hard to find Lucy Cavanaugh. Wearing dark aviator sunglasses and a large straw hat, her glossy ponytail swinging behind her, she might have been off to chat up her new film on the Croisette. If I didn't know her, I would have hated her on sight. I stuck my grubby hand through the moonroof to signal to Lucy, and she sashayed over in impossibly high sandals, with a train case and a collection of tiny shopping bags bouncing on either side.

She leaned in the passenger-side window.

"I brought my entire medicine cabinet. Whatever you need, I've got."

"Hop in first. The natives get restless at any breach of train-station etiquette."

She did a brief show-and-tell of her pharmacopoeia and saved the strongest medicine for last—Belgian chocolates, which I pronounced too beautiful to eat.

"We'll see, Miss Holier-Than-Thou Health Freak,"

Lucy said. "You manage to squeeze booze and coffee into your diet. How big a leap can it be to the really hard stuff?"

A blast from somebody's horn broke up the girl talk.

"The light was green for two seconds." Lucy turned around and gave the driver one of her best withering looks.

"As someone told me recently, we have everything here they have in the big city."

The car behind us passed on the right, and the driver flipped Lucy the bird. "Including assholes, apparently," she said.

She dug through her shopping bags until she found the item she was looking for. "This you're gonna love . . . and it has zero calories."

I was dubious.

"It's a watch with a heart-rate monitor. I saw it and it screamed Paula. I bought one, too. I've been addicted to it since I bought them. You can even see how many calories you burn while you're having sex."

"That must come in handy when your mind wanders."

On the way back to my place we caught up. Mostly gossip about former colleagues—who's changed jobs, who's sleeping with whom, who's getting fat injections.

"Make yourself comfortable," I said, unloading bags in the hallway. "I'm gonna take a quick shower."

"Good idea," Lucy said. "I thought it smelled a little horsey in the car."

Fifteen minutes later, I'd changed, but my tiny deck was positively transformed. Filled with candles, pillows, and two artfully thrown pieces of Provençal fabric Lucy had bought on her last trip to Cannes, it looked like a scene from the *Arabian Nights*. Music was playing, the wine was breathing, and Lucy had snipped a few daffodils from my back garden and stuck them in a tall blue glass.

"You're gonna make somebody a damn fine little wife one day."

"I'm still trying to get you to come to Cannes with me for the next festival. Eat fatty foods, drink to wretched excess, ward off the advances of swarthy foreigners? Sound good? There'll be exercise, too. . . . You can climb up that damn hill to the old part of town two or three times a day."

"I can do all that in Connecticut and not have to deal with the cheese and the chain-smokers. Not this year," I said. "Halcyon is a make-or-break opportunity for me. And it's gotten off to a rocky start."

"To say the least. And I'm here for you, pumpkin." She patted my hand.

"I'm glad to hear you say that, because I desperately need you this weekend." At this point, I thought it wise not to mention it was for manual labor. I poured her some wine and gave her all the gory details of my find.

She voted for Dorothy Peacock as the mother. "I took care of a sick relative once. When I wasn't feeling like a martyr, I wanted to strangle her. Believe me, it's draining. The old girl probably just needed to kick back a bit, got caught unprepared, and had an unfortunate accident. Then the baby didn't make it. *Muy trágico,* but I think it happened a lot in the old days. High infant mortality rates back then."

"I don't know. From what I've read about her, a rebel, sure, but not crazy enough to bury a baby in the backyard with the pachysandra."

"All right, what do *you* think's going on in Cabot Cove, Jessica?"

"There's something going on, but I'm not sure what."

I sipped my wine. "I bet that woman I met could tell some tales. The mystery lady with the shawl."

"Yeah, yeah. What about the cops? Spill."

"Well, one of them is kind of cute. My type. Smart, funny. The tubby one."

"And?"

"And nothing. We've exchanged—" I paused, searching for the right word.

"What? The secret handshake? Precious bodily fluids?"

"No, you idiot. Meaningful glances," I said carefully. "Badinage," I said, dragging out the word for effect.

We were laughing by then and were more than a little toasted. Lucy polished off the rest of the wine while I went in the house for another bottle.

Inside, I realized I had the munchies, so I threw together a quick meal—cheese and crackers, tofu, and olives, and balanced them on a large painted tray.

"Want to give me a hand in here?" I yelled.

"Sure," she said, opening the slider. "How's the wacky neighbor? Seems quiet."

"I'm almost afraid to say it, but he's not so bad this year. I think someone is showing him some love."

I put the tray down, and we started to pick.

"That's all he needed, a little nooky?" She poked through the olives for a juicy Sicilian.

I shrugged. "Who knows? There are still loud bursts of music, but less often and for shorter periods of time."

"So he's either making the naked pretzel or just dispatching his victims more quickly."

My ex had said only twelve-year-old girls needed to squeal every time they jumped in a pool. Chris thought the neighbor was a perv. I simply assumed he was a jerk.

"Let's get back to your body," Lucy said.

"One hundred and sixteen pounds, body fat twelve percent. Higher than it used to be."

"Has anyone suggested that you might be getting just the tiniest bit obsessive about this fitness regimen? I meant the *dead* body, not the annoyingly lean and toned one I'm looking at."

I reached daintily for an olive.

"What about sex in the big city? Don't I get to hear about that?"

"I don't kiss and tell."

The wine nearly came out of my nose. "Since when?"

"I don't know—more meaningless, bouncing-off-the-walls sex? Who needs it?"

"Didn't you just say a little nooky works for most people?"

"Did I? Well, you know I'm not most people."

Now *we* were giggling like twelve-year-old girls, and it barely registered when an engine started, a car sputtered and quietly crept away.

CHAPTER 10

Lucy's face was inches from my own.

"There's a strange woman downstairs," she whispered, leaning over me, eyes wide.

"Some would say there are two strange women upstairs," I said, raising myself onto my elbows.

"This one has two black eyes."

That got my attention. I sat up.

"Anna? *¿Está aquí?*"

Anna responded in the slow, third-grade-level Spanish she knew I could understand.

"That's Anna Peña," I told Lucy.

"Annapurna?"

"Peña, you idiot. Let me get up."

Lucy had been up for hours, plowing through a month's worth of *Hollywood Reporter*s that she'd brought with her, while I slept off a hangover. She looked crisp and polished in a New Yorker's idea of country gear—corduroys, turtleneck tucked in, with a belt. By way of contrast, I looked and felt rumpled, like I'd been on a bender.

"Why does she have two black eyes?"

"She's had her eyelids tattooed."

"Ouch."

"Make some coffee, I'll meet you in the kitchen."

I dressed quickly, avoiding the mirror as much as possible.

"You've turned into a lightweight," Lucy said, pouring coffee as I stumbled into the kitchen.

"I just don't put away three bottles of wine on a regular basis anymore."

"My condolences. Here, drink up." She handed me a mug. "I know," she said nostalgically, "our ranks are dwindling. Everyone's so healthy these days, it's depressing."

"Anything else depressing you?"

She shook her head. "I'm fine," she said, but her face had darkened.

"Bull. I know how *I* feel when I say I'm fine, and it's rarely fine."

"Work. All the same people, hawking all the same stuff. I did an enormous amount of work on that kids' show and then it fell through. Kaput. So then you end up pitching another remake of some classic you hated in school or, worse, reality shows. Sometimes it all seems so stupid. Plus . . . I'm not the cutest little girl in the room anymore."

"Sure you are," I said in true sisterly fashion. "And you definitely are this morning," I whispered, "compared to me and Anna. It's just preshow anxiety. You're worried you won't find the next big thing, but you always do." That cheered her up.

"We'll go to the Paradise," I said. "I guarantee you'll feel better after you meet Babe. She's my new role model."

Just then Anna walked in. She did, indeed, look strange. A large woman, she was partial to stretchy, pastel leggings and tiny jeweled slippers, whatever the weather. Her denim jacket was bedazzled in elaborate patterns.

But what had startled Lucy were Anna's eyes. They were tattooed with two stripes of permanent eyeliner, one black and one green. And her eyebrows were filled in in solid chocolate brown, giving her a look of perpetual surprise. Then came the lips—*bee-stung* is a word that's often used—these looked more like rattlesnake bites. Until all the swelling went down, she'd look like a Maori who'd been in a fight and lost big.

I told Lucy I needed five minutes more to regroup before we left for the diner, then took my coffee and left the pair of them to what would undoubtedly be an unusual conversation.

Five minutes was wildly optimistic. My face was puffy. I hadn't had a good haircut in months. Roberto, astronomically priced stylist to the mid-level media types in New York, kept canceling my appointments. I should have known it was a mistake to leave a phone number with anything other than a New York area code.

I was fanatical about working out, but all that maintenance stuff—manicures, pedicures, facials—I hadn't done any of that for ages, and it showed. Thank God for Stila. I concealed, blushed, curled, and was back in the kitchen in fifteen minutes.

"Loaded for bear?" Lucy asked, after eyeing the paint job. "Do we happen to be stopping by the police station, or is all this for Felix, the handsome, brooding groundskeeper?"

"Too much?"

"No, I like it. And it beats the hell out of that American Gothic look you were sporting yesterday."

Lucy seemed to be her old self again.

We watched Anna waddle back downstairs to the

office, comfortable in her skin, her light, sweet coffee in one hand and a bag of buttered Portuguese rolls in the other. "She may be *my* new role model," Lucy said. "The mythical woman who doesn't think she needs to lose ten pounds I've heard tell of. And why don't *I* have someone who wants to help me and not get paid for it?"

"C'mon, let the games begin," I said. "I want you to meet the cast of characters."

"Sure, we can figure out who the baby is this weekend. Last night, I decided the mother was Dorothy Peacock. Now I'm leaning toward the next-door neighbor, this Congressman Fifield as the daddy."

"And why do we think that?"

"He's a congressman. Need I say more?" Close to perfect, Lucy fluffed her hair, blotted her lipstick, and was ready to go. "Lead on."

The Paradise Diner's new thought for the week was IT'S DIFFICULT TO LOSE A SPOUSE—BUT NOT IMPOSSIBLE. Catchy. The place was half-empty.

"Health department been here again?" I asked, sliding onto a counter stool in front of Babe.

"Bite your tongue, Ms. Green Jeans. You look good. What happened?"

"Ms. Green Jeans? Where'd that come from? Oh, let me guess—*Mom?*"

"You should be flattered. Not everyone gets a cop nickname. Someone must like you."

"Someone must *like* me? I must be having flashbacks to junior high school. This is Lucy. She's an old friend, helping me with the garden; the valuable fashion and makeup tips are a bonus."

"You do nice work. I can see an improvement already," Babe said, looking me up and down.

"Just how bad do I usually look?" I asked, not really wanting an answer.

"I'm helping with the garden? I thought I was here for a Ralph Lauren weekend. Read the paper, sit in a hammock, maybe get to wear all these tweedy duds I buy and never take the tags off."

"What'll you two have?" Babe asked.

"Turkey on rye, no mayo, and an iced coffee for me."

"You're having a turkey sandwich for breakfast?" Lucy asked.

"It's not breakfast, it's *brunch*. And it's never too early for turkey. It's one of God's perfect foods."

"To each his own." Lucy was more adventurous and went for the blueberry pancakes with ham and Pete's special potatoes.

"I like to see a girl with a healthy appetite," Babe said approvingly. "You're not going to throw it up after, are you?"

"Of course not. I've *cleansed,* but I've never *barfed* intentionally," Lucy said, offended at the suggestion and making sure we saw the distinction. Lucy leaned over the counter and grabbed a copy of that morning's *Bulletin,* skimming the latest articles for mentions of me.

"Look at this." She laughed. "There was a candy wrapper stuck in with all the paper in the box you found. Have you been sneaking junk food on the side?"

"Let me see that." I took the paper. It was true. Crumpled in with the rest of the packing material was a Cadbury's chocolate wrapper.

"So it was murder?" Lucy said. "Death by chocolate?"

"You're cracking yourself up, aren't you? A stray, crumpled piece of paper that probably has nothing to do with this matter." Still, it was odd. And maybe a tiny clue. Other than that, there was little new information on the case, just a packaged statement from Win Fifield's office.

As we ate, Lucy launched into her theories from the night before. Convinced she'd found the father, she peppered Babe with questions about Congressman Fifield. Did she know him? How old was he? What kind of kid had he been?

"Easy, tiger. Babe may not even know him."

"Oh, I know the little pisher, all right. He's in his forties now. Terrible *brownnoser* as a kid. Even worse as a teenager. The Young Prince," she added for emphasis. "Thought all the girls should be tickled pink to jump into the backseat of his convertible. I hear more than a few did, and they were sorry afterward.

"When he first ran for office, he tried to park himself here, to glad-hand and kiss babies. Tried to use my boys as campaign props since he didn't have his own kids. I changed the marquee outside to read IF CON IS THE OPPOSITE OF PRO, IS CONGRESS THE OPPOSITE OF PROGRESS? That kept him away."

"Your boys?" Lucy asked.

"I've got twins. Dylan's in Colorado, studying to become a meteorologist. Daltry's in LA, trying to make it in the movies." She grabbed a few menus and left to seat some new arrivals.

"Dylan and Daltry?" Lucy whispered, making a face and playing air guitar with her fork.

"I saw that, honey," Babe said over her shoulder, smiling. "It could have been a lot worse; we were gonna call them Rainbow and Democracy."

"They did luck out," Lucy said, digging into her carbfest. "Your congressman sounds like a slug, but I may be wrong about him. If one of the sisters was the mother, we might have to eliminate young Mr. Fifield. He may be a sleazoid, but I don't see a stud like him going after sixty- or seventy-year-old booty."

"I'm not convinced it *was* one of the sisters," I said.

"If that baby was mummified, the mother could be anyone. The list of suspects can go back five years or fifty. Unless the body was tested, it would look pretty much the same. And if it had been moved it might not even have anything to do with the Peacocks."

"That's right. Your cop friend didn't know, did he?"

"Nope."

Babe came back with more coffee.

"Did they make Cadbury's fifty years ago?" Lucy asked.

"I was starting to like you," Babe said. "Am I supposed to have firsthand knowledge of that?"

I explained about the candy wrapper found with the baby. "Just another thing the cops don't know—to go with the mother, the father." I counted off the question marks that remained. "They don't know much. But someone must. Someone always knows."

"Like who?" Lucy asked, sopping up the last puddles of maple syrup on her plate.

I sipped my coffee and looked around, frustrated with all these idle theories. A woman with a stroller struggled with the door; I almost got up to help her. When she finally cleared it, she held it open for the person behind her.

"Like, like—her," I said, stunned.

CHAPTER 11

The woman sat at the first table near the long picture window in the Paradise Diner. From there you could see the lake and whatever wildlife happened to be visiting, but she ignored the view, concentrating instead on unwrapping her shawl so that it didn't graze the sticky condiments on the tiny pedestal table. She looked around frequently, as if expecting someone.

I motioned for Babe to come down to my end of the counter. "Do you know the woman in the corner?"

"Never seen her before."

"That's her—that's the woman I met at the house!" I hoped I was whispering, but I couldn't be sure.

"Go across the street and get O'Malley," Lucy said to me. "I'll check her out." She grabbed a menu and a pad, as if to take the woman's order.

I pretended to go to the ladies' room but dashed out the side door, across the street, and up the stairs to the police station, nearly getting creamed by an SNET truck in the process. O'Malley watched through the mini blinds.

"I could ticket you for jaywalking, you know."

"She's there," I said breathlessly, pointing to the diner.

"Who's where?" he said casually.

"The woman I saw at the Peacock house is across the street at the Paradise. I thought you were a cop. Are you guys really cops," I said, looking around, exasperated, "or am I channeling an old *Barney Miller* episode? Where's the Asian guy who looked like Robert Mitchum?"

"Calm down," he said, leading me to a small private office in the rear of the station. The other cops looked amused. "She was just in here to make a statement," he told me, closing the door. "I didn't realize we had to notify you every time we interviewed someone."

I sat on the sofa, refusing the coffee he offered me. "Outburst over?"

"Can you at least tell me what she said?" I asked.

"Why don't you ask her yourself? Ms. Gibson's a lovely woman. C'mon, I'll walk you back."

He gripped my arm as we walked down the steps and crossed the street to the diner. "Now you've got me jaywalking. You're a bad influence, aren't you?"

Babe and Lucy looked up as we came in.

"That's right, Officer. Paula ran out before paying her bill. You gonna lock her up?"

I looked around. The lunchtime crowd was going strong, but the mystery woman was gone. Lucy gave O'Malley the once-over.

"Maybe I'll get her to perform a little community service," O'Malley said. "I need to determine whether or not she's a repeat offender first," he added, somewhat suggestively.

"I love it when people talk about me as if I'm not here." I pulled my arm away from his.

I rejoined Lucy at the counter, where my untouched turkey sandwich was still sitting.

"Go ahead," Lucy said, motioning to the sandwich.

"Eat. Babe and I will fill you in. That was Hillary Gibson. Her identity was confirmed by her old sweetie, Gerald Fraser, your new diner buddy and, coincidentally, the person she was waiting for. Here are her numbers," she said triumphantly. She wiggled a slip of paper in the air and handed it to me with no small measure of satisfaction.

"You almost got away with the sneaky exit, but that truck driver had a few choice words for you which we all couldn't help but hear." She pointed to a lummox hunched over a mountain of food. "He's over there. I'm sure he'd be happy to repeat them."

"Maybe later."

"Anyway, Hillary decided this might not be the best place for a quiet tête-à-tête with the old flame, so they split. She said you could call her. They did drop *one* piece of news you should find interesting. Hillary and Gerald don't think the baby belongs to either of the sisters, and do you know why?"

"I've got a pretty good idea," I said.

"I'm not sure we should have this conversation here in the diner," Mike said.

"We've already had some of it," Lucy continued. "They were both very fond of Dorothy and Renata, and they're concerned that people are thinking the worst of the two women. Which is a hell of a lot worse than the truth."

I'd been on the receiving end of Lucy's dramatic reconstructions since we were fifteen and knew this could take a while. Besides, I thought I knew where she was going. I took a bite of my sandwich during her pregnant pause. Pete the cook had struck again; tough as shoe leather.

I swallowed hard and put down the sandwich. "They

weren't sisters, were they? Babe, can I have a little Russian dressing on the side? Fat-free, if you have."

"Would you mind repeating that?"

"Russian dressing. Fat-free?"

She gave me her are-you-kidding look, and handed me a paper cup of gelatinous orange goop, then just stared.

"All right, Miss Marple, how did you know?" O'Malley asked.

"No, no, no, no, nooo, too old," I said, referring to the nickname. "Try again." I dipped a tiny corner of my sandwich into the orange goop. I remembered this stuff. It wasn't as bad as it looked.

Now *I* was milking it. If this wasn't "Colonel Mustard in the kitchen with a knife," it was damn close. Through the window, I could see Officer Guzman trying to get O'Malley's attention. I let him know and reluctantly he got up to leave.

"To be continued," he said.

As the door slammed behind him, Babe said, "He's taken the bait. Now it's just a matter of reeling him in, isn't it?"

"I told you, I'm not interested in him. Not in that way."

There may have been people who wanted more coffee, or their checks, but Babe wasn't moving. "Talk," she said.

"Dorothy's sister was christened Rose. She goes to visit Dorothy in Italy and returns calling herself Renata. That alone might have been a tip-off, but the locals apparently considered it a youthful affectation."

"She was so taken by all things Italian, she was *reborn*. I can dig it," Babe said. "After my first trip to Mexico, I called myself Juanita for months."

"And it was hardly the hot issue in 1934," I added. "Their parents had died; people were just glad she wasn't closing the family business. You guys ever hear of the Depression?"

Even more telling were the clippings I'd found at the Ferguson Library. Although similar, the faded images of Renata, before and after the trip to Italy, seemed to reveal two different personalities. Before the trip, the younger sister could always be seen with a big crooked smile, hanging on to her older sister's hand or watching lovingly from the sidelines. After they returned, there were fewer photographs. And Rose/Renata always seemed to have her face turned from the camera or covered by a heavy veil or shadowed by a wide-brimmed hat.

"Maybe she was just growing up and at an awkward age, or maybe she didn't *want* to be photographed," I said. "And all the trips, the secrecy, the mysterious illness?" I continued. "Whatever it was, I wouldn't mind getting it—she lived well into her eighties. I'm guessing it wasn't Rose. It was a different woman, and she and Dorothy were lovers."

"Well done," Lucy said. "Hillary called it a Boston marriage; she didn't elaborate. Why didn't you say something?"

"It was just a guess. Besides, it wasn't up to me to out them."

"Well, they may have been gay, but it doesn't mean one of them couldn't have had a child," Lucy said.

Babe broke in. "David Crosby's not that old. We're not talking Melissa Etheridge. We're talking *the love that dares not speak its name,* not the love that gives interviews. Those days, straight or gay, women didn't just go off and have babies on their own, even if they were financially independent enough to do it. It wasn't so easy being a little different in the thirties and forties. Not that I was there, of course."

"Either one of those women was raped—," Babe continued.

"Or it really *was* someone else's baby. And it's sounding less like an indiscretion and more like a crime," I added.

CHAPTER 12

"Are you going to do anything about it?"

"About what?" I asked, keeping my eyes on the road.

"The sisters?"

"Let O'Malley handle it. My attempts to be helpful have gotten me nothing but wisecracks and condescension. If I wanted that, I could have stayed in television. Besides, I've got a garden to restore, and I've given myself sixty days to do it. Speaking of which . . ."

We pulled into the driveway at Halcyon, where once again my helpers had preceded me.

"Just like my place," Lucy said in amazement.

Behind the house, the true scope of the job revealed itself. In the distance we saw Hugo and Felix working.

"This place is huge. You do need help."

The compost bins had been built, and Hugo and Felix had already cleared away most of the large fallen branches and debris. Guido Chiaramonte's borrowed chipper hummed in the background.

"*Buenos días,*" I yelled.

Hugo kept working, but Felix jogged over to greet us. Despite the cool morning, he wore just a sleeveless T-shirt and well-fitting black jeans, which showed his athletic body to full advantage.

"Oh, my," Lucy purred.

"*Días. ¿Qué tal?*" he asked. He wiped the sweat from his forehead with a bandanna. Lucy looked like she wanted to make soup with it.

She had morphed into something I'd seen on the Nature Channel—the blue-footed booby pointing to the sky to signal her interest in a potential mate. I was irrationally annoyed. And, just as irrationally, relieved when the object of that interest made a few polite noises in Lucy's direction, then left.

"Very nice," she drawled as he walked away.

"I really hadn't noticed."

"Right. I can say this now. I was a little worried you'd lost your mind—burying yourself up here in *Green Acres* land—all compost and Arnold the pig—but I was wrong. This place is like daytime television, a *cauldron of seething passions*. Who needs the New York bar scene? One guy carries a weapon and the other is good with his hands—nudge, nudge, wink, wink."

"Keep it down. These guys work for me."

"And that's a whole *other* dimension . . . Mistress Paula."

She lowered her voice. "All right, all right. I'm just beginning to see the attraction to country living, that's all. What am I doing here, anyway? Can I really help or did you just want to show off Don Felix?"

I assured Lucy her help was desperately needed, and led her over to the brick terrace and a large green nylon bag held open by circular wires on the top and bottom.

"This is a tip bag. You pull the weeds from in between the bricks and throw them in the tip bag."

"And when I'm bored in five minutes, then what do I do?"

"Then you find the Zen in weeding. You'll love it."

I tossed Lucy a foam knee pad and a pair of gloves,

and set about finding the Zen in cleaning out the herb-drying cottage. A shallow porch held an old-fashioned bistro table and a pair of ice cream chairs. Inside, hanging from the rafters were last season's herbs, tied into bundles and labeled with names and dates. How the old girl got them up there at her age was beyond me. Drying racks, strainers, baskets, and quart jars lined the walls of the thirty-by-thirty-foot cottage. Apart from a fine mesh of cobwebs, Dorothy might have been coming back any minute.

Five hours later, weed and cobweb free, Lucy and I packed up, sent the boys home, and drove back to my place.

"I don't know if I burned any calories, kneeling for hours on end. Are you sure that's a workout?"

"Check your monitor."

"Shoot, I forgot to set it for workout." She inspected her biceps in the mirror, looking for a pump.

"Three hundred calories per hour," I said, "trust me. Next weekend I may let you mow. That's four hundred calories."

"No can do," she said, still checking out her arms, not yet convinced of gardening's therapeutic benefits. "Going to Cannes, remember? But you've got me tomorrow, and if you ever need a firm hand with Senor Felix, I'm always available." A true friend.

After a second day of calorie-burning garden work, I deposited Lucy at the train station, extracting her promise to come back in a few weeks for the Historical Society's fund-raiser.

"Sure. Keep me posted on your baby, okay?"

"Not my baby. Not my job, remember?"

I took the scenic route home from the train station, stopping at Halcyon for one last look. Despite forty-eight hours of grumbling, Lucy had done a thorough job and even managed to weed most of the stone planters dotting the terrace. Hugo and Felix had raked, chipped, and sorted the debris into various piles, all of which would see active duty elsewhere in the garden, and near the maze a haphazard pile of rough-hewn flagstones had been turned into an informal stacked-stone retaining wall.

I hadn't given the greenhouse much thought, but now that the path was cleared, I ventured inside. It smelled of damp and rotting vegetation but in a not entirely unpleasant way. The glass panels were filthy, a few were cracked, and the chains that lifted open the heavy glass ceiling were encrusted with gunk.

Potting tables were littered with pot shards and faded plant tags and seed packets, and everything was covered with cobwebs. A three-foot copper stand with spikes on the top looked like a gladiator's mace, but turned out to be nothing more sinister than an antique sprinkler.

In one corner stood a small cedar hutch. Instinctively I stuck out my hand to open it, then drew back—but what were the odds of finding another corpse?

Cautiously I turned the handle on the door, and pulled it open. Stillness, then a faint fluttering sound turned to Hitchcockian birdlike flapping. Hundreds of moths flew out of their resting place and into my face and hair. My scream caused one of the moths to be sucked into my mouth; I spit it out and flailed my arms spastically, falling on my butt, scattering pots and tools and knocking over a table, which hit the door and caused it to slam shut.

"Thank god there are no witnesses," I said out loud, feeling foolish and shaking off the few remaining moths. Most of them flew to the domed roof, out of my reach. I made a futile attempt to dislodge them with a broom but decided to deal with them the next day when I could borrow a ladder.

I had about forty-five minutes of daylight left. I swept the floors and the tables, organized the pots by size, inventoried the usable hand tools, and tried to ignore a family of mice I'd sent scurrying when I moved a large unfolded tarp. They'd elicited another involuntary yelp.

Around eight o'clock, in the fading light, I decided to pack it in. I was suddenly overcome by a wave of fatigue, and I was fantasizing about a nice hot bath and a glass of wine, not necessarily in that order.

I slung my backpack over my shoulder and reached for the door handle. It was stuck. And no amount of jiggling would unstick it. I looked for a tool or screwdriver to take the doorknob off—nothing. I searched the greenhouse from top to bottom. There were a few cracked glass panels, but none missing—nothing I could wriggle out of. And the foundation was solid stone.

Forty minutes later, it was pitch-black, getting colder, and I was running out of options. Despite my embarrassment, I decided to call Babe at the diner, to see if she or Chloe could rescue me. Dead battery. So much for that idea. One of the unintended consequences of rarely using your cell is that it will inevitably run out of juice without your noticing. Until you need it.

I didn't trust myself to break any of the glass panels without bringing the whole damn house crashing down around me. Besides, despite its condition, it was exquisite, so, bone tired, I did the only other thing I could think of. Using my backpack as a pillow, I crawled onto the potting table, pulled the dusty tarp over me, and succumbed to what someone once called "the divine stupidity of sleep."

CHAPTER 13

Something brushed my face, and I drowsily flicked it away. Then I remembered where I was and jumped up, throwing off the dirty tarp. My four-legged roommates fled, and I scrambled into an upright position.

"Who's there? Is someone there?" I worked hard to keep the fear out of my voice, only marginally succeeding.

"It is me . . . Felix." He playfully shone a flashlight under his chin, the way we did when we were kids and wanted to scare someone. "I was driving by and saw your car was still here."

"Thank goodness," I said, relieved. "I got locked in." I slid off the table and dusted myself off. "What time is it?"

"About eleven. Have you been here all this time?"

"Well, I did some work, then I couldn't get out. I didn't want to break any of the glass—probably cost a mint to replace." I tried to sound as if it was perfectly reasonable for me to be sleeping in the greenhouse.

"Why didn't you call someone?"

"Phone's dead." I closed my eyes and rotated my head, working out the kinks that had set in from sleeping on the damp wooden table. I rubbed my hands up and down my arms to warm myself while I gave Felix a long look.

"I should go home," I said.

"I'll escort you."

"You'll *escort* me? You're not exactly who you appear to be, are you?" I said.

"Who do I appear to be?"

"Don't be cute. I'm a little cranky right now."

"You're probably hungry. I would suggest that we get something to eat, but you may want to freshen up first," he said tactfully.

A glimpse of my reflection in the greenhouse glass told me I had what Lucy heartlessly referred to as stroke face. I fluffed out my flattened hair and tried to inconspicuously rub out the sleep wrinkles on my face. Felix reached over and plucked something out of my hair.

"What was that?"

"Nothing. A small passenger," he said.

Felix followed me home, where I'd clean up and we could have a bite and talk. Once there, I pointed him toward the bar and told him to help himself. After a quick shower, I joined him in the living room.

"I never realized your hair was so long. You look quite different."

"I usually wear it up in the garden or under a hat," I said awkwardly, feeling suddenly female. "It's just easier that way."

Felix showed me the bottle of wine he'd chosen. "I wasn't sure if I should open this one. I didn't know if you were saving it for a special occasion."

"Go ahead. I'm clueless when it comes to wine. After the first glass, they all taste the same to me. If that's a good one, someone must have brought it over."

Felix uncorked the bottle and explained in great detail what the wine was and how it was made, while I put water on for pasta. Ordinarily, I find oenophiles obnoxious, but Felix wasn't trying to impress me with his worldliness; he was simply giving information. I got out some bread and olive oil to munch on while we waited for the water to boil.

"So you're a famous Mexican restaurant critic, just up here reviewing dining options in Fairfield County?"

"Not exactly."

"I'm listening."

"Well, I *am* from Cuernavaca, near Temixco, Hugo's hometown. I *did* know him there, and our fathers *did* know each other."

"You're going to have to do better than that," I said, ripping off a hunk of bread and swishing it in the olive oil.

Felix and Hugo did meet when they were kids, that much had been true. Then he told me the rest. Hugo's father, Ruben, was, and still is, the driver and mechanic on the Ontivares estate.

Felix's dad, Oswaldo, sold sodas from a wagon as a kid. He grew up to become a successful soft-drink distributor; then he branched out into beer, wine, and groceries. Several years ago Oswaldo Ontivares died of a heart attack in the arms of his underage mistress, who had just shown him the *00, 00* she'd had tattooed on each of her butt cheeks in his honor. Mexico's president attended the funeral.

Grief-stricken, Felix's sister Maria Angela vowed to abandon her jet-set lifestyle to take over the family business, and, to everyone's surprise, she revealed not just a talent for food and beverage distribution but a broader business sense as well. She even managed to parlay her close personal friendship with a famous telenovela star into a controlling stake in one of Mexico's fast-growing media companies, nearly doubling the family fortune.

"And you kept busy and fit, not by mowing lawns and weeding, as I'd assumed, but by playing tennis and polo and swimming in your indoor Olympic-sized pool?"

"I wasn't a complete ne'er-do-well. I was pre-med at Rice for a year," he justified. "When Maria started to do so well, my competitive side took over. I returned to school as a business major at the University of Texas at Austin. Got my MBA there," he added.

"I was visiting business associates in Greenwich. After a party that went pretty late or, I should say, early, I dropped some friends off at the train station in downtown Springfield. I stopped for coffee and saw a huge crowd of men milling about on the corner. Someone asked me if I wanted to work. I graciously declined, but the next morning I went back and looked up Hugo."

I wasn't sure I believed him. "Of course," I said, "it makes perfect sense for a handsome, wealthy Mexican MBA to be mowing lawns in Connecticut. I don't know why I didn't see it."

"Don't be too hard on yourself. You saw more than most. We are invisible to most people north of the border. We mow your lawns, clean your pools, wipe your kids' runny noses, and half the time you are mispronouncing our names or don't even know them. You don't know if we are from Mexico, Guatemala, or the Dominican Republic. We could disappear like a puff of smoke and never be missed because the next crop of workers would be there to replace us." He blew through his lips as if extinguishing a candle.

"Most people don't even bother to learn the most basic phrases in Spanish," he said, holding his glass carefully by the stem and taking a sip of wine. "That's why I find it so charming to hear you mangle the language of my ancestors."

I took a big swallow of my wine. I was prepared for some revelation but not a sociology lesson from a trust-fund liberal with a string of polo ponies. "Look, we can have a nice long chat someday about the class system in both our countries. You're right, it sucks, but it doesn't seem to have hurt you any, and, uh, you haven't exactly answered my question. What am I missing here?"

"Do you know how many Mexicans come north for work every year?" he asked, not waiting for an answer. "There are six million in the States right now, and almost all of them left family members back home. It's an integral part of the Mexican experience. Everyone knows someone who's made the trip to el Norte. Since I accidentally got the opportunity, I thought I'd see it firsthand."

"You sound like you're running for office," I said, taking another swig. "Wait a minute—that's it, isn't it? You're planning to run for office in Mexico, so you wanted to see how the *little* people live? Who's in *Upstairs, Downstairs* territory now?"

"Would you prefer that I remain the poor but proud laborer?" he teased. "The noble savage?"

"I'd prefer you not be the spoiled playboy who's slumming. And to be totally selfish, I'd prefer you be someone I can count on. I have a job to do. I have commitments."

"Don't be angry with me. I never intended to deceive anyone. This whole thing was an accident. I came here for a bachelor party. But it's been a valuable learning experience for me; I'm glad I stayed," he said. "I give you my word I will stay to finish the garden. And I will get some of the other men to give us hours—I'll pay them from my campaign war chest," he joked. "Future constituents."

"Let's not get crazy." The water was bubbling over onto the stove, so I jumped up to turn down the heat.

"Can I help?" he asked.

"Sure."

Felix found dishes, napkins, and place mats while I finished cooking. When it was ready, he encrusted his pasta with red pepper.

"Sure that's hot enough?"

"It won't be. Now I will tell you two things that will make you angry all over again."

I looked up and waited for the other shoe to drop. He's married with five kids? *"¿Cómo fue ahora?"* I asked cautiously.

"Hugo speaks English better than I do. He taught me how to read it when we were kids."

"You're kidding?"

He shook his head. Then he reached into his pocket and took something out. A green plastic tie, about twelve inches long.

"I'm out of bread?"

"This was on the door handle. Your greenhouse mishap? It was not an accident."

"Someone tried to kill me with a piece of twist tie?"

"Not kill you. Scare you. Or at least put you out of commission for a while. And it's not a twist tie."

It wasn't. It was a thick plastic tie, the kind used to secure electric cords on factory-packed appliances. The kind you can't pull apart.

"Don't be silly. It must have already been on the door handle and got caught when I fell down in the greenhouse," I said reasonably. "Besides, who'd want to scare me? A rival gardener? If one of them really wanted to scare me, he'd bring over a bucket of banana slugs. Have you ever seen them?"

"Okay. Here. Keep it as a souvenir." He finished his wine and pushed away from the table. "Now it's late, and I have a new, very demanding boss to answer to."

"You didn't eat much."

"Well, midnight is a little late for dinner, maybe not for Brazilians, but it is for humble Mexican laborers. I'd appreciate it if you don't tell anyone my little secret just yet."

He took his time walking downstairs. At the door, he brushed my still-damp hair away from my face and kissed me on the cheek. Then he bent down again, aiming for the lips this time. I tensed a bit, but let it happen.

"*Buenas noches, maestra.* Don't forget to charge your phone."

I closed the door behind me and let out a deep breath. I was dying to tell Lucy. I plugged in my phone, but it was too late to call without either worrying her or interrupting something, so I went online on the outside chance she'd be surfing. No luck. I deleted the daily messages from that pain-in-the-ass reporter from the *Bulletin,* and forty-seven junk e-mails. Although it's as risky as unprotected sex, sometimes I take a chance and check out the unsolicited gardening or fitness ones: *Build a pond in two hours! Check your body mass index.* I took a flyer and clicked on *Free garden plans!* and waited for the message to load. . . .

Framed by squiggly lines meant to look like electricity, it was a picture of a shovel inside a red circle with a slash through it. *Here's a plan . . . be careful where you dig.*

CHAPTER 14

The smell of French toast and frying bacon hung in the air like smog; it was warm and welcoming. I was getting to love it. After only two hours' sleep, I climbed on the counter stool slowly, carefully, like an old person afraid of breaking something. Without my asking, Babe brought me a mug of coffee and told Pete to fix me the morning-after special.

"What happened to you?"

"You want the long version or the short version?"

"Start with the short version."

Counting off on my fingers I said, "Worked like a dog yesterday, got trapped in the greenhouse, got rescued by Felix, got kissed by Felix, got no sleep—except for a few hours on a moldy potting table. Oh, yeah, and I got another dozen messages from that jerk at the *Bulletin* and a weird e-mail."

"Does the 'no sleep' mean what I hope it means?"

"Dream on," I said, twisting my torso in a long stretch. I could hear the bones and muscles creak.

"I know a great massage therapist who can fix that."

We both waited for the caffeine to kick in.

"Since there doesn't seem to be anything juicier, tell me about the kiss," she said.

"It was friendly. Mostly." I guzzled the coffee like it was a drug.

"Tongue?"

"Have you ever had a friendly tongue kiss?"

"Yes, as a matter of fact, but that's my story. I want to hear yours."

I told Babe about the previous night, leaving out Felix's family history. If it was true, it wasn't up to me to blow his cover, and if it wasn't, I'd feel like less of sap for having believed him. "He followed me home to make sure I was okay. We talked, had some wine, a little food, and then, as he was leaving"—I leaned in, and lowered my voice—"he kissed me."

"Bodies touch?" she asked.

"I didn't film it. It was fast. . . . They may have touched. A little. They touched a little."

"So, now that he's followed you home, are you going to keep him?"

"Hey, the only things I want to keep right now are my house, my business, and my sanity. The last thing I need is another complication. Ever since the baby . . ." I sputtered. "Finding that body has been like *having* a baby." I looked around surreptitiously. "Last night Felix suggested I was locked in the greenhouse intentionally. And I got a stupid crank e-mail from someone trying to scare me. That'll teach me to leave my business card just anywhere. Now I'll have to change my e-mail address, and that'll be another pain in the ass." Even I knew I was escalating into hysteria.

"I'm just as curious as the next person," I said, breathing deeply to calm myself, "but if Springfield's finest think there's no case here, there's no case, right? People around here are getting carried away."

"Settle down. Someone might think you're one of the people getting carried away."

Mercifully, the food came. Who knew cinnamon toast had such curative powers? It was no substitute for a hot tub and a good night's sleep, but it helped bring me back to center. And if my mouth was full, it reduced the chances that I'd have another meltdown.

Babe plucked something from the Paradise bulletin board and dropped it near my plate. "Despite the fact that you've maligned my bulletin board, I'm gonna give you this. Here's the name and number for that massage therapist. Make an appointment, honey. You need it." She patted my hand and went off to chat with other more rational customers.

I did need it. And I needed something else I didn't like to admit. Sex had never been all that great between Chris and me; there were more than a few nights I was left staring at the ceiling thinking *clematis* when I should have been thinking *clitoris*. Especially toward the end. Even so, when you don't have it, you damn well miss it.

Exercise helped, but recently working in the garden had taken the place of serious weight training, so I was also missing *that* endorphin high. I decided to go back home and pump some iron before heading to Halcyon.

"Babe, I don't know what Pete put on this bread, but I feel a lot better already."

"Who knows? He's been watching the Food Network for two solid days." She motioned to the business card near my toast. "You gonna call my pal or what?"

I looked at the card—tasteful aqua and cream—

NEIL MACLEOD
Licensed Massage Therapist

Swedish • Shiatsu • Reflexology

I nodded and pocketed the card.

"Yes, ma'am. After a nice, long workout. I'm taking the morning off."

"That's my girl."

For the first time in a week, I was doing exactly what I wanted. Back home, I put on some music and wiped down my tag-sale bench and weights. For the next sixty minutes, I sweated, grunted, and thought only about my body in terms of muscle groups—chest, arms, back, and legs. I finished up by hitting the Fat Boy punching bag for thirty minutes. Then I dug out MacLeod's card, called him, and arranged to meet him at his place later that day.

I showered, dressed, and took a cup of green tea down to my office to catch up on paperwork. After an hour, my billings were in order and I was feeling pretty good. If my few measly clients paid on time this month, I'd be in good shape.

The Peacock job wasn't going to make me rich, but I was gambling it would land me at least one other big fish. My biggest client to date was Caroline Sturgis, a blond, velvet-headband type, who was plump despite her many hours on her newly landscaped tennis court. Maybe it was all those trendy drinks between sets. Caroline was a glacially slow payer and still owed me for work done last fall. It had been my largest, least-interesting job—over a thousand bulbs lining her court, and another hundred on the berm beside it in the shape of two crossed rackets. I warned her it was going to look like hell in June, but she didn't care.

"We'll just change them all to white and blue ageratum, and red impatiens in time for the U.S. Open!" she said, thrilled with her own design skills.

Yeah, *kemo sabe*. *We*. Still, it was all but a guarantee of a future job, since the dying leaves from those bulbs would make her tennis court look like a diseased cornfield by Wimbledon fortnight.

I made a note to sic Anna on her for payment, then it was time to hit the road. I still didn't know Springfield that well, and I'd have to hunt to find the Nutmeg Apartments, where Neil MacLeod lived, so I packed up my stuff, left Anna Peña my favorite deadbeat's phone number, and took off.

The Nutmeg Apartment complex was a cluster of modest, two-story buildings, barnacled with postage-stamp-sized terraces uniformly furnished with Astroturf and molded plastic chairs.

When he opened the door, I recognized him immediately from the diner. Neil MacLeod was in his thirties, with closely cropped brown hair and long sideburns. He wore a metal stud in one ear, and I would have bet good money there was another piercing somewhere on his body. Incense mingled with the sweet smell of almond-scented massage oil in the tiny, immaculate apartment, and lest you think you were in the hands of a nonprofessional, a blue velvet curtain sensitively set off the massage table and two stacks of meticulously folded towels.

"Thanks for seeing me on such short notice," I said.

"Rust never sleeps. Besides, I'm a Glaswegian. We take the work when we can get it."

I undressed behind the curtain and climbed on the table as he reeled off a laundry list of ailments and conditions. "Any recent surgeries, injuries? Any particular problems? Are you pregnant?"

Only one of the conditions applied to me. My face was squished and my answer was muffled by the sheepskin face cradle on his massage table. "Stress, I suppose. A lot going on," I mumbled, "and I haven't been working out enough, although I may have overdone it today."

"Can I come in?" he said.

I mumbled yes. I heard him moving about the room and felt another towel being folded over my legs with origami-like precision.

"You have to stretch after, as well as before. Most people don't unless they're in a class. Any parts you'd like me to focus on or stay away from?"

"Stay away from my toes. I'm kind of funny about them."

Neil asked what kind of music I'd like to hear, but other than that, he said little, which was good. Buck naked, I didn't exactly feel like having an animated conversation. Despite his slight build, he was deceptively strong, as I found out a short time later, facedown, with only a thin sheet covering me from the hips down.

"Let me know if it's too hard."

I was already on Planet Paula. After a few minutes, I drifted off. Too soon, I felt his hand on my shoulder.

"Take as much time as you need."

Behind the curtain I dressed. I heard him turn his phone back on and fill a teakettle. Over tea with a splash of milk, I learned how he and Babe had met.

They had the band experience in common. Neil MacLeod had been the massage therapist for a perennial opening act called the Downward Dogs. Who knew *that* was a job? The Dogs toured for five years, then broke up when the lead singer, a free spirit named Skye, ran off with a classic car salesman from New Jersey. Unable to replace her, and getting tired of life on the road anyway, they divvied up their dough and belongings and scattered to the winds, right after a gig at UConn.

Neil was telling this story to the sympathetic woman at the diner and decided it was kismet, or karma or something, so he settled down where the Dogs had barked their last. Now he lived near the university, teaching yoga and Pilates at the UConn Fitness Center and seeing private clients in his apartment.

"What's that you're burning?" I asked, tying my shoelaces.

"Is the smoke bothering you?"

I shook my head.

"It's a smudge stick—copal resin and rosemary. Copal is sacred to a lot of Central and South Americans. I smuggled this in from Belize, but you can get it online now. It's used in some Mexican churches, too. It's supposed to call in the spirits of health," he said. "I can't guarantee that."

"I like it. Do you know much about this stuff? Herbs, I mean."

"A bit. I've read a few books."

"The house I'm working on has an herb garden and a drying cottage."

"I know. I've been there."

"You have?" So, *he* was Babe's friend who'd known Dorothy.

MacLeod told me he'd been in the local food co-op a few years back looking for borage. They didn't stock it, but another woman overheard the conversation and suggested he contact Dorothy Peacock.

"I left a note in her mailbox, and she invited me over for tea. At first, I thought she was daft as a brush—

most of the time she talked as if someone else was with us—but she knew her stuff as an herbalist. I'm an amateur compared to her. Seemed a bit lonely; I didn't find out till later that her sister had just died. After that, she told me I was welcome to harvest herbs anytime I liked, as long as I was careful. I only went a few times, more to visit her than anything else; the co-op carries just about everything these days."

We talked a bit more, then I sensed I was cutting into his free time between clients, so I got up to leave.

"You really are tight, you know. And your left trapezius is pretty knotted. You carry your bag on that shoulder?"

"I just slept funny last night. Listen, I may need some advice about the herb garden. Okay if I call you?"

"Sure. We can '*gather the enchanted herbs*.' "

"Excuse me?"

"Shakespeare."

CHAPTER 15

Good do-bee that I am, I felt too guilty not to stop at Halcyon to see how Hugo and Felix were making out. I didn't want my mental health day to leave us too far behind, and I didn't want Felix to think one kiss from him had sent me into a swoon.

When I got there, I saw three vans in the driveway and a small army of Mexicans pruning, raking, nipping, and chipping, ignoring most of my borrowed tools in favor of their own rusty rakes and *coas*. A traditional Mayan tool, the *coa* has a sharp, curved blade and a wooden handle, like a scythe. It's been used for centuries in the Yucatán, and it's the tool of choice for many of the Latin American gardeners up north, who do everything but pick their teeth with it.

"*¿Qué pasa?*" I yelled to Felix nervously. "What's going on? Who are these guys?"

He sauntered over to me, as if he were the boss and I was his helper. "More of Hugo's cousins," he teased. "They're friends—just helping out for the day. As a favor to me."

"Are you the Godfather in your little village? I can't afford to pay all these people," I whispered, stress level rising again. "My budget isn't that big. . . ." I started to protest further, but Felix held up his hand to stop me.

"I told you: it's a favor. Think of it as the Felix Ontivares Bracero Program. I know I should have asked you first, but I wanted to surprise you. I didn't want you to worry because of what I told you last night."

I couldn't argue with that; I had been a bit worried, but the men had come in on their one day off and done an amazing job. Most of the dead shrubs were gone, and once we trucked in compost, we'd be ready to plant.

Felix told the men to pack up. They collected their things, doffing their hats to me, nodding to Don Felix, and piling into the vans that would take them back to the inexpensive, crowded rooms and apartments they shared while they did their time up north. We walked to the back of the house.

"So, what's a bracero program?" I asked lightly, trying to forget the feel of his tongue in my mouth and keep things professional.

"Braceros were Mexican field-workers imported into the United States in the forties, fifties, and sixties to help with the harvests. Most of them went to California, Texas, and Florida but some drifted up the East Coast."

"I'm not sure I like the sound of that. Weren't most of them exploited by unscrupulous companies and practices?"

Felix stared at me. "I was teasing you. You need to relax."

"I just had a massage. This is as relaxed as it gets."

We continued our inspection tour, with me finally checking things off my to-do list instead of adding to it.

All this time, nothing in his manner suggested he had planted a wet one on me last night; I started to think I'd imagined it or misinterpreted its meaning.

"Hugo fixed the door to the greenhouse . . . in case

you decide to sleep there again tonight," he added play-fully. At the greenhouse, Hugo was just finishing up.

"*¡Tu hiciste un gran trabajo! Gracias,*" I said lamely. Then I remembered how good Felix said Hugo's English was, so I dropped my pitiful Spanish.

The greenhouse sparkled. Glass panels and wooden potting tables had been thoroughly hosed down and years of soot, grime, and mouse droppings washed away. The antique sprinkler had been scraped clean, and Hugo spun it around to show me that it was still in working order. The chains and hardware had been oiled, and the roof panels had been opened—something I'd been too afraid to do—to air out the place. An iron plant stand organized empty pots and planters, all the wildlife had been evicted, and smack in the middle of the central table was a mason jar holding a bunch of yellow tulips.

"They're only from the supermarket," Hugo said, "but we thought they might cheer you up."

I thought I might cry. Obviously, those closest to me had seen the meltdown coming.

"You guys . . ." I fumbled for the right words. "Why are you being so nice to me?" Hardly adequate but all I could think of.

A muffled sound and slight vibration in my backpack interrupted. I hunted for the phone and found it just before the outgoing message would have kicked in.

"Hello? Is she all right? Of course, we'll be right there." I hung up and shoved the phone back in my bag.

"It was Mike O'Malley. Something's happened to Anna."

Hugo and Felix were talking too fast for me to understand them, but I could guess what they were saying.

"I don't know what happened; she's not hurt. Looks like maybe someone tried to break in to my house," I said. Hugo turned pale.

The three of us sped to my place, where two silver-blue Springfield police cars sat in the driveway. I sprinted past them into the house and up the stairs to my living room, where Anna was daintily sipping a Diet Coke, and holding court for five of Springfield's finest, including Mike O'Malley.

Anna got up when she saw me, and we hugged. Her blackened, tattooed eyes welled up, and she dabbed at them gently with a hankie.

"What on earth happened? Are you all right?" I squeezed her chubby hands and told her to sit down.

"*Sí, sí.* I am all right, Miss Paula."

"Shaken up, mostly," O'Malley said.

Hugo and Felix joined us in the living room. The veins were popping out on Hugo's neck and forehead. *"Dios mío. ¿Qué te paso, mi bella flor? Dime quién te hizo esto,"* he spat. *"¡Yo lo mato!"* Felix calmed him down, but Hugo's eyes were wild and his fists clenched. I'd never seen him like that.

To make matters worse, Hugo hadn't seen Anna since her questionable beauty treatment, and seeing her two black eyes and puffy lips, he thought she'd been savagely beaten. Anna did nothing to disavow him of this notion. She stoically looked down and quietly refolded her embroidered hankie.

"Tell us what happened."

"Like I tell the police. I finish my office work quickly." She took another sip of soda. "By the way, Mrs. Sturgis brought over a check. Then I go outside to tidy up the toolshed."

Good grief, how did she wheedle the money out of Caroline Sturgis so fast? I hoped threats weren't involved. And she was ambitious; my toolshed's a wreck.

"Good girl. Go on," I prodded.

"I hear something out in the woods. At first I think it

is just the deer, but then the sounds came slowly, more de-li-be-rate-ly." She said it carefully, pleased with her new word. And why not? I don't know how to say *deliberately* in Spanish.

"They start to sound more like footsteps, and they were coming closer. I call out. Maybe it's you," she explained, "or Senor Hugo," she added sweetly, fluttering her swollen eyelids.

"I become frightened. I feel someone behind me, so I grab the first thing I can get my hands on, and I swing around and hit him in the face. Then he run away, and I run inside, lock the door, and call the police."

"That was smart. He didn't hurt you, did he?" I asked.

"No. I lose my balance when I hit him and I fall, but I have a lot of padding." Looking at Hugo, she stroked her extra-large mint-colored leggings seductively.

"Well, you're very brave," I said to Anna, hugging her. "Somebody will think twice before messing with you again." Felix and Hugo joined Anna on the sofa, where they comforted her in Spanish.

I got up and pulled O'Malley into the kitchen, where they couldn't hear us. "You're the cop. What do you think?" I whispered.

"She wasn't hurt and nothing was taken. Probably not a serious burglar. A vandal, maybe. Sometimes they take tools or patio furniture—anything left outside can be a temptation once the weather gets nice. Usually they're just kids raising a little hell." He looked down at his notes. "From the description it could have been anybody. Skinny, dark hair, about one hundred and fifty pounds, age unknown—twenty to whatever. You know, since you found the body, you've acquired a certain notoriety. . . ."

"Do you think they're connected?" I pressed.

"Hugo and Anna? I'd say."

"Not them! This, and what happened last night. Could they be connected, for god's sake?"

"Well, since I don't know what happened last night, I couldn't say."

Of course he didn't. I gave him the edited version, omitting the good parts.

"Why didn't you call someone? Me, for instance?"

"To tell you that I'm clumsy?" I felt stupid for letting my phone die, and I had no intention of volunteering the fact that Felix had rescued me.

"Never mind."

His beeper went off. "I've got to go. But we should talk. I don't see any mass conspiracy here, but I understand how you might be concerned."

"That's very understanding of you. As long as you're here, I've got a question about the Peacock case. . . ."

"Ms. Holliday, there *is* no Peacock case. Besides, I thought you didn't want to get involved in our *local ghost story.*"

Great. He'd been in the diner during my tantrum.

"I don't. I was just curious. Forget it."

In the living room, Hugo and Felix were still soothing the victim.

"Hugo and Anna, who knew?" I whispered as we walked toward them.

"Love is all around," Mike said. "You know, if she really did make contact with the intruder's face, he shouldn't be hard to find."

He pointed to something on the floor that looked like an instrument of torture from the Spanish Inquisition— a pair of dirty, steel-spiked aerator sandals.

CHAPTER 16

My mother is a wonderful woman, but she knows as much about gardening as most women who live in apartments in Brooklyn. She buys azaleas at Easter, mums in the fall, and poinsettias at Christmas, and watches their slow decline from the moment they enter her overheated apartment until she inevitably pitches them down a chute where unwanted items in New York miraculously disappear.

That's how I came to own a hedge trimmer (I have no hedges) and high-priced Wellington aerator sandals (I have no lawn). Those sandals had been hanging, unused and rusting in my toolshed, until Anna Peña presciently decided to clean up the shed, arming herself in the process.

For the uninitiated, aerator sandals can best be described as cleats on steroids. You strap the spiked soles on over your shoes then walk around Frankenstein-like, sinking the three-inch-long spikes into your lawn. This is supposed to break up thatch and aerate the soil, thereby letting in water, nutrients, etc. You can also, as Anna learned, hold the flat side against your hand and scare the bejesus out of someone with even a kittenish swipe in their direction.

I wasn't somebody who saw conspiracy everywhere, and weapons of mass destruction in every garage, but something was starting to smell fishy to me, even if it didn't to O'Malley. Was there something more mysterious here than a dead woman's old heartbreak and a suburban kid with too much time on his hands? Or was I turning into a hysterical female? I gave myself the benefit of the doubt.

After the law enforcement types and my Hispanic friends cleared out I sat down at the computer, ready to do a different kind of digging. I'd already learned one of Dorothy Peacock's secrets online; who would my next victim be? I started with Lucy's favorite suspect, Congressman Win Fifield.

The screen filled with Fifield links. I dismissed his official Web site as pure propaganda and clicked on the more interesting "Loser" Fifield home page. His head appeared full frontal and in profile, like mug shots.

It was almost too easy to dislike Winthrop "Winner" Fifield. The unauthorized Loser Web site told the tale. Rich kid, faked his way through school. Bought out of half a dozen scrapes—that the papers knew of—before the age of twenty. Probably more that Daddy's money and position were able to bury, pun intended.

Early pictures show him unlined, always smiling, exposing more teeth than the rest of us have. He ran for class president at Fairfield Prep, and his Ken-doll looks helped him get elected by unanimous vote; apparently even his opponent voted for him. That's when people started calling him Winner. At twenty-eight, Winner slid effortlessly into Connecticut's 53rd congressional seat finally vacated by eighty-four-year-old Warren Chamberlain, who one morning decided to sleep at home instead of in the House.

Since then, Winner had an inauspicious career,

avoiding the tedious subjects of health care, education, crime, and rebuilding inner cities in favor of two burning issues—supporting recognition of quasi–Native American groups for casino development and extending the bow-hunting season. His position on Native Americans was well crafted by his aides, but in a rare moment when his handlers weren't watching, Winner committed to the bow-hunting faction, mistakenly thinking it would get him in solid with the Indians, who, of course, couldn't care less.

Now the clock was ticking for Winner. If he was ever going to have a national presence, it had to happen soon, and message boards were betting it was going to be in a scandal rather than because of some ground-breaking legislation.

Still online, I called Babe. She gave me an earful about Winner and one of his "scrapes." Apparently, he got a girl "in trouble," as they used to say, and she refused to have it "taken care of." Whole family moved away, relocation paid for by the Fifields.

"That must have set them back a bundle," I said.

"I don't think so. They were just a decent, working-class family. . . ." She sifted through her memory to find a name. "The Yampolskys. Seems they were more concerned about preserving the family honor than extorting money from Loser. Don't know what happened to them or the baby."

"How long ago was that?" I asked.

"Twenty, twenty-five years."

The timing could be right, but why come back here to bury the baby if you've already left town? Still, it was a place to start. While she talked, I continued with my snooping. More unflattering photos of Congressman Win Fifield appeared on the computer screen.

In addition to his lousy record in and out of the

House, Winner was not aging well. Only a vestige of the boyish good looks remained, just enough to make him look like a child actor who's outgrown his cuteness. The endless comp meals and drinks had added thirty or forty pounds to his once-athletic frame. In another twenty years it might lend him an air of gravitas à la Ted Kennedy; right now, it gave Winner a sweaty, overinflated look to go with his perpetually worried but trying-not-to-show-it look. Not attractive.

"Okay, we have a flabby congressman of questionable character," I said. "Alert the media."

"But your friend Lucy's instincts were right: he *is* a loser," Babe said. "I gotta go; the after-theater crowd is coming in. Did you, by any chance, look up Cadbury's?" Babe asked. "She ticked me off with that question, but now I'm kind of curious."

"Forgot. I'll see you in the morning."

I keyed in Cadbury's chocolate, and a page loaded. And another, and another.

CHAPTER 17

"Did you know that Good and Plenty candy is the oldest branded candy in the United States?"

"I did not know that."

"Yup. The Quaker City Confectionery Company in Philadelphia started making them in 1893."

I closed the door of the Haviland police substation behind me and strolled over to Mike O'Malley's desk.

"Fascinating," he said. He motioned for me to sit down, but I was already settling in.

"And Milk Duds were originally supposed to be perfectly round . . . but they kept coming out lumpy—*duds*, get it?"

"Before you move on to Whoppers and Goobers, want to tell me what this is about?"

"Just like a man. No sense of . . . buildup, anticipation. Never mind."

I fished around in my backpack and pulled out my candy research papers; I enjoyed spreading them out and messing up his unnaturally tidy desk.

"Cadbury's has been around since the 1820s, but didn't merge with Schweppes until 1969. If we can get a closer look at the package that was in the box with the baby we might have a better idea when the body was buried. And we wouldn't need anyone's approval—no medical examiner, no missing relatives—just another look-see at something we've already seen, right?"

He stared at me blankly.

"Okay. It's not carbon dating but it's a clue. You don't seem to have many of those. If the sisters are ruled out because of the candy wrapper, maybe we can make a case for DNA testing of the body."

"Let's see, where did I put it?" He patted his pockets, opened his pencil drawer, then pretended to look in the garbage for the candy wrapper. "For someone who doesn't want to get involved, you sure do stick your nose in a lot."

"I've printed out a whole list of milestones in the history of Cadbury's Chocolates—Dairy Milk Bars were introduced in 1905, Roses in 1938 . . ."

He held up his hands to silence me. "It's good. Very clever, really, but it's unlikely to rule them out completely," he added more thoughtfully, "unless—"

"Unless what? What do we do next?" I interrupted.

"*We* do nothing. I'll make a few phone calls. I'm not even sure where the wrapper is. It may still be in New Haven."

"Why New Haven?"

"Chain of custody. I think the Forensic Science Center still has everything. I'll look into it."

He seemed ready to send me on my way.

"How long do you think it will take?"

"Sweet Jesus, you're impatient. This isn't the big city, you know."

"My point entirely. Have you found any other bodies around here lately?"

He picked up the phone and hit a button.

"It's Mom. I've got Paula Holliday here. The woman who found the body? She's got a notion related to the Peacock matter. Okay if I put you on speakerphone?"

I was annoyed by his use of the word *notion*. He pressed the mouthpiece of the phone to his chest.

"I'm on with Marian Lyle. I took some of the pictures at the crime scene, but she took the ones that came out."

I told Marian my Cadbury's theory. I couldn't tell if her silence meant she was considering my suggestion or covering the phone and laughing her ass off.

"All the pictures I took are on a disk," she said finally. "I can send them to your computer, Mike, but I don't recall spending much time on the candy wrapper other than to record its existence. I was more interested in the necklace the baby was wearing. Took a lot of shots of that. Thought it might help with the ID."

"And *I've* been kicking myself for not having taken a closer look at that medal," I added.

"It was something in Spanish; I couldn't quite make it out," she said.

"Send everything here," Mike said. "My home computer, too." He hung up.

"So now that we're, sort of, partners, are you going to tell me what happened to Dorothy's sister?"

"Number one, we are not partners. Number two, Dorothy Peacock's sister died four years ago. Check Morning Glory Cemetery if you don't believe me."

"Right. And Jimmy Hoffa is alive and well and in the witness protection program." I got up to leave, taking my research with me.

"Where's the other Hardy girl?" Mike asked.

"Lucy? Home. Working. Like I should be, instead of wasting my time here."

"If anything comes up, I'll call you."

"Sure you will. Thanks a lot, Sergeant," I said, silently vowing not to share anything else with that guy until I could rub his nose in it.

CHAPTER 18

I was on my hands and knees, weeding, when Hugo and Felix pulled into the Peacocks' driveway in a thirty-foot U-Haul truck. As soon as they parked, the back door rolled up and five other men piled out and immediately started off-loading the shrubs and trees they'd been riding with.

Hugo stayed with the men, acting as foreman, while Felix joined me at the perennial bed. He dropped to his knees alongside me and sat back on his heels.

"Hi, boss. Hugo thought you would want to plant these today," he said, motioning to the shrubs. "He says it will rain tomorrow and if we get them in the ground today, they'll get off to a healthy start."

"Smart thinking."

"He may even turn me into a gardener—always good to have something to fall back on if the president thing doesn't work out. He looks after you. You've been very kind to him and to Anna."

"They're good people," I said. "I didn't realize they were a couple. I guess that's why she comes over so often."

"That's not the only reason. She likes you. We all like you," he said. I realized our knees were almost touching, and scrambled to my feet, losing my balance and nearly falling over into the bed. Felix stayed on the ground for a minute, looking up at me. Then he got up, too, calmly brushing himself off. Hugo joined us and bailed me out of the awkward moment.

"My knight in shining armor. I see you brought in the cavalry again," I said, referring to his helpers. "We'll need them."

"The men are happy to do it," Hugo said. "For you and for Don Felix. And for the baby. Some of the men consider it a blessing that you found it."

"I don't know how much of a blessing it's been for anyone. I just seem to be annoying people and raking up a lot of old stuff."

"Perhaps it's like turning the compost pile," Hugo said. "The material takes a while before it is ready to be used."

I hadn't seen Anna since the incident at my place, and it was unlike her to disappear for days, unless more cosmetic enhancements were involved, which was entirely possible. Now that the cat was out of the bag I asked Hugo how she was doing.

"She is good. Very busy, but she will be back to work this week."

"You two should have told me," I said, and he actually blushed.

"Anna wanted to," he stammered, "but I am a very private person, and old-fashioned. There are traditions to be followed, from my family and my village. It will take some time, but we will be married," he said proudly.

Two men came over to us, awaiting more instructions. Balled and burlapped trees were dragged to the spots that Felix and Hugo had previously prepared. Nursery pots were placed where they'd eventually be planted—starting with fifty small boxwoods on either side of the oyster-shell path that separated the herb garden and the white garden.

"Is this everything from the nursery?" I asked, getting back to business.

"Only the evergreens. I didn't think we'd have time to plant everything today. Better to let the nursery's men water them until we get them in the ground than to have to do it ourselves. *Excave los hoyos tan hondos como las bolas de las raíces,*" he told the men.

"*¿Qué estás diciendo?*" I asked.

"I was just telling them to dig the holes as deep as the root-balls."

The men operated like an assembly line, and the work went quickly. Dig, place, fertilize, backfill, water. The allée was finished. Five large rhododendrons replaced those that had had to be severely cut back in the front of the house. Luckily, two twenty-foot viburnums on either side of the porch had survived and would serve as a backdrop for the rhododendrons until they filled in and re-created the lush hedge that had once been there.

Woolly adelgid, the sticky white critters ruining the hemlocks in Connecticut, had done a number on the trees marking the property line shared by Halcyon and the Fifield home. The men planted a dozen new ones. Staggered, they'd look less like puny replacements and more like offspring of the larger ones. At least, I hoped they would.

My biggest challenge had been finding mature cypress trees to fill in Halcyon's Italianate hedge that lined the far side of the Peacocks' stone wall and separated the garden from the lawn and Long Island Sound beyond. These were grown in Oregon, and were a remarkable match for the ones Dorothy Peacock had planted.

The men dug a long trench on that side of the wall.

The cypresses would be evenly spaced along the length of the wall, providing shelter and privacy, which I now understood was a priority for Dorothy and Renata.

We stood on the brick terrace, telling the men where the trees should go—this one to the left, this one to the right.

"Perhaps we measure the space and plant them equidistant," Hugo suggested, no longer feeling the need to hide his exceptional English.

"That's a good start, but they're not all the same size. We'll have to eyeball it, too." I squinted into the sunlight and motioned for the last one to be moved closer to the edge of the wall.

"The third one from the left must be turned around to face the terrace," someone said decisively.

It was Guido Chiaramonte.

"Mr. Chiaramonte, how are you?"

Arms folded, he inspected our work but didn't answer. "It looks good, not bad. I'm surprised, with the level of help you have. *Scusi,*" he said, barely acknowledging Felix and Hugo's presence. "These boys, they don't work hard, and they think you should give them chicken every day for lunch. You have to keep after them, or else they'd sit around all day taking siestas."

Hugo bristled but said nothing; Felix wisely pulled him away.

"That hasn't been my experience. My partner and I have worked with some very good men, very knowledgeable, too."

"Partner, eh?" He laughed.

"That may be a little optimistic on my part, but I certainly hope Hugo will be my partner on future projects."

I'd had my fill of Guido, with his sexist and racist cracks, but I still had his garden tools and equipment, so I was obliged to suffer his company a little longer.

"Will you be coming to the Historical Society's event?" I asked, changing the subject.

"Absolutely. There will be beautiful women there. That Anna is a beautiful woman. But she shouldn't waste her time with a skinny runt like that," he said, gesturing in Hugo's direction. He said it loud enough for Hugo and the other men to hear. He leaned in and whispered what he'd like to do to her. I marveled at the acrobatic details.

"I'm just trying to make you jealous." He chuckled and touched my forearm. "She's delicious, but she's not you."

Oh, goodie. I was still number one. I wriggled out of his oily reach.

"You're too much of a gigolo for me. I couldn't keep up with you," I said. Couldn't keep from *throwing up* with you, I wanted to say.

"Don't say that. I'm a very sensitive man. I know how to take care of a woman." He flashed a little bit of tongue. If that was supposed to convince me of his desirability, it had the opposite effect.

"Mr. C., I have a small struggling business. I've really got to get back to work." *Or go do my hand washables or get a root canal or anything to get away from you, you slug.* "I'll make sure all your tools and machines are returned by the end of the week," I said, anxious to be out of his debt.

"Come yourself. It was naughty of you last time to send your boys. Forget about that Hugo. I can be a very good partner. We can have a drink to celebrate your new venture." He patted my cheek and left.

Yikes. Did he have much success with that shtick?

Hugo had been watching us the whole time, waiting to come to my aid if I needed him. I gave him a thumbs-up to let him know everything was okay, and we got back to work.

After a few minor adjustments in placement—Guido was right about the tree—we backfilled and tamped down the soil around the cypresses. What would have taken a week on my own took just one day with team Mexico.

When we finished, all the trees and shrubs had been watered in, and Felix and Hugo loaded the men back into the U-Haul.

"Do they have enough air back there?" I asked.

"*Sí, sí*. The roof is open." Hugo backed out of the driveway. He looked up at the overcast sky. "With the weather tomorrow, I don't think you will need us here. There is a new bank going up downtown and they need many workers. And I have a few personal things to attend to, so you will be here on your own then."

I nodded, and watched Felix leave, flashing a smile that I realized I was going to miss.

CHAPTER 19

The extra manpower had put us way ahead of schedule. I took the opportunity to get back to the quiet, anti-social side of gardening that I loved. Just a girl and her trowel.

My tiny budget for Halcyon was long gone, spent on things Richard Stapley and I couldn't beg or borrow. One of the society's members was the owner of a chain of seafood restaurants, so we scored two truckloads of free oyster shells and clamshells to line the garden's paths. In this light, the mother-of-pearl paths glistened against the rich brown of the newly turned beds like the bleached bones of a skeleton.

Richard had been feeding me weekly updates on ticket sales, and the numbers were strong. Our little wine and cheese party had blossomed into a full-fledged social event, at least by Fairfield County standards. Once I knew tickets were selling, I'd ordered the more expensive trees, shrubs, and perennials and, with Richard's approval, had the bills sent directly to him.

Three nurseries provided the plants—Lee's for shrubs and woody ornamentals, Gilbertie's for herbs, and Guido's for annuals. Guido wasn't thrilled he wasn't getting more of the business, but even he had to admit Lee's had the best shrubs; and Gilbertie's had been around so long, they may have provided Dorothy with her original herbs.

The herb garden occupied the same amount of space as the white garden but at the opposite end of the allée. In each corner of the large square was a triangular bed that probably had held taller perennial herbs like yarrow and bee balm. A round central garden, with a raised bed, was surrounded by four curved beds with spaces in between so Dorothy could tend and harvest the herbs. Again, the paths were covered with crushed shells, and they evoked the sea and fresh herbs, even though most of the vegetation was long gone.

My plan was to install Halcyon's herb garden last; that way it wouldn't be damaged by any late spring frosts. The newspaper photos weren't much help, but, judging from the vintage Comstock, Ferre seed packets I'd found in the greenhouse, the sisters had made some eclectic choices.

Neil MacLeod, my massage therapist and Dorothy's erstwhile student, agreed to work on the garden with me, so I was relying on him to fill in the missing pieces.

According to the copper plant markers I'd found and scraped clean, the most common herbs were all represented, but so were pennyroyal, feverfew, tansy, rue, and others I assumed were either fashionable in the thirties and forties or were personal favorites of the sisters'. The lavender and oregano still flourished; once the dead foliage was cut back, they'd fill in. Wisely, the mint and lemon balm were in concrete containers, to control their aggressive roots; tiny clusters of lady's mantle peeked out in the newly cleaned beds.

Everything else had to be replaced. No problem,

though; my list didn't raise an eyebrow at Gilbertie's. They had everything, even the hard-to-find ones, like the borage Neil had been looking for.

In the interest of saving a few bucks, and getting to use the newly cleaned greenhouse, I'd started a few plants from seed. I don't usually, because, as it's been noted, I'm not that patient, but basil, nasturtium, sage, and parsley are so easy, it's just plain lazy not to do it. If the seedlings survived, I'd transplant them when they hardened off. Flats of herbs from Gilbertie's would form the bulk of the garden, and they filled the largest of the tables in the greenhouse.

Since my unintended nap there, I'd learned the greenhouse was an Amdega, the Rolls-Royce of greenhouses and conservatories. I'd seen one on top of a building on Sutton Place on the East Side of Manhattan—and supposedly Queen Elizabeth had one—so I was doubly glad I hadn't smashed any glass to get out that night. Hugo had fixed the latch on the door, but I nudged a broken concrete planter between the door and the jamb, just to be on the safe side.

Everything looked healthy, and the nasturtiums had shot up another two inches. I was thinning out the crowded basil seedlings with a pair of cuticle scissors when I heard a tap on the glass.

"Anybody home?" It was Stapley.

"Richard, in here." He seemed in a fine mood, looser than I'd ever seen him.

"I thought I'd stop by to deliver the news in person. As of today, ticket sales have put us in the black."

"That's wonderful," I said. I offered him a seat on an upturned whiskey barrel Hugo had brought to the greenhouse to use as a step stool.

"It was slow going at first, but I called in some markers," he bragged, trying to get comfortable yet still maintain his dignity on the uneven surface of the barrel.

With the raffle items and silent auction, SHS would cover its costs, pay me, and maybe even deliver the bonus that Richard dangled but didn't promise when we made our handshake deal. I gently reminded him of it.

"I guess I shouldn't have told you the good news," he joked. "We're not there yet. We'll see what happens the night of the party." I knew he still had hopes of prying checks out of some guests at the event.

I gave him a quick status report on the garden, and saw his eyes start to glaze over. *Good, you raise the money, and I'll handle the garden.* I preferred that arrangement to one where the client was constantly second-guessing my decisions. He listened politely, but his mind was elsewhere, and I wasn't surprised when he rode off, presumably to share his good news with Margery.

Now I was in a good mood, too. Not only did I have a realistic shot at the bonus, but if the restoration came off as planned, Lucy's idea of a Garden Channel feature might not be that crazy. I still had connections. I'd documented and photographed all of the major improvements. Why not? There were plenty of stupider things on television. That was the fantasy I was indulging when I heard another tap on the glass. I thought Richard had forgotten to tell me something, but it wasn't him.

Felix Ontivares toed the concrete planter away from the door and closed it behind him. Instead of his usual work clothes he wore jeans and a gray V-neck sweater over a white T-shirt. He smelled delicious—a little sweat, a little Armani. He walked toward me slowly, finally backing me up against the edge of one of the empty potting tables. Without uttering a word, he bent down

and gently slipped his tongue into my mouth. Whatever I was holding fell out of my hands, and I wrapped
my arms around him, sliding my hands up and down
the muscles I'd been eyeing for weeks.

His mouth still on mine, he reached behind me and
lifted me onto the table. Then he peeled off his sweater
to make a pillow.

"Someone might come," I said, breathless.

His lips brushed my ear as he whispered, "*Espero
que asi sea*. I certainly hope so."

Felix's hands were on my waist, rolling up my thin
T-shirt and stopping only to unhook my bra.

"Wait a minute. I can't do this."

"Afraid I'll accuse you of sexual harassment?"

"I'm sorry. I can't start sleeping with—"

"The *help*?" He laughed. "What if you don't pay me?
Am I still the *help*? Or is it something else?"

"Of course not."

He searched my face to make sure I was serious.
Then he rolled down my T-shirt. "*Está bien, maestra*."
He gave me a fake salute and left me in the suddenly
chilly greenhouse.

CHAPTER 20

By the time I pulled into my garage, the first snowflakes were falling, but I was reasonably warm, thanks to the sweater Felix had left in the greenhouse.

I'd nearly broken one of those unwritten rules. Thou shalt not go food shopping when you're hungry; thou shalt not commit DUI (dialing under the influence); and the biggie, thou shalt not make the beast with two backs with someone who works for you.

I had mixed feelings. True, I'd risen above my animal instincts, but feeling virtuous never seems to last that long, and it's generally a lot less fun than feeling guilty. It'd been a long time since the earth had moved for me. On the other hand, the image of me, half-dressed, flailing about, and kicking over the nasturtium seedlings was not one I would have been particularly proud of. I only hoped Felix didn't think my resistance was because he was Mexican. There was something in the way he called me *boss* in Spanish that suggested he did. I consoled myself with an obscenely large bowl of mint chocolate chip yogurt.

I tried to put Felix out of my mind and enjoy the last of my firewood—and hopefully the last snowfall—of the season. Before settling in, I scanned my bookshelf for something I remembered picking up at a tag sale. I routinely bought old garden books despite the fact I hadn't read half the ones I already owned. There it was— *Culpeper's Complete Herbal.*

Culpeper's is a six-hundred-page tome first published in 1653. My copy was an inexpensive paperback reprinted in the 1970s during the last big wave of interest in alternative medicine. After the author warns the reader about bootleg copies, in the seventeenth century, no less, he starts with *Amara dulcis,* which "is excellently good to remove witchcraft both in men and beasts." Always useful.

From amara to yarrow, Nicholas Culpeper explains where to find and how to grow the herbs, trees, and plants he claims could treat common illnesses. Most of the plants were new to me—ladies bed-straw, for example, which was "good to bathe the feet of travellers and lacquies." Mustn't forget the lackeys. And duck's meat, which could be applied to "the breasts before they be grown too much." Cheaper than breast-reduction surgery, I suppose.

I leafed through to the entry for one of the Peacocks' less-common herbs, pennyroyal, which was described as being "so well known unto all . . . that it needs no description." Wonderful. This was going to be a productive read. Then, under Culpeper's heading of *virtues,* I saw a number of applications for pennyroyal related to fainting and swooning in women and the more intriguing "provokes women's courses."

I flipped back to his description of feverfew.

"Venus commands this herb and has commended it to succur her sisters (women) and to be a general strengthener of their wombs, and remedy such infirmities as a careless midwife hath there caused."

The next two snowy spring days I spent at home,

buried in *Culpeper's*. When I didn't hear from Felix, I shrugged off the disappointment, telling myself it served me right for being so stupid. Then his flowers were delivered, and I softened. *A family emergency requires me to leave town for a few days. Take care of yourself, and my sweater, until I return. Felix.* Like a teenager, I'd slept in the damn sweater the first night, then balled it and threw it into a corner of my closet when he didn't call. It was still there.

In Felix's absence, I worked hard to keep my mind on business. Remarkably, there wasn't much that was new in the world of botanica medica. Another book extolling the virtues of newly fashionable echinacea, ginseng, goldenseal, and black cohosh was published over a hundred years ago. Roots, bark, berries, vines, and flowers of certain plants had been cultivated for their medicinal properties for centuries. Aristophanes refers to them as early as 421 B.C.

Unable to work in anyone's garden, and not wanting to obsess about Felix, I was off on another tangent. One that would probably lead to nothing more nefarious than the Peacock sisters' fondness for potpourri, but what the hell. I needed a reality check. And food. The cupboard was just about bare. Can't put condiments on condiments.

I pulled the Jeep in to the far end of the Paradise parking lot, honking to displace a group of ducks sunning themselves on a mound of dirty snow. They plopped back into the lake.

"Hey, stranger," Babe yelled. "Where've you been hiding?"

"Not hiding, just housebound. Doing research mostly. Neil was great, by the way. I don't think I ever told you. I should factor the cost of a massage into every job I get from now on." I stretched like a cat on the counter stool.

"Massage is a beautiful thing. Keeps people out of watchtowers," Babe said.

"You heard about Anna?" I asked.

"Old news. Some kid, right?"

"Maybe."

"You've reached celebrity status in our little burg. Lotta kids around here with nothing to do and all the time in the world to do it. I haven't seen you, or Felix, for a while. I thought maybe you two eloped."

Was the woman clairvoyant? "No." I laughed nervously. "I think he's out of town. And I've been swamped. We're getting to the homestretch on the Peacock job, and I still have the Caroline Sturgises of the world to deal with. Those monthly guys pay the bills . . . that is, when they pay the bills."

"Well, you haven't been gardening in this weather. What else have you been up to?" Babe pressed. She poured me some coffee and brought a menu.

"Taking a crash course in this." I reached into my backpack and held up *Culpeper's,* my new bible.

"You be careful with that stuff," she warned. Not the response I'd expected from a former flower child.

"People have killed themselves not knowing what they were doing with that shit. That stiff I told you about? The backup singer? Stupid kid drank something she was supposed to make tea with. What was the name of it? Neil would know. What the hell was it? It was like a woman's name. Kurt Cobain wrote a song about it—not about her, about the herb."

I was not a huge Nirvana fan, so nothing instantly leaped to mind. I held the menu, but my mind was running through the list of Nirvana songs I actually knew until the jingle of the cash register snapped me out of it. Babe took a five-dollar bill from a customer and waited while he fished around in a small cardboard box on the counter—*Leave a penny, take a penny*. And the penny dropped.

"Pennyroyal?" I asked.

"Bingo," she said, slamming the drawer shut.

CHAPTER 21

"Decoctions, concoctions, infusions, extracts . . . It all sounds a little eye of newt, tail of frog to me."

"You wouldn't be the first to feel that way. People used to be burned at the stake for practicing that stuff. It's not that mysterious. It just has to do with how much water you soak the plant material in and for how long," Neil said.

He handed me a cup of tea. "It's *toe* of frog, by the way. Good Scottish recipe."

"Any toe of frog in here?"

He shook his head, smiling. "Straight from the Food Emporium. It's honeybush tea from South Africa.

"After my first visit to Dorothy's," he said, sitting at his desk in a swivel chair, "she let me do some harvesting on my own. She was very knowledgeable, and I quite enjoyed her company. I went over a few times, early in the morning, after the dew had dried and before the morning sun wilted the plants. Dorothy was careful about that sort of thing."

He leafed through some papers on his desk and handed me one. "I made a list for you. Things I remembered seeing there. My memory's pretty good, but her notebook probably has all of these in it."

My blank stare told him I didn't know about any notebook.

"It was an old black bookkeeper's ledger, with sketches and notes. She even pressed specimens in it. I don't think it was for the whole garden, just the herb garden."

"I haven't found anything remotely like a journal or notebook. I've been relying on ancient news clippings and anecdotes from octogenarians." I groaned.

"C'mon, let's go," he said, taking my cup and putting it in the sink. "I haven't been there for over a year. Maybe going back to the scene of the crime will help me remember."

On the way, he told me more: how Dorothy believed in working by the phases of the moon, how she'd harvest only during certain signs of the zodiac, and pick only certain parts of the plants during certain quarters of the moon.

"I guess that's why she needed the journal," he said, "to keep track of all that stuff."

When we arrived at Halcyon, we could see Guido Chiaramonte and his men next door at the Fifields'. It was impossible to avoid him. He waved and, uninvited, walked toward us through the spotty line of trees that separated the houses.

"Something wicked this way comes?" Neil whispered.

"No planting today. Too wet," Guido pronounced, dusting the nonexistent dirt from his hands as if he'd actually been working.

"No, just a little planning. Neil knows a lot about Dorothy's herb garden."

"Is that so? You don't look like a gardener," Guido said in his usual dismissive tone.

"Too bad we don't have her notebook," Neil said,

inspecting the beds and doing his best to ignore Guido.

"A notebook?" Guido asked. "For what?"

"Apparently she kept a record of her herb garden. I didn't even know there was one until about an hour ago," I said.

"A record. What a good idea." Guido tapped his forehead. "But the old lady, she was a little funny at the end, *stunad*. Who knows what nonsense she may have scribbled?" he said, shrugging. Then he returned to his favorite subject. "So many years in the same house with only her sister. It's no good for the woman to be without the man. That's what I keep telling my little friend here," he said, looking back and forth between us, trying to figure out if Neil was his rival for my affections.

I motioned to the Fifield property. "What are your men working on?" I asked, hoping he'd get back to it soon.

"We are turning on the signora's fountain. It is my crowning achievement in Springfield. Eight tons of Carrara marble," he said proudly. "I commissioned two of the statues myself. We blow out the pipes in the fall and restart the system in the spring. We're late this season. Signora Dina has been away for a month, and she likes to be here when we do it," he cackled, pleased with his clumsy innuendo.

"It's chilly today. Can I take you for an anisette to warm you up?" he asked, trying again.

I'd never be that cold. I begged off politely, blaming Neil and the work we still had in the herb garden.

"Eh," Guido said, not believing me. He returned his attention to his workers at the Fifield house. "I must go back. Otherwise those lazy boys will be standing around sunning themselves."

I said nothing about the fact that they all looked busy and the sky was overcast. I was too anxious for him to leave so that Neil and I could look for that journal.

CHAPTER 22

"Is this what you Americans call breaking and entering?" Neil asked.

"We're not going to break anything," I whispered, "and this is more like . . . trespassing." Still, unflattering images of people holding cardboard numbers under their chins flashed in my head. (Winona Ryder? Robert Downey, Jr.? Frank Sinatra?)

Neil and I had first checked out the herb cottage, a safe distance from Guido and his men. No such luck. Since Neil knew what the journal looked like, and I didn't, I thought we'd have a better shot at finding it together in the rambling old house. Otherwise I might spend days and still come up empty. I dialed Richard's number at SHS to see if it was okay for us to go in the house. Inez answered.

"Richard's in Hartford for the next few days," she said. "Some big doings about a painting for the Wadsworth Atheneum." She started to elaborate, but I cut her ramblings short, telling her I needed to get into the house to look at Dorothy's garden books. She hesitated.

"Well, I suppose it'll be all right." She paused again.

"There was one door that never had a lock; it probably still doesn't."

"That's hard to believe. I wonder why."

"Things were different in the old days," she said softly. "Safer. Springfield was a small town; everyone knew each other. I'd be very surprised if Dorothy ever bothered to put a lock on that door." Her voice trailed off, and I had to lead her back.

"Which door was it?"

"To the left of the French doors on the back terrace. Well, let's see, that would be if you were in the house. To the right, near the statue of the woman holding the basket." I looked across the terrace and saw a narrow door practically obscured by a climbing hydrangea. If you didn't know, it would have looked another tall window.

Hugo had scrubbed the moss and dirt from all the statues at Halcyon: the stone dogs, a respectable copy of Diana the huntress, and the little peasant woman I'd barely noticed before. She wore a full skirt and petticoats, and a scarf held back long curly hair. On her shoulder was a basket filled with wheat, and she stood guard outside the door I hoped was still unlocked.

The door handle squeaked from disuse but clicked open. Neil and I bent down under the hydrangea and entered a small mudroom with an old Formica table, a sink, and floor-to-ceiling shelves. The shelves were empty, except for a few mildewed needlepoints. An inner door led to the main house. It, too, was unlocked.

My first impression was of a hodgepodge of stuff. Different styles, different eras, giving it the appearance of an upscale flea market. The Peacock house was furnished in an idiosyncratic style not unlike its garden: mostly New England, some Italy, a touch of France.

We tiptoed around, as if there were someone there to disturb. In the main entrance, at the top of the stairs, a stained glass window featured an ornate vase overflowing with pink cabbage roses. To the left were various bedrooms and sitting rooms. To the right was the room we were looking for.

The library had a large bay window, with a window seat overlooking the entire garden. A great wooden table in the middle of the room was covered by a patterned dark green velvet throw, moth-eaten in spots. A dusty floor globe stood in one corner.

More framed needlepoints shared the shelves with Dorothy's books, which were in no order I could instantly recognize. Most were gardening books ranging from 1840's *Mrs. Loudon's Gardening for Ladies* to *Martha Stewart's Gardening*. They even had a copy of *The Temple of Flora*, a very rare nineteenth-century book of flower illustrations. I wondered if Richard knew about this small gem.

"'*What shall we do for our sister? Come into my garden, my sister.*' Sounds familiar," Neil said, reading two of a series of needlepoints.

"Not to me."

In the same way one's eyes eventually adjust to low light, my eyes adjusted to the unique arrangement of the books—some by author, some by subject, some by country of origin. After a while, it made sense.

Then I found them: two bays devoted to herbs and herbal remedies. One entire shelf held books with the words *Materia Medica* in the title. There was a hardcover copy of the ginseng book I'd read about and a personally inscribed first edition of Jethro Kloss's classic *Back to Eden*. Alongside *King's American Dispensatory*, I saw the *Culpeper's*. Unlike my cheap paperback edition, Dorothy's was a well-thumbed, leather-bound copy printed in 1906, and stuffed with bookmarks and crumbling sprigs.

We searched every inch of the library for Dorothy's journal, but found nothing.

"I've got to get back. I have a client at five," Neil said, checking his watch.

"I'm leaving, too. And I'm borrowing this," I said, shoving the *Culpeper's* in my pack. "I don't think Dorothy will mind."

CHAPTER 23

When I got home, I found O'Malley on my doorstep. Given my recent, unauthorized exploration of the Peacock house and the book I'd snatched, I thought he was there to read me my rights. Then I noticed the grocery bag, a plastic bag from Shep's Wines and Liquors, and a ten-pound bag of charcoal leaning against the door.

"At the risk of sounding inhospitable, why are you here?"

"You didn't strike me as a gas grill person."

"You must be a detective. Let me take something." I reached for the charcoal, but he handed me the smaller bag.

"Salmon okay? Wild, not farmed."

"Is this an official call?"

"Officials have to eat, too."

Upstairs, he unloaded everything onto the island in the kitchen. I dumped my stuff in the bedroom, buried the book under my pillows, and went back to see what Mike was up to. I watched silently while he made himself at home, unpacking bags and whipping up a respectable sesame-soy-ginger marinade for the salmon. He stuck it in the fridge, then opened the wine, picked up the charcoal, and started for the deck.

"I'm a sucker for anyone who wants to cook for me, but is there a legitimate reason for this visit?"

"Got a laptop?" he asked.

"Do bears go in the woods?"

"Get it. I'll start the fire and meet you back here in ten minutes. And bring your candy notes."

Uncharacteristically, I did as I was told, retrieving my laptop from my office, and clearing a spot for it on the kitchen counter. Mike came back with a flash drive and a detailed picture log, presumably so I wouldn't have to look at any of the more graphic shots.

"Candy, little girl?"

Instantly, a picture of the crumpled candy wrapper appeared. "Okay, you're on," he said.

Even at 500 percent magnification, it was impossible to see a date on the package, but we were able to see one thing clearly: Cadbury. I shuffled through my research.

"Okay, Cadbury merged with Schweppes in 1969, so this package predates that."

"Can you make out the name on the bar?"

It was difficult to read; the wrapper had spent the last few decades crumpled in a box, and the cops' efforts to flatten it out only served to hasten its disintegration.

"I don't know," I said. "It looks like one word, starting with a *P.*"

"Does it say *Paula*?" he asked, leaning in.

"Idiot. It probably says *Picnic*. If the package says *Picnic,* and doesn't say Cadbury *Schweppes,* it was made and buried sometime between 1958 and 1969. If the mother was a teenager when she gave birth . . ." I noodled with my next calculation.

"Let's say, for the sake of argument, the childbearing years are fifteen to forty, all we have to do is look for a woman who was born between 1918 and 1953.

Your candy wrapper may tell us who isn't the mother, but it doesn't tell us who is."

He did the math so fast it made my head spin.

"If the child was buried in 1958," he explained, "and the mother was forty, she would have been born in 1918. If the body was buried in 1968, and the mother was only fifteen, she could have been born as late at 1953. Too large a group. Why are you smiling?"

"Nothing. My aunt Jo used to say, 'and if my Grandma had wheels she'd be a trolley,' or something like that."

"There's a rude version of that."

"Aunt Jo knew that one, too. So virtually every woman in Fairfield County over the age of forty-five is a candidate. That narrows things down." I tried to sound optimistic. No one's as optimistic as a gardener.

"And why limit it to Fairfield County?" he said. "She might have moved. She might be dead. Look, it's an interesting exercise but it doesn't prove anything."

"Someone once said that when you have eliminated the impossible, whatever remains, however improbable, must be the truth."

"Was that Aunt Jo again?" he asked.

"I think it was Arthur Conan Doyle—Sherlock Holmes, wise guy. Any ideas about the other stuff?" I asked.

"More annoying than dangerous. Anna's encounter could have been a prank. And bunking down in the greenhouse isn't life threatening, even if it isn't fun."

No, but it could have been, I thought.

"What is it? Has something else happened?"

"No, no." If O'Malley knew about my near miss with Felix, he did a good job of hiding it.

"We don't know that your incidents are remotely

connected to the body. It could be a business rival or someone who's ticked off at you."

O'Malley might have had something there. I didn't think there were a lot of people who wanted to see me dead, but there was no shortage of people I'd pissed off. Once a year they all met in Yankee Stadium.

"Too large a group," I mimicked.

"What about the ex?" he asked, for the first time venturing into personal territory.

"Not that crazy. Look, maybe we should take a break," I said, steering him away from the subject. "Didn't you promise me a gourmet meal?"

"I did indeed."

After dinner, we sat on the deck. Mike fiddled with the grill's dying fire, and then settled in across from me on an old rattan loveseat.

"You haven't talked much about yourself. All I know is you were some big television honcho, and now you're in the garden business. How did you come to be a gardener? Don't most city folk have one houseplant they either neglect or overwater?"

"Hardly a honcho, just a cog in the machine. But I've been a gardener since grade school. One day my second-grade teacher had us bring in avocado pits for a class project. I didn't even know what an avocado was—they were not on my mother's shopping list. She cooked vegetables no one in my class ever heard of—escarole, broccoli rabe, fennel, stuff like that."

"Holliday isn't a very Italian name."

"You *are* a detective. I'm half-Italian, on my mother's side. It was strictly an Italian menu, except for corned beef and cabbage once a year."

"I should have let *you* cook."

"I'll ignore that. Anyway, we planted the avocado pits in cut-off milk containers, and I checked them every morning for signs of life. I've been hooked ever since."

"Are you good at it?"

"That's an astute question. A good gardener," I answered slowly, "knows what to put where. And not just aesthetically—it's the zone, the microclimate, the soil, a lot of things. So, yes, by those standards, I am a good gardener."

"Ever married?"

"That's a switch. Nope."

"Not interested?"

"Bad timing, mostly. I was in a relationship that ended a few months ago. We met cute and parted ugly."

"Sorry."

"That's okay. What about you?"

Mike was single. That helped him avoid the twin occupational hazards lots of cops succumbed to, alcoholism and divorce. He spent most of his spare time kayaking and renovating a cabin in northern Connecticut. Dad was a cop, uncle was a cop, most of his friends were cops. I got the picture.

"Dad and I are a couple of grizzled old bachelors. I thought he might remarry after my mum passed, but it never happened. We live just a few blocks apart. Some nights he cooks, some nights I do. I just stopped smoking—eighteen months ago; so mostly I'm battling the weight I put on. Walking the dog helps, but I need to get back in the gym."

"What do you have?"

"A border collie. Her name's Jessie. Guzman looks after her while I'm on duty."

Guzman again. Were they a couple? Then what the hell was he doing here with me? And what the hell was

I doing? For the second night in a week, I was sitting in the dark, getting cozy with a man I barely knew. Either I was lonelier than I thought or hornier. And he's apologizing for his weight, which means he's somewhat interested.

A blast of music from the other side of the woods ripped through the night, nondescript rock, the kind you'd get on a cheap drugstore party CD.

"The noisy neighbor, I presume?"

"Comes with the springtime; all the slugs come out. He hasn't been too bad lately. At least there aren't any squealing bimbos frolicking in the hot tub."

"Still, it is late for a school night," Mike said, glancing at his watch.

I used it as a cue to end the evening—before bachelor number two decided to make *his* move. "Excellent point," I said, standing up. "I don't know about you, but I have a full day tomorrow." I walked him down to his car, and watched him pull away in the direction of the music. *Heh, heh, heh, that'll teach my noisy neighbor.*

CHAPTER 24

Back in the kitchen, the old laptop's screen saver showed a haunted house, inhabited by digital bats and screeching cats. (Who remembers what significant documentary I was working on when I chose that one.) I'd barely touched the mouse when the phone rang.

"Jesus, you scared me!"

"Is that the way you answer the phone? When was the last time you got a call?" Lucy said.

"I knew it was you—I saw it on caller ID."

Lucy filled me in on France, and I filled her in on Springfield. Mid-conversation, she forced me to put down the phone and set the house alarm. "What if there *was* a connection between Anna's attack and your greenhouse incident? Why are you still up there? Stay at my place until this is sorted out."

"Can't. I have to work. Besides, Mike's right—it's probably nothing."

"Oh it's Mike now—no more Mayberry jokes? What am I thinking? Is he still there? Don't answer, cough. Then I'll know you're not alone."

"No one else is here. But there *has* been some action on that front." With little encouragement, I gave Lucy the broad strokes on my encounter with Felix.

"I always say the best way to get *over* someone," she said, referring to my ex, "is to get *under* someone. Too bad you weren't ready. And where is *he*?"

"Mexico, I think. Family business."

"Wow. My rejects rarely feel the need to leave the country, but I suppose a clean break is best. Is that why his backup was at your house so soon? You're not turning into the town slut, are you?"

"Please. Tonight was all business." I told her about the pictures on the flash drive and reeled off the shorthand descriptions on Mike's photo log.

"Hmmm. *Babhdbck.* What's that?"

"I'm guessing baby's head, back."

"I think I can skip that one," she said. "Anything about the necklace?"

I didn't know if I was supposed to be looking at the other pictures, but why not? By accident or by design, Mike had left the drive. I scrolled down to the necklace images and waited for the first to load. It was a tiny medallion on a slim chain that might have been silver. On the front was the worn image of a female saint with a border of horizontal lines emanating from her robe to the edges of the medal.

"It's the Virgin of Guadalupe," I said, "the patron saint of Mexico. In 1531, she revealed herself to a poor Indian named Juan Diego on the outskirts of what's now Mexico City. Her image miraculously appeared on his cloak and supposedly it's still there after almost five hundred years. They're talking about making Juan Diego a saint, too."

"I'm impressed. How do you know this? Don Felix?"

"I worked on a documentary called *Religions of the World.* Besides, you've been to Mexico. She's everywhere, on guest soaps and shopping bags. When I was there I bought a Virgin of Guadalupe devotional candle, the thick glass kind you find in bodegas in the Bronx.

"Anyway, the Virgin told Juan Diego to climb this hill and cut some flowers. Even though it was December, and Juan Diego couldn't believe there would be flowers growing in the winter, he climbed the hill. When he got to the top, it was covered in roses of Castile. He took them to the doubting Thomases in town, who fell to their knees at the miracle. When he dropped the flowers, the Virgin's image was on his cloak."

"You believe that?" she asked.

"I didn't say I believed it. It was a souvenir. And the candle was cheaper than the Zapata T-shirt."

"Come to think of it, I bought soap on Bourbon Street once that was supposed to wash away evil spells. I had to repeat this one line over and over while I was lathering up. Is there any writing on the medallion, you know, like a prayer or incantation?"

"You bought spell-removing soap at Marie Laveau's and you're giving me grief about someone twenty-six popes have recognized? Let me see." The front was easy, *Con ella todo, sin ella nada.* "With her, everything, without her, nothing." The back was trickier, a lot of microscopic writing. I squinted at the tiny, imprecise lettering. I zoomed in on the picture.

"Something she was supposed to have said to Juan Diego. *'Let not your heart be disturbed. Do not fear the sickness. Am I not here, who is . . . your mother?'* Holy shit."

"It says *that*?" Lucy asked.

"Up to the holy shit part. Don't be afraid, little baby? Am I not here? Your mother? Some poor Mexican woman buried her child with this medal. Someplace she knew it wouldn't be disturbed. A place that wouldn't cost her anything, that she could visit as often as she wanted."

"Did the Peacocks have any regular help?" Lucy asked.

"Not inside, only garden help. And even that stopped as they got older."

"That's not much help," she said. "Ever find out what became of the real sister?"

"No. I can't believe I keep getting suckered into telling O'Malley stuff, when he volunteers nada."

"What did Hillary say?"

"I haven't seen her. I have been working, you know. I'm more likely to bump into Gerald Fraser at the diner."

"That reminds me. Dave Melnick knows him. Well, not really. *Knows of*. Dave's at the Cop Channel now. I bumped into him and he asked about you, so I told him about your case, and he e-mailed me some stuff. Your Fraser's some kind of hero cop. I don't think they're going ahead with it, but he was researched for an episode on a missing girl. Want me to forward what Dave sent me?"

"Great." Maybe I'd try to see Hillary and Gerald this week.

"Jeez, '*Am I not here . . . who is your mother?*'" Lucy repeated.

"Yeah," I said, "but where?"

CHAPTER 25

Only one eye was open when I heard the door downstairs. If Anna was here already, I'd overslept.

"Meez Paula?" she called.

"Up here," I mumbled. A steady rain had fallen all night and was falling now. Maybe subconsciously I knew gardening was out, so I slept in.

Still in my jammies, I made my way to the kitchen and, zombielike, started the coffee. Anna put down her voluminous handbag and her packages and just stared.

"Don't you need to grind those beans first? Why don't you let me do that while you get dressed?"

I yawned and nodded. Fifteen minutes later, I was back. The smell of the coffee stoked my appetite. When Anna offered me one of her four heavily buttered Portuguese rolls, I wolfed it down.

"This is delicious," I said, mouth stuffed.

"You need to eat more. You are too skinny."

I repeated my mantra. "I'm not, I could lose a few."

"Says who? Some magazine?" She pushed another roll toward me, but I passed.

"When the man holds the woman, he doesn't want to feel bones. It's true." She nodded sagely, and who was I to question the words of an experienced courtesan?

Revived by the caffeine, my brain was functioning again. I reached for more coffee and noticed the time on the coffeemaker—6:34.

"Anna, isn't this a little early for you?"

"I got a ride. I was waiting for the bus in the rain, and someone offered me a lift." She mumbled something in Spanish and looked agitated.

"Is there something you want to tell me?" I asked.

"It is nothing," she said. Anna lifted the coffeepot and offered me more, launching into the nonstop Spanish she knew I couldn't keep up with. One thing I was able to understand, *"Boca cerrada, no entran moscas."* Loosely translated it means, "Flies can't enter a closed mouth." Or "keep your mouth shut." She retreated to my office and closed the door behind her. I kept my mouth shut; maybe she and Hugo had had a spat.

With all this rain, gardening was definitely out; tramping around in the muck isn't good for the soil, and anything planted in this goop probably wouldn't survive. Instead, I decided to tackle a less pleasant but necessary task.

Guido Chiaramonte's heavy machinery—the chipper and the riding mower—had already been returned, but I still had a lot of smaller items that belonged to him. Hand tools mostly—dibbles, augers, *coas*—many more than I had reason to own in my one-woman operation. I dreaded it, but I'd bring them back myself.

It was too early to leave for either Halcyon or Guido's, and I'd started to regret Anna's buttered roll, which was already settling on my hips, so I embarked on another less pleasant but necessary task—cardio. By my calculations and according to the heart-rate monitor Lucy had given me, I'd need fifty minutes on the rowing machine to work off that baby, and I dreaded it. Cardio was boring. The best experience I'd ever had on a rowing machine was the time I accidentally caught *Ben-Hur* on television and did my workout to the chant of ramming speed, but I didn't own the movie and thought it unlikely I'd get lucky twice.

I bailed after thirty minutes and went a few rounds with the punching bag. The smack of leather hitting leather brought Anna out, armed with a heavy-duty stapler—God knows what damage she could inflict with that thing—but she quickly retreated when she saw it was just me and not a return visit from our prowler.

She was still sequestered in my office by the time I was ready to leave. My anorak hung over the banister. I grabbed it and my keys and yelled to her that I'd be back after lunch. I rooted through the backpack to make sure I had the cell.

"If Hugo or Felix calls they can reach me on the cell, okay?"

"*Sí, sí, sí,* but I am leaving soon." Then more Spanish too fast for my gringo brain to decipher.

The rain had eased from blinding to driving. At Halcyon, a black Lincoln I recognized as the Stapleys' was parked at the side of the house. I called out for Richard a few times, but was eager to get out of the rain, so I hustled over to the greenhouse and started packing up Guido's tools. Early on, Hugo had cleverly suggested we put colored tape on the handles of anything we'd borrowed to make sure it was returned to its rightful owner. I picked through two large Rubbermaid containers for tools with orange tape on the handles, Guido's color. I peeled off the tape, and gave them each a swipe with an oiled rag before loading his into a single container.

The rain had picked up again, and the sound of it on the greenhouse roof was like artillery fire. Or what I imagined artillery fire was like. But I still had an hour to spare, and nothing more to do, so I ran from the green-house to the never-locked back door. Inside the mud-room I shook off the anorak and stamped the rain from my shoes, checking the time again. Not enough time to start a new project but too much time to spend with Guido Chiaramonte.

Looking around the tiny room for a second time, I noticed the small framed needlepoints were bordered with roses. I made a mental note to look up the quotes; even without knowing their origin, the sentiments about sisterhood were moving.

I went inside the house and up the stairs to Dorothy's library. As soon as I entered, I could sense something was different. The fine layer of dust that had covered everything when Neil and I were there was disturbed. Not cleaned, just . . . handled. The library table, the globe, the books themselves, everything was slightly askew. Then I noticed one of the needlepoints was miss-ing. So were three or four books.

I'd mentioned to someone there might be rare books here but couldn't remember to whom or whether I might have been overheard. I searched for *The Temple of Flora*. Right where I left it. Since that was arguably the most valuable book in the library, robbery didn't seem a likely motive. Was there really a journal as Neil seemed to recall? And was something in it someone wouldn't want found? I walked to the bookcase where the shelf had been cleared out, and hunkered down to see.

"Looking for something?"

I turned around quickly, slamming my shoulder into the solid oak bookcase.

"Richard! You startled me. I didn't hear you."

"Horrible weather. I'm surprised you're out in it." He shook out his hat and rolled down the cuffs of his pants. Standing there quite still, face dripping wet, he made me nervous. He seemed to be waiting for an explanation.

"I was just getting in out of the rain," I said, rubbing my shoulder. "I'm on my way to Chiaramonte's, but I had some time." He stood motionless and said nothing.

I worked my way around the library table to the side near the door. "Have you seen this?" I pointed to *The Temple of Flora.* "It's amazing. I understand there are only twenty or so in the world. The original plates were destroyed after an auction. To make the books more valuable," I babbled.

"That's a clever investment strategy. Anything else of interest?"

"No. I just happened to notice the book because a copy was on display at the New York Botanical Garden. I kept meaning to go see it. I thought maybe the Peacocks had a journal or diary—you know, like *The Country Diary of an Edwardian Lady,*" I joked.

"You know, strictly speaking, we never discussed your needing to enter the house."

I started to explain that I'd called SHS, then decided I didn't want to get Inez in trouble.

"I hope it's not a problem." He didn't answer.

"The insurance company isn't scheduled to come for another few weeks, but I've been downstairs all morning trying to inventory anything of value. China mostly. I just ran out for a coffee before starting on this room." He thumbed through the copy of *The Temple of Flora.* "Thank you for telling me about this, although it's likely just a reproduction," he said, turning the book over in his hands.

Richard's cheery manner from the other day had vanished, and in its place was the clipped, supercilious tone I'd experienced that first day at SHS. Okay, maybe he was bipolar. Maybe he thought I'd stolen something. I thought of the book I'd borrowed and wondered when I could sneak back in to replace it without Richard's knowing.

"Don't let me keep you," he said. "And give Chiara-monte my regards."

CHAPTER 26

Compared to other nurseries in southwestern Connecticut, Chiaramonte's had a decidedly retro style. He didn't carry five different types of basil, and he didn't sell resin Buddhas, Japanese stepping-stones, or tranquility chimes. Most of Guido's shrubs looked like they had set down roots right out of their nursery pots, and he eschewed all other bedding plants in favor of red and white impatiens. Not even New Guinea impatiens. How he stayed in business was baffling.

I opened the door to Guido's shop, displacing two of the nursery's many cats, and the fresh-faced clerk behind the counter seemed stunned to see a customer on such a miserable day. She was chair-dancing to whatever pounding music was pumping through her headphones and hand-lettering one of the crude, self-promotional signs Guido wanted me to place at Halcyon. I'd have to nip that baby in the bud. I told her why I was there.

"He must be in the back," she said, removing her headphones and wearing them as a necklace. "I just got here. I haven't seen him yet." She sifted through the clutter on the dirty counter—Bag Balm, watering worms, and sell sheets for deer fencing. "We have these walkie-talkies. They're kind of lame, but would you like me to try him?"

"Sure, give him a buzz."

I lingered near the electric space heater while she fiddled with the buttons on the walkie-talkie, which she apparently rarely used, since her strategy was to push every button and yell hello. Hanging from the beams in Guido's shop were baskets of all shapes and sizes, and Styrofoam hearts, crosses, and wreaths. Maybe that was it. Guido catered to the cemetery crowd. As long as people kept dying, Guido would stay in business.

"He's not answering, but he doesn't always carry his walkie-talkie with him. The car's here though, so he must be around."

"No problem, I know where the office is. I'll drive around to the back. If he's not there, I'll just leave the tools and a note."

That would be a break, not having to actually interact with His Oiliness. I pulled into the pergola-covered parking area that separated Guido's trailer from the rest of the nursery and crossed the wet gravel to Guido's office. The door to the trailer was open and I could hear the crackle of the walkie-talkie as the girl kept trying to reach him.

I knocked on the door frame. "Guido? Mr. Chiara-monte? It's Paula. I've brought back the rest of your tools."

I stepped into the trailer, trying to make as much noise as possible. With Guido's reputation, I didn't want to catch him in flagrante anything. Catalogs and plant labels were everywhere. On top of a gray metal file cabinet was a plaster model of the Fifields' grotesque fountain.

"Guido?"

I ventured farther inside and detected a subtle shift in the decor—from messy office to sloppy love nest. A saggy, stained couch conjured up images of Guido and his women. A boom box and a handful of audio-cassettes—Jerry Vale and Dean Martin, as I expected, and a generic opera compilation—sat on the plain pine coffee table.

Ooooh-kaaay, I thought to myself, *time to hit the road.* It would be just like Guido to be standing behind me with a bottle of wine and a head full of crazy notions.

I was about to leave when something on the floor caught my eye. White and fluffy, at first I thought it was another of Guido's cats. It didn't move, but something else did. A huge fly, feeding on the pool of blood the head was sitting in. Guido Chiaramonte was facedown on the floor of his trailer—a long-handled Mexican *coa* protruding from his back.

CHAPTER 27

EMS was there in six minutes. The girl and I sat in the shop, waiting for the cops. She was numb.

"What's your name?" I asked, trying to pretend things were normal.

"Tanya."

"Tanya, do you want to call your parents? Or someone to pick you up?"

"I don't have a cell. My folks won't let me have a cell yet. And Mr. C. doesn't let us use the phone for personal calls." She was shaking now, making noiseless sobs.

"I think just this once it'll be okay."

Tanya was in the process of leaving someone a long-winded, disjointed message when Mike O'Malley and the other cops arrived. They told us to sit tight, then they headed for the trailer. Twenty minutes later, O'Malley came back to the shop. He questioned me first.

"Why is it you're the only one to find bodies in this town?" he whispered, not wanting to frighten the girl.

"Maybe you're not looking," I snapped. "Besides, he's not a body. He's still alive, right?"

"Barely. It's a miracle with all the blood he lost. Good thing you came along when you did."

I shuddered; if Richard hadn't interrupted me in the library, I might still be there, reading. And Guido might be dead. "I came here, saw Guido on the floor, and called the police. End of story. That's all I know."

O'Malley turned his attention to the girl.

"This is Tanya," I said.

"Tanya—Richardson," she added. "I have to pick up my little brother from his piano lesson at four."

"Don't worry. We'll be finished long before then," Mike said gently.

"Mr. C. doesn't let us have the keys. I don't know how I'm supposed to lock up." She began to blubber again; I handed her a tissue. "Is—is he going to be all right?" she asked.

"He's in good hands now. And don't worry about the shop; we'll take care of it. I just need you to tell me everything that happened this morning."

"Nothing happened. Nothing. I can't believe I switched days with LaToya. I wasn't even supposed to be here." She shredded the tissue in her lap.

I put my arm around her for support.

"Just tell me everything from the minute you walked in the door," O'Malley said.

"I got here at eleven. Mr. C. wasn't around, but that's not unusual. He gets here at the crack of dawn, so sometimes he's eating lunch and listening to music when 'his girls' come in. That's what he calls us," she sniffled, "me, and LaToya Kidd. LaToya doesn't like it, but I don't mind. He's a harmless old geezer." She blew her nose loudly. "I didn't have one customer all morning. Until this lady." When did I change from *girl* to *lady*?

"Not even someone who didn't buy anything?" Mike asked.

"Nobody."

"No phone calls?"

"None. Well, one, but it was a hang-up. I figured it was a telemarketer who didn't realize he'd dialed a business."

"You remember what time it was?"

"Maybe eleven fifteen, right after I got here. Honest, I didn't see or talk to Guido or anybody until this lady came."

When O'Malley finished with Tanya, he asked if she'd like a ride home.

"Are you kidding? If my neighbors see me coming home in a police car, my parents will ground me for life." She looked at him as if he were titanically stupid.

"I can give Tanya a lift, if she wants."

She nodded enthusiastically.

"I may have a few more questions for you," O'Malley said to me.

"I'm not skipping town. You know where to find me."

"That I do."

I hadn't been in the diner for five minutes before O'Malley slipped into the booth opposite me.

"Jeez. You don't waste any time."

"I hadn't quite finished with you, but I didn't want to scare the kid any more than she already was," he said.

"Me neither," I said. "That's why I drove her home. I tried to reassure her, I even suggested it might have been an accident—but she's a smart girl, I don't think she bought it."

"You think she's okay?" he asked.

"She's all right. What's that thing people always say about kids . . . they're resilient? I love that. She was more concerned about putting on a good face for her little brother. I called the hospital; Guido's still unconscious," I said.

"Yes, I know."

I'd intruded on his turf. "Sorry. Any suspects?"

"Apart from you? How much time do you have? They're not exactly putting up any statues to Guido in Mexico or Guatemala or Colombia. Or here, for that matter. A lot of his workers have probably wanted to do the same over the years."

"But actually doing it, that's something else."

Mike looked down at the six dishes on the table. Babe and Pete saw the fuss at the police station and had heard about Guido. They'd been plying me with comfort foods since I walked in; dishes were lined up in formation from one end of the table to the other.

"You should have the soup before it gets cold. Cold matzo ball soup is not a good thing," he said. "Will you be eating that muffin?"

I slid the plate over to his side of the table.

"No one in the neighborhood heard anything unusual," he said. "Someone saw an old rust bucket parked on the block that morning. No plates, no ID. There's no guarantee it's anything, but we're checking it out." He sliced the muffin into quarters, furthering my suspicion that we had nothing in common; I'd have picked off the top first.

"The weather was not our friend," he went on. "The rain kept most people indoors, except you, so there aren't a lot of witnesses. You'd think the rain would help with tire tracks or footprints in the nursery, but what wasn't gravel or mulch was a swamp. Primordial ooze. As it is, we've only got yours and some wheelbarrow tracks. What's most telling, as you may have noticed, my budding sleuth, is that there was no sign of a struggle. Guido casually turned his back on his assailant, and was stabbed. We've got a few leads. Not many."

Which he wasn't inclined to share with an amateur in a crowded public place. He poked through a bowl of condiments until he found a foil thimble of jelly that met with his approval.

"You'd have to be pretty pissed off at someone to plunge a knife into his back, wouldn't you?" I said. "There isn't the anonymity of dispatching someone from a distance. I imagine shooting someone would be a lot easier than feeling a knife go through someone's flesh."

"I guess that lets you off the hook. Personally, I'm glad to hear you say that," Mike said, reaching for my knife. "Have you given this much thought or is this all gleaned from repeat screenings of *The Godfather*?"

"Guido may be a terrible boss. But few people really kill their employers, even if they fantasize about it. Someone must have *really* hated him."

"Maybe it was the last straw, one insult too many, one salacious remark too many," Mike said, meticulously layering jelly on his wedge of muffin. I knew he was leaning toward one of Guido's workers.

I shook my head. "I know these guys. I can't believe any of them could do this. A lot of them don't even realize how objectionable Guido can be, because of the language difference."

"You know them? Is that so? You mean like Hugo and Felix?"

He had me there. How well did I really know any of them? They came, they pruned, they left. They could all be mass murderers or nuclear physicists in their own country for all I knew. I was starting to worry. I hadn't known about Hugo and Anna and I hadn't been able to tell that Felix wasn't a garden-variety leaf blower. And I hadn't seen either of them for days. Were they really working elsewhere and managing the family fortune in Mexico, or were they hiding out?

"Speaking of which. Where are Hugo and Felix? You were joined at the hip a few weeks ago."

Well, not quite, pal. Maybe O'Malley did know about that night in the greenhouse. I mumbled something about the new office building, and steered him away from my missing workers.

"I just don't see Guido enraging one of the workers this much. A good *screw you* maybe, but a knife in the back?"

He brushed the crumbs from his fingers, and smiled at the simpleton sitting across from him. "As I said, we're following up on a few things."

O'Malley got up to leave just as Babe returned with two portions of red Jell-O.

"Off so soon?" she said, putting the plates down. "This is my speci-*al*-ity."

"Thanks for the muffin. She's buying." He turned and left.

Babe sat down and helped herself to one of the Jell-Os.

"O'Malley thinks one of the workers did it," I whispered.

"What do you think?"

I tried to erase the image of Hugo's purple face when he thought Anna had been attacked, and his anger over Guido's racist remarks; I only hoped he hadn't overheard any of the smutty comments that followed. And I hoped the rust bucket that had been spotted at Chiaramonte's nursery hadn't been Hugo's.

"None of his workers stays with him long enough to hate him that much. But who else could come and go unobserved?"

She nodded in agreement as she sliced her spoon into the Jell-O. "I haven't seen Felix in a while. You two have a lovers' spat?"

"I'm not even going to dignify that with an answer." I didn't bother protesting, since Babe seemed to know everything and probably knew about our aborted roll in the mulch. "I think he's in Mexico."

"That's a helluva commute."

"I don't know if he's coming back."

"C'est la vie. Stabbing," she said, taking another poke at the quivering dessert. "That's serious hate. That kind of hate takes time to develop."

With the spoon halfway to her mouth, Babe stopped and stared right at me. We'd had the same thought.

"Maybe years. Maybe forty to fifty years?"

CHAPTER 28

I didn't know how nervous to be. The next morning I got to Halcyon early. I jogged around to the back of the house and was relieved to find Hugo working on the pear trees near the stone wall. He saw me and waved me over, but I stood motionless, rooted to the terrace, watching the sun glint off Hugo's shiny new *coa*.

He sensed something was wrong and started toward me.

"What is it?" he asked.

"Do you know about Guido Chiaramonte?"

"I do."

"Hugo, where is Felix? And where were you yesterday?"

"I can't. *En boca cerrado.*"

"Don't give me the *boca cerrado* line. This is serious. Hugo, you might be in a world of trouble."

He said nothing.

Hugo's well-known dislike for Guido, his unfortunate display of temper in front of the cops the day he thought Anna was attacked, the money owed, and Guido's salacious cracks about Anna. And now the squeaky-clean *coa*. I didn't believe he was capable of it, but the cops were going to treat Hugo, and possibly Felix, as suspects in the stabbing of Guido Chiaramonte.

The three Springfield police cars pulling in to the Peacock driveway confirmed my suspicions. Mike O'Malley walked straight over to us, barely acknowledging me.

"Hugo Jurado? We'd like you to come down to police headquarters to answer some questions related to the attack on Guido Chiaramonte. You have the right to remain silent. . . ."

He continued to read Hugo his rights, while I stood there in shock.

"Sergeant O'Malley, Hugo's English is not that good. Is there any reason I can't come along as a translator, before he retains counsel?" I asked.

O'Malley continued with his note taking. "Officer Guzman can translate." He turned to face me. "If that's even necessary. By the way, Mr. Jurado's vehicle has been identified as the one seen near the Chiaramonte nursery on the morning of the assault."

I was about to protest when O'Malley held up his hand to stop me, adding, "And his fingerprints were found on the weapon." That silenced me.

Finally Hugo spoke. "Ms. Paula, I will finish the espaliers on the wall when I return. Some of the wires are coming down; you should take a look at them. And, please, let my Anna know that I am all right, and I will call her as soon as I am able." Hugo was led away by the cops, and I was alone.

Not long after the cops left, I got a frantic call from Maybel Peña, Ann's daughter. I barely had time to scribble down her garbled directions before she ran back to her mother's bedside. The Peñas lived in Somerville, a modest neighborhood of bodegas, hair salons, and storefront churches. Their apartment was in a tidy white-washed building with colorfully painted iron gates on all the windows and seedlings growing out of lard cans on the steps.

Anna's daughter opened the door. Maybel was every Japanese businessman's dream date. Golden skin, soft curves, masses of ringlets, all wrapped in the white knee socks and seductive plaid uniform of St. Agnes's Girls School.

"I'm sorry to have bothered you, Miss Holliday. My mother is very upset. She's been like this for hours, and she won't tell me what's wrong." The kid broke down. "She keeps insisting only you can help her, so that's why I called—"

"You did the right thing. I'll talk to her."

Maybel led me through the kitchen, where her homework was spread out on the table, to a small bedroom in the back of the apartment. Anna was lying in bed, fingering a rosary and staring at the ceiling. I knocked on the open door, and she hoisted herself onto her pudgy elbows.

"Oh, thank God, you are here, Meez Paula. Maybel, sweetheart, go finish your studies. The grown-ups must talk alone. And close the door, like a good girl." She waited until her daughter was gone before continuing.

Anna Peña had just found the perfect lace mantilla when the cops walked into Dona Maxi's Bridal Shoppe on Calhoun Street and escorted her to the police station for questioning. "Meez Paula, he didn't do it. The police don't believe me."

She spit out something in Spanish. "*Dios mío,* this will kill his mother. If I don't do it first. That silly woman. He is so superstitious—they both are. And now that I tell the police, he thinks it will bring him more bad luck."

"Worse than being arrested for attempted murder?" I asked thoughtlessly.

She rolled over and mumbled into her pillow, something I couldn't quite make out.

"Anna, I'm sorry. That was insensitive. What did you tell the cops?" I asked.

"The truth," she wailed plaintively, as if that was the dumbest thing she could have done.

The truth was that Anna had given Hugo a new set of tools, including the spanking-new *coa*, as an engagement present. And she talked him into going to Chiaramonte's the morning Guido was stabbed to collect the money Guido owed him.

"I never should have forced him to go. It's all my fault. But that was hours before they say Guido was stabbed. We were already downtown by then, getting the marriage license." She collapsed into tears again.

She recovered, and continued. "He didn't even tell the police, because he thinks it's bad luck if his mother isn't the first to know. So *I* told them and he was angry with me. What could I do—let him go to jail?" And now he was there anyway.

Anna told me how the happy couple waited seventy-five minutes for their number to be called at the license bureau. According to the cops, that was more than enough time for Hugo to drive back to Chiaramonte's, stab Guido, and return to the office in plenty of time to sign on the dotted line.

"Weren't there witnesses? There must have been a roomful of people if you had to wait that long."

"Have you ever been in love, Meez Paula? There was a roomful of people staring into each other's eyes. I couldn't see anyone else there but my Hugo. What if no one can identify him? The police say they will look, but I am scared. Meez Paula, he didn't do it."

"What can I do?" I said lamely.

She bolted upright. "You can help us. You must. That police officer likes you—he'll listen to you."

"He's liking me less these days. He's mad I didn't tell him about Hugo's car, so now he thinks I'm hiding something." She looked at me, pitifully. I'd dashed her only hope.

"I may know some other people who can help," I said.

CHAPTER 29

They both had gates to keep out undesirables. Otherwise, Chestnut Hill, New York, was as far away from Somerville, Connecticut, as you could get, the kind of place where every few years some yahoo caused a stir by trying to park his Cessna on his front lawn.

As I drove on, the houses got bigger and more elaborate. It reminded me of that old joke. A guy gets a flat in an upscale neighborhood. He doesn't have a jack, and it takes him a while to walk back to the last house to borrow one. It starts to rain, and he's muttering about his bad luck, his crummy car, and the undeserved affluence around him, and by the time he rings someone's doorbell, he says, "Screw you and your jack."

An unseen person buzzed me through the wrought-iron doors that then swung closed behind my car. I continued around the well-tended circular drive to the front door of a huge Tudor house, where Hillary Gibson came out to greet me. She wore a blue cashmere sweater, a white shirt with the collar turned up, and wide-legged pants. She extended her hand.

"Ms. Holliday, please come in. I rather thought I'd hear from you sooner."

I left the car where it was and followed her up the short steps to the house. The center hall was large, with a sweeping staircase off to the right. To say it was simply decorated was an understatement. It was practically empty. Just a few Oriental rugs and lots of plants. She anticipated my reaction.

"I know," she explained. "Friends tell me I really need to get some furniture. My former husband's taste was so execrable that when he left I couldn't wait to get rid of everything. And I've taken my time replacing things. I like it sparse."

"So do I," I fibbed, thinking of my own tchotchke-crammed house.

Hillary's former husband had made a fortune in insurance. Dubious business practices had earned Randall Adams an eighteen-month stay in a minimum-security prison in Danville, Pennsylvania. As expected, Hillary stood by her man during the scandal, but they parted quietly shortly after his release. She kept the house, and a ton of dough, most of which was hers anyway; he got to disappear, probably avoiding further prosecution, with his twenty-three-year-old surgically enhanced secretary. Hillary didn't seem to mind and, in fact, couldn't wait to jettison the Adams name and have it chiseled off the stone pillar in the front of the house, which remained tellingly blank.

Her low heels clicked on the marble tiles as she led me through a garden passageway to a P-shaped conservatory overlooking a small stream. The conservatory was classic Victorian—all mahogany and leaded glass with solid brass handles and fittings. The roof vents were automatically controlled but had a manual override to let the air in on cool, sunny days. Hillary raised them as we entered.

The room held three enormous date palms. A

bird's-eye maple vanity with a triple-paned mirror served as a sideboard, where tea and cookies were waiting for us.

"Please sit down." She motioned to a grouping of mis-matched faux bamboo furniture and, without asking, started to pour the tea.

"What a wonderful space," I said, taking the cup. "Doesn't the humidity ruin the furniture, though?"

"The greenhouse hasn't really been used for years. It's been my sitting room. That may change."

"Well, it's lovely. Perfect," I added.

"Not quite," she said, "but almost."

I wondered what she thought was missing. "I see you're something of a gardener yourself," I said, eyeing the landscape outside.

"I've always enjoyed the peacefulness of the garden and the beauty, but not the work. Gerald was always the hard worker of the two of us."

Hillary's family had lived on the same block as the Peacocks for years; some distant cousins had even married. For as long as she could remember, though, it had just been the two women, Dorothy and Renata. As a child, Hillary was treated to the best side of her sometimes antisocial neighbors. She had the run of the gardens and the maze, which she'd mastered by the age of seven. Only the herb garden was off limits.

By the age of twelve, Hillary was old enough to realize others thought her friends strange, but she didn't care. Especially that summer, when Adonis appeared in their garden, in the form of Gerald Fraser. He was handsome, tanned, terribly serious, and, at fifteen, an older man. Despite her parents' protests, their friendship evolved, eventually deepening into love.

"Your parents didn't approve of Gerald?" I interrupted.

"He was poor and they were snobs," she said matter-of-factly. "Gerald worked harder and studied more than anyone I ever knew. He got a scholarship to study art abroad," she added with pride. "Gerald was all set to leave when his father had a stroke. Eventually, his father recovered, but Gerald's mother never did. She was as helpless as a child, didn't even know how to write a check. It took all the money Gerald had saved for the family to get back on their feet."

She took a sip of tea and broke off a small piece of cookie but didn't eat it.

"Dorothy Peacock pleaded with Gerald to take a gift or a loan from her, but his father wouldn't hear of it. So Gerald stayed here, helped his family, and commuted to Teachers College. Eventually I went off to Vassar." She sounded guilty, even after all these years.

"One day," she continued, "just before I left for school, Gerald and I were strolling through the maze, daydreaming about the future and what we might do. Exiting the maze at the white garden, we came upon Dorothy and Renata. They were . . . embracing. Only then did we realize why they'd been so reclusive and why there was this fiction about Renata's frailty when she always seemed perfectly healthy to us."

"So they were lovers. Ms. Gibson, do you know what happened to the real sister?"

"The real Rose Peacock *was* frail; she'd suffered from rheumatic fever as a child, and it weakened her heart. She never fully recovered. That's why it was so easy to convince people the woman they *thought* was Rose was sickly.

"As soon as Rose arrived in Italy, she fell ill and was confined to her bed. Rose never even learned of the accident that killed their parents; she died soon after.

"Renata was a wealthy English girl studying art in

Florence. She and Dorothy were close before, but inseparable after Rose's death. When Dorothy decided to return to America, she convinced Renata to join her—as Rose."

"Why not as herself?" I asked.

"It was an accident, really. Renata used Rose's return ticket onboard ship. The purser knew, of course, but everyone else thought the two were sisters. They decided to continue the ruse after arriving in Springfield. That way they could live together and no one would suspect."

"Nobody noticed?"

"Their social circle was small. They didn't see the butcher and the mailman every day the way you or I would. And William was such a small child when Rose left, he wouldn't have known."

"And when they had their annual party," I added, "Renata stayed indoors, watching from the library." That part I'd read in the papers. "Which was the reason everyone believed she was sickly."

"Just in case," Hillary said. She took a deep breath. "Lesbianism wasn't chic in those days, the twenties were over and the seventies hadn't arrived yet. They said William was crushed when he found out. He was only a boy, fourteen or fifteen when he left Springfield, bitter, confused, and vowing to never return."

"Did he ever return?"

"He might have come back once—I can't say for sure. I was rather young at the time. The sisters always spoke so fondly of him. They kept thinking he'd show up one day, and then their little family would be complete."

"People seemed to think he went west."

"That's possible; a lot of people did in those days."

"It can't have been easy to keep up a charade like

that for so many years. I feel rather sorry for them," I
said.

"They had each other and friends, I believe, in other
cities."

"That would account for the trips to out-of-town
specialists."

"Yes. Everyone's life is different," she added a little
sadly. "Don't feel too sorry for them. They brought
each other a lot of joy. Not many heterosexual couples
stay together for over sixty years." She straightened up
in her chair, possibly thinking of her own unhappy
marriage.

"There were some in town who knew, or suspected,
but they kept quiet—after all, it's nobody else's business. It was courageous of them to defy convention like
that at a time when most folks didn't." She briefly disappeared into her own thoughts.

"In any event, the sisters were wonderful to us,
which is why Gerry and I don't like hearing the assump-
tions people are making."

"Ms. Gibson, something even more serious has happened. Guido Chiaramonte has been stabbed and Hugo
Jurado has been arrested."

She hadn't heard.

"No one who knows Hugo would believe him capable of that. I think it's possible the baby I found may
have something to do with Guido's stabbing." I trod carefully. "Since you don't think either of the sisters was
the mother, have you any thoughts on who the mother
might be?"

"I'll assume you're including me on your list of suspects, but you can cross me off. I can't have children."

I hoped I didn't look too disappointed. And I hoped
she was telling the truth. "It sounds like not many

strangers had access to the property, so it was very likely someone they knew," I said.

"Over so many years that could be a hundred people."

"A special friend or art student?" I suggested.

"Not that I can recall."

"Someone who worked there, maybe in the garden?"

"They didn't keep live-in help, but I couldn't say for sure. After all, I haven't been a local for almost thirty years."

"Oddly enough, that may be just the right time frame."

"Guido Chiaramonte." She shook her head. "A thoroughly disreputable man. I probably shouldn't say it, but it's a wonder somebody didn't stab him years ago."

Perhaps Hillary knew another candidate? "Did you see much of him when you lived in Springfield?" I asked, wondering if she could have been another of his old flames.

"I wouldn't say much. Let's see, I was away at school when he moved here, so I suppose it was when I was home on holidays. He always seemed to be there at the Fifields', hovering and leering. I don't think he suspected the sisters' true relationship," she said. "That would have been beyond his comprehension.

"I'll give it some more thought," she said, "but you should talk to Gerry. He has some very different ideas on the subject. I said as much to Sergeant O'Malley. He was here yesterday."

The sound of a vehicle crunching gravel in the driveway brought the interview to a close. "You'll have to excuse me now," she said, getting up. "That must be my architect."

"Thank you for seeing me. I will call Mr. Fraser."

She walked me to the door.

"It's a wonderful house," I said politely. "What are you having done?"

"I'm putting in an elevator. A friend of mine has trouble with stairs."

CHAPTER 30

From the porch of the Sunnyview Nursing Home, a resident would have a good view of both Morning Glory Cemetery and the Springfield Recycling Center. I wondered if the old folks appreciated the constant reminders that we're all future compost. Gerald Fraser saw me pull into the driveway, and he waved me over to where he sat, tapping his gimpy leg to keep the circulation going.

It was a far cry from the picture I'd gotten of him last night. On the passenger seat of my Jeep, stuck in between nursery receipts and old copies of *Garden Design,* were the attachments I'd finally printed out from Lucy's e-mail of the week before: two articles from the *New York Times* and two from the *Bulletin.*

The first *Times* article had a cropped picture of Gerald Fraser's graduating class at the police academy, with Fraser's head circled. Wrestler's body, thick brows, superhero jawline, and million-watt smile. Full of testosterone and good intentions. The headline read: CT COP SAVES JOGGER IN PARK.

On March 17, 1976, Fraser and some other local cops had been in New York for the St. Paddy's Day Parade. After a busy day marching and partying, Fraser and a few of his buddies were watering some bushes in the north end of Central Park when they surprised two guys attacking a woman. Fraser zipped up the fastest and took off after the assailants. He managed to subdue them both but not before being stabbed in the leg so viciously the doctors thought he'd never walk again. And never be a cop again. They were only half-right. The second *Times* attachment was one line in the Metro Briefing section, **HERO COP GOES HOME.**

The *Bulletin's* headlines were almost as intriguing: **FORMER COP REPRIMANDED** and **FORMER COP TAKES 1ST PRIZE AT BIG E ARTS FESTIVAL.**

"Come on up," he said, putting his paper down. "Hard to believe all this is coming back. And then some."

I took the stairs two at a time and settled in next to him on one of Sunnyview's green-and-white-striped gliders. "I appreciate your seeing me." An attendant brought us a pitcher of iced tea and two glasses.

"Thanks, Genevieve. I love to watch her walk away," he said to me, looking at her. "I don't get many visitors. Except Tom Robbins, the kid from the recycling center. He brings me scrap metal for my sculptures and slips me the occasional *Victoria's Secret* catalog for inspiration."

"I'd like to see them one day," I said politely. "The sculptures," I clarified. "I was surprised when Babe told me you lived here. If it's not too presumptuous, you don't seem old enough."

"I'm not. Some developer offered me a ton of dough for my property, and I couldn't refuse. I like to think of this place as a bad hotel I'm temporarily booked into until I find the right piece of land to build on."

"Did you say something, Officer Fraser?" a nearby worker chirped.

"I was a detective." Under his breath, he added, "Half-wit.

"My wife had just passed away," he said, returning to me, "and the kids had scattered. It was too much house for me and too many memories. The last few years were tough, especially with the kids so far away, but she didn't suffer. At least, not according to that quack doctor. You know 'Dumbo' Parrish?"

I shook my head.

Robert "Dumbo" Parrish had been the class clown when he and Gerald were kids, but he gave up his plans for a career in stand-up comedy when a minor surgical procedure corrected his protruding ears and changed his life. Impressed by his doctor's power, he decided to devote his life to medicine, but fifty years later—and with no evidence of his previous deformity—many still referred to him as "Dumbo."

"Well, I see your memory's still good," I said positively.

"It's my curse. Take me to lunch. You'll be rescuing me from the week's culinary atrocity, chipped beef on toast. That way I can tell you what I know away from Nurse Ratched here." He motioned inside to a perfectly pleasant-looking woman whose name tag actually bore the unfortunate name Ratched. I agreed and we made our way haltingly to my Jeep.

"It just stiffens up a little if I sit too long," he explained. "My leg, that is."

"I feel like I know them already," I said, holding the car door open for Gerald.

"Who?" he said.

Maybe he was older than I thought. This was going to be a long afternoon if he couldn't remember who we were talking about. "The Peacock sisters," I said gently.

"Sure, sure, kid. We'll talk about them. But the person you really want to know about is Yoly Rivera. I wouldn't be surprised if she's the mother."

CHAPTER 31

Yolanda Angelina Grace Rivera was born in Mexico in a dusty, corrugated shack held together by bottle caps. Her mother was a worn-out woman of twenty-three, and by the time Yoly was sixteen, she realized her life would be no different from her mother's. So one season, when the men went north for the harvest, she stuffed a few things in a nylon shopping bag and left her small town to go with them.

In El Paso, the group contracted for agricultural work on the East Coast, picking crops in Florida—beans and tomatoes mostly. Rickety buses and trucks took them from one state to the next, one crop to the next, through the Carolinas, up to Virginia, then to New Jersey and New York. In New York she learned about the tobacco crop in Connecticut, and when the rest of the group drove south to start the cycle again, Yoly headed east.

She worked the tobacco fields for a year, then got work as a nanny for a crew leader with five children. She wasn't much older than the kids she was looking after, but it kept her from the backbreaking work in the fields, and Yoly loved the kids and dreamed of one day having her own family in this quiet Connecticut town. When the season ended, and the crew leader moved on,

Yoly stayed. In her last letter home, she said she was engaged to be married to a very important, very wealthy man, *un hombre de renombre*. Yoly's mother never heard from her again.

Fraser unfolded a familiar-looking piece of paper and handed it to me.

"This is the missing persons flyer I saw at the police station, I said."

"No one wants to be the one to take it down. It would be admitting defeat."

"So you think she's dead?"

He nodded. "I bet her mother wrote a hundred letters, looking for that poor girl," Gerald Fraser said. "The department never even answered her. Chief Anderson just threw those pitiful letters in a drawer, said we had no time to chase down 'some little wetback.' Nowadays the mother would go on TV and on the Internet. They'd find the kid like *that*." He snapped his fingers. "Like I said, though, probably dead." He pushed his coffee cup to the edge of the table and signaled Babe for a refill.

"Those days Chiaramonte had the only nursery in town. He'd hire illegals who were too scared to complain if he treated them badly. He denied it, but I felt sure that Guido and Yoly had met. What if they more than met? What if the baby is Yoly's and Guido's?" He sat back, a satisfied grin on his face.

"Even if it's true, what's the connection with the Peacocks? Did Guido work for them?"

He shook his head. "The sisters didn't like him. But he did work next door. And he was there a lot more than any gardener needed to be."

"Still, who would try to kill him now, after all these years?"

That was a question neither of us could answer. If

my naive plan had been to save Hugo by finding the real assailant, it was backfiring badly. If Guido was connected to this missing Mexican girl, and she was connected to the baby, that could be a motive for Hugo, or some other Mexican, to have attacked him. And I didn't want to think about who that other Mexican might be. A lot of *ifs,* but this was a small town—even smaller thirty years ago. Anything was possible.

"I just can't believe Hugo's involved, even if this Yoly is somehow related. Millions of Mexicans have come to the States. They don't all know each other."

"Ray O'Malley, Mike's dad, and I were out drinking one night. We took some heat for it afterward, but we wrote to the mother in pidgin Spanish. You should have seen the two of us, with no more Spanish than you'd get off a bottle of Dos Equis. It didn't matter, though—the letter came back marked undeliverable. Not that we had any answers for her. We just hated to think of that poor woman sending these letters off into the void, and no one having the common decency to reply. Then this happened," he said, slapping his leg, "and I got sidetracked."

"You don't happen to remember the town she was from, do you?"

"I can do better than that," he said. He pulled a tissue-thin, pale-blue airmail envelope out of his breast pocket.

"The postmark's illegible, and unfortunately I only put the month and date on the letter itself, but Phil Anderson was chief at the time, and he didn't get promoted till 1973. This would have happened a year or two after that."

"You think Ray O'Malley might remember?"

"I doubt it. They're not calling it Alzheimer's yet, but he's got all the signs."

I held the envelope with both hands.

Sra. Celinda Rivera, c/o La Palapa Hotel, Alpuyeca, Mexico

"Can I have a friend of mine take a look at this? I promise to return it."

"Be my guest. But remember, you'll be raking up something that's been buried a long time, and, chances are, whoever stabbed Guido isn't going to like it. If I think of anything else, I'll give you a holler," he said, easing out of the booth. "Don't get up. I'm going to walk back to Sunnyview. The exercise will do me good."

Once standing, he looked as fit as he did in his academy picture. He strode to the door of the Paradise with just the barest trace of a limp. If you didn't know, you might not have even noticed. He must have felt me staring, because he turned to me just as he was leaving. "This doesn't count. You still owe me lunch, kid."

Back home, I checked my atlas. Alpuyeca wasn't even on the map, but an online search showed it was uncomfortably close to Temixco, Hugo Jurado's hometown.

I didn't know if Felix was back—or if he had even really gone away—and I didn't have his phone number, so at 6 A.M. the next morning I headed for the downtown corner where the day laborers congregated, on the outside chance someone there would know how to find him.

Dozens of them, maybe a hundred, clustered at the coffee shop, dressed for work. Some knew who they were waiting for; most just showed up and hoped. They hoped they'd get picked, they hoped the work was safe, and they hoped they'd get paid what they were promised. These were the people who fixed roofs, laid tile, put up walls, planted trees—and we called them unskilled workers. Most of the men *I* knew didn't know which end of a hammer to hold.

I was the only woman in the coffee shop, except for Gina. At least that's what was written with a black Sharpie on her uniform. It may have been the last girl's name. She was barely visible behind a hill of plastic-wrapped rolls. In Spanish, I asked if she knew Felix. She shook her head quickly and moved on to a paying customer. *That went well.*

A young man shyly approached me to offer assistance. He identified himself as one of the small army of men Felix had brought to work at the Peacock house. I managed to get a cell number for Felix and reached him right away.

"*Hola, maestra.*"

"Are you still in Mexico?" *Damn—that came out too fast.*

"Yes. I had to attend an emergency board meeting and I also agreed to deliver an important package for a friend. Don't get nervous—I'm not a drug dealer. It was a letter to Hugo's mother and a present for her. He didn't want to entrust it to the mail."

I moved away from the throng of men, smiling and trying to pretend I was having a casual conversation. "Hugo's been arrested for stabbing Guido Chiaramonte." A ripple went through the crowd at the mention of Hugo's name, and the men moved away from me, either to give me privacy or to distance themselves from a potential legal problem. I gave Felix the details. "They have Hugo's fingerprints on the weapon and they think they have a motive. The cops may not know it yet, but Gerald Fraser may have uncovered something even more damning." I told him Yoly's story.

"Do you think Hugo could have known her?"

"Everybody knows somebody named Rivera in Mexico. Close your eyes, spin around, and touch someone.

It is like hitting a piñata: every third person is named Rivera."

"Gerald has a letter he wrote to the mother. It'd be more helpful to have one of Yoly's letters, but this is better than nothing. Maybe her mother worked at that motel. It's the La Palapa in Alpuyeca. We can at least check to see if the place still exists."

"Oh, it still exists."

"How do you know?"

"I've passed it a thousand times. It's the only two-story building in Alpuyeca. It's on the main road from Cuernavaca to the coast."

"You're kidding. Well, then we can just call them and see if they know how to contact her."

Before the words even left my mouth, I knew how ridiculous that was. Did Babe keep tabs on every waitress who passed through the Paradise? His hesitation told me what he thought of the idea.

"I know it won't be easy, but Hugo needs us. And it may solve a thirty-year-old mystery—two, if the baby and the missing girl are connected. Isn't that worth a few phone calls?"

"It's unfortunate you weren't there thirty years ago when Yoly Rivera went missing. It might have spared her family a lot of heartache." He chose his next words carefully. "We must be careful not to reopen old wounds if this has nothing to do with Celinda Rivera's daughter."

He was right about that part. Why break some woman's heart all over again?

"My Spanish is good enough for me to get in touch with someone at La Palapa. Maybe there were stories in the Mexican papers. Any chance of you getting info from your media contacts down there?"

"I'll see what I can do. And I will arrange for Hugo

to have the best attorney in southeastern Connecticut—
one of those sharks who handles all your white-collar
criminals. You'll see. Everything will be all right."

"I wish I had your faith in the judicial system."

The thought of media contacts reminded me of
Jonathan Chappell, that pest from the *Bulletin*. Maybe
I'd break down and talk to him . . . if he'd agree to do
something for me.

CHAPTER 32

The dark, shaggy head bobbed up and down, fumbling for something on the front seat of the old white sports car. Leaning toward the passenger window of the tiny car, Jonathan Chappell looked up at me. "I was beginning to think you were avoiding me," he said.

"Whatever gave you that idea?"

"I don't take it personally. Most people hate to talk to the press, even a small fry like me."

Well, at least he didn't have any delusions. He was scrawny, bookish, and, judging from the fresh acne scars, younger than I expected. He looked as if he should have been writing for his college paper instead of the *Springfield Bulletin*. A scraggly beard, probably grown to make him look older, was just filling in. He pulled his car around to the right-hand side of the Peacock house.

"Nice wheels."

"Thanks. Got it on eBay. Still needs a little work. So, your highness," he said, hands on his nonexistent hips, "why did you finally decide to grant me an audience? You must want something pretty bad."

So much for being cagey. "I have some stuff I'd like

to show you. There's a cottage in the back. We can talk there."

"Okay. Great place," he said, looking around as we walked across the terrace to the herb cottage. I could see him trying to calculate the property's value. "Helluva job you've done here. It was a dump." He turned to me. "Were you here that first day when the Mexican guy said you weren't?"

"Of course not," I protested, although I *had* been there the second time he stopped by, crouching in the maze until Felix assured me the coast was clear.

Inside the cottage, we brushed off the rickety chairs and sat down. I started to empty my backpack onto the old wooden table Dorothy must have used to prepare her herbs. Then I stopped. "You have to promise me something."

"Conditions? I don't like this already. Where's the trust?"

I wondered if I should go ahead. "The only reason I'm talking to you is to clear Hugo Jurado's name. I have a feeling the baby I found *and* a missing girl may be connected to Guido's stabbing." I was having a hard time spitting it out; you'd think I was coming out myself. "There's something about the Peacock sisters . . ."

"You mean that they were carpet munchers?"

I winced. "Do you kiss your mother with that mouth?"

"We went back and forth on that at the paper," he said, trying to sound like a grizzled veteran. "To me, news is news—'All the print that fits,' as my junior high school paper taught me."

Chappell claimed his editor yanked all his best stuff. **CRAZED LESBIANS SACRIFICE BABY. HOW MANY MORE DID THEY KILL?** I couldn't tell if he was kidding.

"I knew he'd never let those stories run. Hypocrite.

He said it was like putting in all the gory details of a child murder—who needs to know? 'The *Bulletin's* not the *Enquirer,* you know. When does it stop being news and start being pandering?' " he said, mimicking the editor I was starting to like. "Damned if I know." He shrugged. "I spent all of my time in ethics class hitting on the girl next to me. Great rack. She wanted to be an anchor—not a reporter, an *anchor*."

I was betting she never gave this weasel a tumble.

"I can't make any promises," he said, "but you should feel better since we already knew they were sweethearts and haven't printed it. No promises about the missing girl either. So now you've got me interested, who is she?"

I hated his style and still wasn't sure I could trust him, but I needed him. I had no choice. I showed him everything: scribblings, notes, and the faded missing persons notice Fraser had given me.

"Pretty girl."

"I think you'll agree it's unlikely one of the 'sisters' was the mother of the baby. Yolanda Rivera disappeared around here sometime in the early seventies. I think she may be connected to the body. And Guido Chiaramonte may be connected to her."

"So the baby was wearing a Mexican necklace. O'Malley didn't tell me that. Probably wanted to keep the crackpots and fake confessors away. And a Mexican girl went missing some years ago. Doesn't this give your amigo even more of a motive?" Jon asked.

"It may give *someone* a motive, but I know it isn't Hugo. He's one of the sweetest men I've ever met. He says he's innocent, and I believe him."

"Touching. What do the cops say?"

"Nothing. I don't think any of them has made the connection yet. Fraser said Yolanda didn't know the

Peacocks. She didn't know many people at all—that's why the original investigation hit a dead end."

Chappell looked at the pictures again.

"He also gave me this." I whipped out Gerald's letter to Mrs. Rivera and showed it to Jon.

"That hotel still exists," I said, pointing to the address. "I spoke to the current manager, Jaime Gutierrez, this morning. Celinda Rivera, Yoly's mother, did work there years ago, and he thinks she's still alive. He didn't know where she was, but he said he'd ask around. I told him to call collect if he found her."

"Not bad. So what is it you think I can do for you?"

Was he dense? I chose my next words carefully. "I don't believe *no one* knows what happened to that girl. Maybe they didn't think anything of it at the time, or maybe they knew exactly what was going on. If you wrote a story on Yoly, it might jog people's memories."

There was no response.

"What? Why are you looking at me like that? This is a good story. Are you too busy working on the sequel to the walnut feature? **THE DARK SIDE OF HAZEL-NUTS?**" I said, exasperated.

"Relax. I'm just jerking your chain. Aren't gardeners supposed to be patient? Of course I'll write the story. That's what I do. We just have to think how we're going to play this."

He took out a small tape recorder. "Start with the day you found the body."

When I finished, Jon said he needed copies of my research, so I suggested a drugstore about three blocks away that I knew had a copier. I scooped up my papers and shoveled them into my backpack.

"Want to walk?" he asked.

"And miss the chance to ride in that snappy vehicle? No way."

"Top down?"

"Of course." The car was a Sunbeam Alpine, white with a red leather interior. I waited while he collapsed the top and tucked it away.

He turned the key in the ignition, and, after a few false starts, the car sputtered to life.

Ehrlich's was an old-time pharmacy. A small sign in the window, next to a glass urn filled with colored liquid, read ESTABLISHED 1872. A woman who could have been one of the original cashiers told us the mimeo machine was located in the back, near the pharmacist's window. While Jonathan figured out how to use the copier, I nosed around.

The store looked as if it had been frozen in time. While most drugstores today carry flash drives, copy paper, and rainbow-colored condoms, Ehrlich's still sold individual hairnets in blond, black, and brown. Hair dye, shoe polish, yellowed greeting cards—everything looked old even if it wasn't. One display did look familiar—Bach Original Flower Remedies. My health food store had the same green wall rack.

Dr. Edward Bach was a general practitioner in London in the 1920s. By 1930, he'd left Harley Street to devote himself full time to research on natural remedies, identifying thirty-eight ailments and the thirty-eight plants and flowers he claimed could alleviate their symptoms. I'd heard about him from a dancer friend who swore by his essences to calm her nerves before performing.

I stood there reading about the different floral essences and how they were used—gentian, for feelings of discouragement; olive, for lack of energy; walnut, to help adjust to a new situation. Bach remedies had been around for seventy years. With more people turning to alternative medicine, I guessed they were seeing a resurgence.

"How's that copying coming?" I yelled to Jonathan, still reading. "Do you have a future as a guy Friday?"

"Don't break my concentration, I'm on a roll."

I felt a tap on my elbow and heard a faint, childlike voice behind me.

"Paula? I thought that was you."

"How are you, Mrs. Stapley? Are you getting excited about the fund-raiser?"

"Oh, yes. So many RSVPs. Richard's had me order more food and party supplies. He's enjoying the fuss. He refers to it as troop movements."

"Sounds like *you're* doing a lot of the work," I said.

"I was very fond of Dorothy. Richard, too. You know he built the stone wall there. No mortar," she added proudly.

"I didn't know that."

Chappell finished his copying and joined us at the cash register.

"Who's next?" the cashier asked.

I motioned for Margery to go first. She had just a few items, so basic as to make me think they were a cover for her real purchase—two small brown bottles of Bach Flower Essences—honeysuckle.

"I was just looking at those. Do they really work?"

"Yes, they do. I'm a firm believer in floral and herbal remedies," Margery answered, her chin lifted. She sounded a little defiant, as if she expected me to contradict her.

She put the two small bottles in her purse while the clerk bagged the other items. "Well, children, I'm off. More errands to run. Richard's bicycle is in the shop. I may surprise him and pick it up."

"There's a sweet lady," I said to Jon, as she left.

"Husband's kind of a prick, though," he whispered. Once she'd gone, he continued. "He was in the war,

Korea. The way he parades around you'd think he'd stormed the beaches at Normandy."

"What did he do before he retired?"

"Big-shot lawyer. He was a partner in Russell, Jenkins and Stapley."

The cashier painstakingly counted out the copies, twice, as if fifteen cents one way or the other would make a huge difference in the day's take. "You two probably never even heard of a mimeograph, have you?" the cashier said.

"Sure—some kind of Flintstonian copy machine," Jon said, putting his change and his receipt in a separate section of his wallet.

I kicked him on the way out.

"Look who's calling someone else a prick," I whispered on our way out. "What'd Richard ever do to you?"

"He squashed a couple of good stories. Didn't squash, really, but he was aggressively unhelpful."

Chappell told me that two years ago there was a heated controversy in town about extending the downtown sewer system. Most residents were against it, except for those who stood to make a profit from it. Stapley helped both sides reach a compromise, but it opened the door for increased development, which had yet to materialize but was threatening.

"Rumor had it Stapley had a silent interest in one of the companies looking to build, and he adamantly refused to be interviewed on the subject. I don't ordinarily hold a grudge, as you well know, but I made an exception in his case."

"Well, you said yourself most people don't like to talk to the press."

"There's a difference between personal stuff and community affairs. The public has a right to know," he said with a straight face.

"Catchy. You make that up?"

"Chiaramonte was probably happy about the sewer deal, too. That run-down nursery of his must have tripled in value—he doesn't need to sell another . . ." He struggled to think of a flower.

"Honeysuckle," I prompted.

The honeysuckle reminded me of something.

"Hold on a sec." I ran back to the drugstore.

When I returned, Jon asked, "So, what's it for? The Bach's honeysuckle?"

"To help 'stop yearning for the past.' And the poor dear needed two bottles."

CHAPTER 33

Despite the efforts of Felix's high-powered lawyer, Hugo Jurado was still in custody, considered a flight risk. Anna Peña dutifully brought him clean shirts and socks. And empanadas, which the Springfield cops let him heat in their microwave since she brought plenty for them, too.

The last word from Felix was that he had a scheme to find Yoly Rivera's mother, but that had been two weeks ago. Since then, I'd heard nothing.

Jon Chappell was also missing in action, but clearly he'd made more progress than either I or Felix. His first article had caused a sensation. And he followed it up. Like a determined terrier he'd dug up any scraps of information on the missing girl and had not let up.

Jon's biggest score had been finding a copy of one of Celinda Rivera's letters to Chief Anderson, which he published on the eve of the Historical Society's party. The story of Guido Chiaramonte's stabbing was relegated to the inside pages, and after thirty years, Celinda and Yoly Rivera were finally front-page news with the not-too-subtle headline WHERE'S MY DAUGHTER? A MOTHER'S ANGUISH. Chappell's editor seemed to be caving in to the younger man's tabloid tactics. I guess it was hard to argue with newsstand sales and with the results—it was all anyone in town could talk about.

The crowd at Penny's Nails was abuzz with gossip and theories. Penny's had six manicure stations and four pedicure stations, and there wasn't an empty seat in the house. The phone was ringing off the hook, and waiting clients were stacked up like airplanes at O'Hare. All in anticipation of that night's soiree at the Springfield Historical Society.

Among those getting buffed and waxed pre-party was Caroline Sturgis. She wiggled a paraffined hand in my direction and smiled before leaning in to whisper to a friend.

I would not have been there, perched in a vibrating pedicure chair with my pant legs rolled up and my whiter-than-white calves exposed, if Lucy Cavanaugh hadn't dragged me in. My heel marks were still visible in the parking lot.

"Real gardeners don't get their nails done between March and October. Between digging in the dirt, moving rocks, and washing up fifty times a day, what's the point?" I said. It made no impression on my well-groomed friend. The night before, Lucy had tossed her bag in the backseat of my car, given me the once-over, and shaken her head in disgust.

"If we had more time, I'd do something about the hair. At the very least, you're getting a manicure and a pedicure. You'll thank me later."

"It's a small-town event. With all that's going on here, I think I can safely say my toes will not be the hot issue."

" 'Mother used to say you could always tell a lady by her hands,' " she quoted reverently from *Gone with the Wind*. "You don't have to look like a field hand. Besides, potential clients will be checking you out. Maybe you should wear a hat. Don't garden ladies wear dramatic hats?"

I nixed the hat but agreed to the mani-pedi, though few things filled me with as much trepidation as having my little piggies manhandled by some stranger. It ran a close second to going to the gynecologist, and usually required a glass of wine first to loosen me up. Hands and feet splayed, only the stirrups were missing, when Mike O'Malley walked by the salon.

"Oh, great."

"What's the problem?" Lucy whispered.

Mike tapped on the glass as if we were puppies hoping to be adopted.

"Which one is that, anyway—number two or number three? It's so hard to keep track of your turnstile romances. I can't believe all the trouble I go to to meet men, and you just stay home and they come to you," she said, eyeing him through the window. "He'd be cuter if he had a little more definition."

The bells on the front door jingled as Mike came in, and the young Korean proprietor fussed over him, giggling as if it were hysterical for a man to be in a nail salon. At least that's what I think she was laughing about; for all I knew he was here every week, getting his knuckles waxed.

I hid behind a magazine and pretended to be immersed in an article on how to wear green eye shadow tastefully. It didn't work.

"Afternoon, ladies."

I hadn't seen him since the night at my place. If he'd learned anything new, he hadn't shared it with me, and I was just as happy to keep my distance from the police station. Like two fighters, we'd retreated to neutral corners.

I peeked over the top of the magazine. "Sergeant O'Malley. What a surprise. Manicure or pedicure?"

"Or bikini?" Lucy added.

"I couldn't get an appointment. I'll be reduced to handling my own grooming," he said, spreading his fingers. "What do you think—cut cuticles or push back?"

"Push back," Lucy said, aghast.

"We haven't seen you in a while." He slipped into the royal *we,* so I did, too.

"We've been busy at the house."

"We?" he asked.

With Hugo languishing in jail and Felix still in Mexico, there was no *we,* but I wasn't sure O'Malley knew Felix was out of the country, and I didn't want to be the one to tell him.

"Neil MacLeod has helped out. And Lucy," I said, recovering quickly. "We're almost finished, but there may be more we can do if we get any additional contributions. Richard's anticipating a few last-minute surprises tonight."

"Looks like your little side investigation is also starting to bear fruit," he said, holding up a copy of the *Bulletin*.

"And there's more," Lucy added. "Tell him what Felix has been up to."

"Do tell," Mike said.

I pushed a button on her vibrating chair and sent her shaking like a washing machine on spin cycle.

"He-e-e-ey." She fiddled with the controls and returned herself to gentle cycle. "What was that for?"

Mike turned to me. "Anything you'd like to share with the group?"

"Nothing yet. I'm still recovering from the psychological letdown of my candy fiasco. When I know something for sure, I'll be sure to let the proper authorities know."

It came out snottier than I'd intended. Like a good pal, Lucy broke the icy silence that followed. "So, will we be seeing you at the big bash tonight, Sarge?"

"Yes, ma'am."

"And will you save a dance for us?" she flirted.

"I don't think there's going to be any dance music. I can bring my accordion if you like."

The young Korean girl tapped my toes and motioned for me to put my feet in the whirlpool bath. I couldn't possibly hold a conversation while I was getting a pedicure; I squirmed too much, and I was starting already. Tactfully, O'Malley turned to leave.

"Well, I'll leave you ladies to your ablutions. See you tonight, then."

"I may want to revise my initial comment." When he was safely outside, Lucy added, "Do you think he really plays the accordion?"

"Why? Are you suddenly developing a taste for ice-skating music?"

She leaned in. "How many men do *you* know who can move their fingers and push in and out at the same time?"

CHAPTER 34

Richard Stapley's silver hair gleamed under the crystal chandelier. I could almost hear the cash register ringing inside his head as he grinned and posed for the videographer who was chronicling the evening's festivities.

Poster-sized before-and-after pictures of the garden were displayed around the grand wood-paneled room, as was an early portrait of Owen Peacock. The walk-in fireplace was filled with fresh flowers; I was camped out in front of it when Richard sidled up to me.

"I don't think we'll have a problem getting you anything else you need for that garden, Paula." He looked around the Historical Society's crowded gallery, doing a silent head count. "I do believe we may even have something left over for that bonus I mentioned." Bending down closer to my ear, he added, "We should have charged fifty dollars."

As it was, for a modest thirty-five-dollar contribution anyone in town could dress up, drink nondescript jug wine, and gossip to their heart's content—and feel civic minded while doing it. They came like locusts—community activists, avid gardeners, and the just plain curious.

Hillary Gibson and Gerald Fraser were there. So

were Caroline Sturgis; the thrift-shop ladies; Richard's wife, Margery; and a couple hundred others I didn't know. The mayor was in attendance, but no one turned more heads than Babe Chinnery and Neil MacLeod. Anyone who thought she lived in jeans and a leather bustier had another think coming. She was elegant in a slinky tuxedo suit, tats hidden, and he was striking in a suit that could have been Zegna. They might have been going to the Grammys.

"I've got to hand it to your development people. This is a fantastic turnout," I said to Richard.

"I wish we could take the credit for it," he said, surveying the crowd and occasionally acknowledging someone, "but I think we both know it was those articles in the *Bulletin*. I believe you know Jon Chappell?" He knew I did.

Jon was standing with a group of people I didn't know, and probably didn't want to—granite-faced corporate types who'd clammed up the minute he joined them. He excused himself and came over to us.

"Jon, I was just telling Paula this is mostly your doing. I suppose I should thank you." Richard gripped him tightly on the shoulder.

"Some people thought you might postpone the party, sir, in light of what's happened," Jon said, praying for a slip of the tongue that he could print.

"What's happened? You mean Chiaramonte?" Richard seemed genuinely surprised, but it had occurred to me, too. "I'm sorry, of course, but he has nothing to do with the Historical Society. He's not even a member. And we have our own responsibilities—don't we, Paula?" Richard finally released his hold on Jon's shoulder and left us, to welcome Congressman Win Fifield and his entourage.

"No thanks necessary, sir," Jon called after him

loudly, for others to hear. He rotated his shoulder. "Quite a grip.

"You clean up nice," he said to me.

I'd taken an old Nicole Miller out of mothballs, one of those little black numbers that'll look good forever; and since no amount of sunscreen keeps all the sun off a gardener, I had a little color.

"Thanks. Please tell me I haven't created a monster."

He pretended not to understand.

"'A mother's anguish'?"

"Give me a break. A month ago, the biggest news around here was the invasive hogweed story. I've earned this. *We've* earned this. I've got my editor eating out of the palm of my hand thanks to you." He gave me a little toast and downed his drink.

"We're sniffing someone out, I can feel it," he said, reminding me I was his coconspirator. "Don't play innocent—you called me, remember? Besides, a little press—it's got to be good for your business."

"Right—landscaping, water gardens, exhumations. I can hear the phone ringing now."

"I'm getting another." He snorted. "Want one?"

"Sure. Red wine."

Jon walked to the bar, and I was briefly alone. I looked around for Babe or Lucy, who'd dropped me off, then gone to park the car. As I scanned the gallery I couldn't help but feel that if we interviewed everyone in the room, we'd have all the answers to the baby mystery, Yoly Rivera's disappearance, *and* the stabbing of Guido Chiaramonte. I felt someone behind me. I turned, expecting to see Jon or Lucy. Instead it was Mike O'Malley.

"I was thinking the same thing myself," he said.

"What?"

"We should just question all of them. Right here."

"How on earth did you know what I was thinking?"

"I'm the detective, remember? Actually, you said it ever so softly. You do know that you talk to yourself?"

"Damn. Another secret out in the open. You won't tell?"

"I'm very discreet. Ask anyone. You look good tonight. Different." He squinted, as if trying to figure out what it was.

It wasn't the dress or the flame job on my toes. It was the blow dryer. At Lucy's insistence, I'd resurrected the dusty Conair from underneath the bathroom sink. Unused for almost a year, it started up like a new car.

It was scary how quickly one could slip back into the tyranny of blow-dried hair. Instead of pulled into a ponytail, plastered against my skull, and stuffed under a hat, my long auburn hair was sleek and shiny and tucked behind one ear.

"No baseball hat, that's it. I don't think I've ever seen you without one," he said.

"It took me an hour to rub the Knicks logo from my forehead," I said, not comfortable discussing my appearance with the cop. What was next? My skin? My boobs? "I don't suppose you've had any success finding a witness to confirm Hugo and Anna's story?"

"I'm afraid not."

Just then, Jon returned with our drinks. "Hello, Michael."

"Jonathan." To me, Mike said, "I'm not much for parties. I just made an appearance to show my community spirit. I'll see you tomorrow around eight, then?"

I had no idea what he was talking about but found myself saying, "All right" as he left to mingle with a knot of people just to our right. Out of the corner of my eye, I found Lucy and signaled for her to join us. She and Jon exchanged CVs and theories; Jon was instantly smitten. As if her looks weren't enough, Lucy's experience in reality-based programming had him lapping at her feet and inundating her with questions.

"Hey, Jimmy Olsen, come up for air," she said. "This is a party, isn't it? Or have I once again been brought here under false pretenses? Make yourself useful and get me a glass of something, okay?"

Jon left to do her bidding before she finished speaking.

"Nice kid," she said, used to having acolytes.

"Maybe."

"Not my type, of course, too young. And there's something peculiar about that beard."

I cut her off because her new servant was back in a flash with her drink.

"I thought the Jeep was big," she said smoothly, as if we'd been talking about cars in Jon's absence. "There are SUVs outside bigger than my apartment."

"Like they all need them," Jon added. "Most of these folks don't do anything more adventurous than going to dinner without a reservation. I've got a Sunbeam Alpine," he said, trying to impress her.

"A Sunbeam? Is that so?" she said, not really caring since she didn't know a Sunbeam from a Sunfish. "I had to park near a bunch of cardboard crosses, too. What gives?"

"That's Arlington Cemetery. Memorial Day is coming." I was about to explain the suburban phenomenon of Holiday Harry when Springfield's illustrious congressman came into view.

Lucy recognized him right away.

"He's even sweatier in person," Lucy said, rolling her eyes in Win Fifield's direction.

Jon chugged some more wine. "And the blonde next to him? That's his *mother*."

"Wow. What's her doctor's name?" Lucy said.

As we made juvenile, mean-girl remarks, a young woman purposefully walked toward us. She had chin-length, blunt-cut hair, apparently requiring her to keep her head at a 45-degree angle at all times. She wore a dark, conservative suit and sensible shoes. The only hint of a personality came from her flaming red lipstick.

"That's Jess Colford," Jon whispered. "Loser's top aide. He'd be operating a car dealership if it weren't for her. Be careful: those ruby lips hide fangs." He dragged Lucy away, ostensibly to introduce her to someone, but I sensed it was to avoid a face-to-face with Colford.

Her eyes followed Jon and Lucy, but she quickly returned her gaze to me. "My name's Jess Colford. I'm an assistant to Win Fifield." Colford had a textbook handshake—not too long, not too short, not too personal. I could imagine her practicing it on herself. "The congressman would very much like to meet you."

The fangs were well hidden, so I thought why not (as long as Fifield didn't think I was going to hop into the backseat of his convertible). The small cluster of hangers-on parted as Colford and I penetrated the congressman's inner circle.

"Ms. Holliday, so pleased to meet you." Win Fifield extended a moist, hammy hand; I fought the urge to wipe mine after we shook. "Richard has spoken very highly of you. Very highly. And I understand from my mother that you've already increased the property values in her neighborhood with the job you've done." What a joker.

So far, he wasn't too horrible, just predictable. Then I noticed Jess Colford watching him like a hawk, as if they had rehearsed even this innocuous little greeting.

Three people from *Nutmeg* magazine converged on us and asked permission to take our picture. I only hoped it was a full-length shot so my freshly lacquered toes would be immortalized; Lucy would be so pleased. Jess Colford deftly plucked the wineglass from the congressman's hand and glided out of the frame.

"Unfortunate business, early on. Tragic, really," he continued, when the photographer left. "And now, of course, this other matter . . . very troubling. An honest, hardworking businessman . . . cut down in his prime, our—my thoughts and prayers go out to his family. . . ."

He was winging it now and babbling idiotic, sound-bite clichés. Chiaramonte was a lot of things, but honest and hardworking were not among them. And he had no family. Not as far as anyone knew. With impeccable timing Colford stepped in to the rescue. "Congressman, you'll want to say hello to Mayor and Mrs. Pilkington. You will excuse him." She pushed him off toward the Pilkingtons, with a few words in his ear, probably reminding him what he was to say to them.

"The congressman is really quite impressed with your work. He's recommending the town turn the empty lot on Brookhaven Road into a small park honoring his predecessor. If it goes through, I feel sure he'll want your advice on how to proceed."

Colford cast a quick look in the congressman's direction and saw that he'd delivered his packaged greeting, so she excused herself and went to bail him out.

"What did Dragon Lady want?" Jon asked when he and Lucy returned moments later, when the coast was clear.

"I'm not sure. If I were the suspicious type, I'd say it was a gentle bribe."

"See, I told you there'd be potential clients here.

Who's that one?" she said, surreptitiously pointing into the crowd. "We saw her at the nail salon."

"She's already a client, Caroline Sturgis." She saw us looking, so I waved, and she and another woman came over. They were working on a couple of martinis, and I had the feeling it wasn't their first round. Caroline's friend loudly claimed to need landscaping advice, so we chatted about that, and I gave her my thirty-second sales pitch and my card.

"PH Factor? Whatever does it mean?"

When that line of conversation dried up, it was strictly party chat. Chappell went to hover around Win Fifield's group, making sure to steer clear of the over-protective Ms. Colford. Caroline and friend moseyed back to the bar for thirds.

"Your buddy Jon?" Lucy said.

"He's not my buddy. Just a means to an end."

"He's got some major acne scars."

"That's very grown-up of you. I've been too polite to stare."

"I can't help it, I'm observant. He's obviously growing the beard to cover them, but you can still see them even though he's using hair dye to fill in the light spots. They looked like that constellation—not the Big Dipper, the other one everyone knows, the crooked *W*."

"Cassiopeia?" I asked, the light dawning. "Or maybe *W* for Wellington. As in Wellington aerator sandals," I said. I was furious. "Where is that little rat?"

Her eyes widened. "Anna's prowler? That sneaky little bastard."

I scoured the room for Mike O'Malley. This was something I did want to share with the group. I saw him leaving and called out across the room but couldn't catch his eye. Coming in as Mike left was a tall, white-haired gentleman in a gray, tweedy sport jacket and denim shirt that hung on his bony shoulders.

A clatter of glasses, then the crash of a drinks-laden tray caused a commotion off to my right.

"Let her have some air."

"Get a chair. Get some water. Where's Richard?"

"Richard!"

Margery Stapley had fainted.

CHAPTER 35

The party broke up shortly after Margery hit the deck and Richard whisked her away. The absence of our hosts gave us all license to leave and begin the business of serious gossiping in the privacy of our homes.

Lucy and I took our postmortem to the Paradise Diner. Jon Chappell had disappeared into the crowd when Margery fainted, and it was a good thing. I was ready to tear him a new one.

"Leave it to you to stare at a guy's pockmarks. What the hell was he doing snooping around my house and scaring Anna half to death?"

"This is the world in which we live. I bet he poked through your garbage, too."

Lucy was eyeing that morning's scones. "You don't want to eat those," I said under my breath. With that glowing recommendation, she got up, put two on a plate as if she worked there, and came back to the booth. Pete, the cook, was in love.

"Well, the air was certainly humming. And we seem to have gotten to the bottom of the Anna incident. What an asshole."

"Y Señor Felix?"

"Nothing. Still in Mexico, I guess. I'll give him one

more day before he goes on the DNR list—do not re-suscitate. For all I know, that entire playboy story was something he lifted from a Mexican soap opera. I thought he'd at least come back for Hugo's sake."

"Too bad. I had high hopes there."

"For . . . ?"

"Why not? He's handsome and possibly rich. And you didn't seem to want him. Stranger things have happened."

"Which leads me to Margery Stapley," I said, dropping the subject of Felix.

"What do you think really knocked the old girl off her feet?" Lucy said, working on her second scone. "I wonder if they got that on video. It could be, like, *Wedding Bloopers,* only *Senior Bloopers.*"

"I bet it had something to do with the older guy that came in just as O'Malley was leaving. The one in the denim shirt and tweed jacket. He had a familiar face. Did you notice him?"

"Just barely. Who'd you think it was?"

"This is probably crazy, but I thought it might be William Peacock, Dorothy's long-lost brother," I answered. "I've been looking at so many old pictures of Dorothy, I thought I saw a resemblance."

The swinging doors from the restrooms flapped against each other, and I felt someone standing over my shoulder.

"That's a damn good guess," Gerald Fraser said, sliding into the booth next to Lucy. "That was William. He was a teenager when he left. No one knew why."

"You think William found out that the woman he thought was his sister was really his sister's lover?" I asked.

"It'd be hard to keep it from him, once he got to that age. At the time, people thought he was just looking for adventure—too young to have been in the war, too old to stay home with his spinster sisters."

"And he never came back?"

"I couldn't say. Hillary recognized him right away, though, from all the pictures the sisters had."

He glanced quickly out the front door, and only then did I notice Hillary sitting in her Lexus.

"I'm gonna try to see him in the next couple of days. Care to join me when I do?" Gerald asked.

"Say when."

Gerald said good night and took off.

Lucy licked her index finger, picking up the last few crumbs from the plate. "At least someone's getting lucky tonight."

CHAPTER 36

The next morning, I dropped Lucy at the train station and drove straight to the police station to see Mike O'Malley. The station was locked, so I jogged across the road to Babe's.

"How's it going?" I asked, looking around. The crowd was mixed—late laborers and early commuters but no cops.

"It's going," Babe said, juggling dishes and menus. "Want a menu or just coffee?"

"Just coffee. I overdid it last night."

"Suit yourself. You're the one who's always saying you shouldn't skip breakfast."

Common sense kicked in. I ordered.

"You seemed distressingly sober. Did I miss something?" she asked, bringing my setup. "Unless you had your own little party afterward." Babe had a vivid imagination.

"After coming here for some surprisingly tasty scones, Lucy and I went home and gossiped till about three A.M. I polished off a container of yogurt, but that was as rowdy as it got. You'll just have to live vicariously through someone else's exploits. What am I saying? From the looks of it, you're not exactly sitting home reading the *Farm Journal* every night," I said, referring to her handsome young date of the night before.

"Yeah." She smiled. "Neil and I thought it was about time we went public. I was convinced we'd be a scandal, but Neil didn't care. Then old Margery conveniently got the vapors and stole the show. I'll have to thank her next time I see her. Anyone know how she is?"

I gave her the flimsy explanation Richard had left on my answering machine the night before, but neither of us really believed one glass of wine was enough to knock the old girl on her keister.

"Something took her breath away and it didn't come from Connecticut's wine trail."

Back at Halcyon, my regular parking spot was taken by a silver-blue Springfield patrol car.

"We did say eight, didn't we?" O'Malley knew I thought he'd meant 8 P.M., but I wasn't going to give him the satisfaction of saying it. He held out a cardboard tray with coffee and what looked suspiciously like half a dozen donuts.

"Don't worry. The donuts are for me—sugar fix. I got you a couple of low-fat blueberry muffins."

"A couple? Have you any idea what's in those things? Besides, I've already had breakfast. C'mon, let's go around to the back. I'll watch you clog your arteries."

We sat on the brick terrace and Mike handed me a coffee.

"I looked for you last night," I said, peeling a triangle out of the plastic lid.

"I'm flattered."

"Don't be. It was about the person Anna maimed with my aerator sandals."

"You mean Jon Chappell?"

The coffee hadn't even made it to my lips. "Am I, like, half a step behind everyone in this burg?"

"This may surprise you, but I am a real cop. After a nutritious, low-fat, omega-whatever salmon dinner not long ago, I popped by your neighbor's place—where the noise was coming from. I gave him a few tips on how to be a considerate suburbanite and was heading back to my car when I noticed a vehicle pulled over onto the shoulder near the bird sanctuary. If Chappell's going to do undercover surveillance work, he really should get a less memorable car. Or at least not announce at a crowded party that he owns a Sunbeam Alpine. Someone spotted a Sunbeam in your neighborhood the day of Anna's incident."

The police had picked Jon up an hour ago, and Anna had already identified him.

"You think he's the one who sent me the e-mail and locked me in the greenhouse, too?"

"He denies it. He's certainly been watching you, though. You might consider drapes."

"I might consider a burka, too, but I'm not going to," I said, a little too fast.

"What is your problem? First, you're annoyed that we're not doing our job, and then you're annoyed because we are. I've got to take things one step at a time. I can't go off half-cocked because some senior citizens have been filling your head with fairy tales. We got the bad guy. Granted, trespassing is only a misdemeanor, but at least we can put your conspiracy theory to bed."

"I'm not talking about finding Jimmy Hoffa. Hugo Jurado did not stab Guido. Certainly not over a hundred dollars and a few racy remarks."

"A few racy remarks? So you didn't know that Anna

had a run-in with Chiaramonte the morning he was stabbed?"

I kept my head down, picking at a few stubborn weeds between the bricks so O'Malley wouldn't see the shock on my face.

"Yeah. He offered her a lift at the bus stop and it was pouring, so she said okay. Apparently, he introduced her to little Guido. She threw hot coffee on the little guy, Guido slammed on the brakes, hit the car in front of him, and Anna had to jump from a moving car. Some people might think that's a pretty good motive.

"Look," he said, blowing out air like a dying balloon. "Got milk?"

"What?"

"Ever read a milk carton? People go missing all the time. It isn't that I don't care, it's just that the more time passes, the less likely they are to ever be found. That's reality. I know it doesn't sell newspapers or make good television, but there it is. And it's extremely unlikely that Guido Chiaramonte was stabbed in retaliation for a girl that went missing thirty years ago. I am sorry about Hugo—and, I agree, it does seem out of character for him—but it doesn't look good. And other than an alibi from his intended, he can't account for his whereabouts the day Guido was stabbed."

"What if he could? I thought of something last night at the party. Maybe someone at the marriage bureau had a video camera. People video everything nowadays. I've been to a civil ceremony. Even though it's just two people signing papers, they bring flowers, throw rice—why not shoot video?" My voice trailed off. "You could ask. Maybe put an ad in the paper."

I knew he was thinking of my great candy evidence, which had gone nowhere. So was I. We were quiet for a few minutes; the only sounds were me pretending to blow on my cold coffee and O'Malley poking around in the donut bag. He took out the muffins and set them on a paper napkin on the terrace, a piece of waxed paper covering them. Then he left.

After a few minutes, I heard three quick taps on a horn and the sound of a vehicle out front. I ran to see who it was, hoping it was O'Malley coming back to tell me that upon further reflection, my idea was brilliant.

It wasn't.

CHAPTER 37

"I've got some explaining to do."

"I agree," I said, standing stiffly, arms folded, in front of Jon Chappell. I was not happy.

"Your friend Lucy's great," he said, unfolding himself from the Sunbeam and trying to make nice.

"I know. She's smart, too. She's the one who spotted the Just for Men hair dye I was too polite to stare at. What the hell did you think you were doing?"

"My job. I'm sorry. I didn't mean to scare anyone. Then I met you and I liked you. I've wanted to tell you a dozen times since then but it never seemed like the right moment."

All the false bravado fell away. He looked like such a kid, I'd already forgiven him but wanted to drive home the point.

"Anything other than stalking you want to confess to?"

He admitted to driving by the house a few times, once when Lucy was there, and following me to the Paradise Diner a few times. As luck would have it, he also knew my geeky neighbor and had borrowed his telescope one night to spy on me.

"See anything interesting?"

"Nothing worthy of publication. Let me rephrase that: nothing I'd write about. You do have great abs, though."

"Stop trying to butter me up, pervert."

We walked around the porch to the back terrace, where the two muffins O'Malley brought me were crawling with ants. I tossed them into a nearby tip bag. Jon sat on the steps and flipped through the pages of his spiral notebook until he found what he was looking for.

"On the Yoly Rivera front. Like most things, there's good news and there's bad news. I found the wife of the crew leader Yoly worked for when she came to Connecticut. Real sweetheart. She called Yoly every name in the book—and some I hadn't even heard of. I'll spare you the more colorful details, but basically she thought our Yoly was a *puta.*" He brandished the word as if it wasn't part of his regular vocabulary but he was considering making it one.

"I thought I'd make her feel guilty by telling her Yoly disappeared, but the only thing she said was 'Whose husband did she take with her?' "

"She could just be jealous," I said, sitting down and leaning against one of the stone planters. "Pretty younger woman. Mrs. Crew Leader sounds like she might have missed the whole feminist sisterhood thing."

"After thirty years, you'd think she'd mellow out a bit. Don't you girls ever let bygones be bygones?"

"Nope. Friend of mine refers to it as sediment. Never really goes away. Scary, isn't it?"

He filed that feminine insight for future use.

"She also thought Yoly might have been moonlighting as a waitress while she was working as the nanny. Nothing permanent—weddings, parties, stuff like that."

He shuffled through some papers. "The crew leader's kids got a postcard from Yoly with a Rhode Island postmark." He looked up at me. "Life before Xbox; the kids collected stamps and noticed the postmark. Mom was thrilled; the farther away the better—she was just sorry the letters didn't come from Outer Mongolia."

"You think she relocated?"

"No. According to Mrs. Rivera's letters, she heard from Yoly twice after that, both times from Springfield. Not much else, I'm afraid. No luck finding Celinda Rivera yet, but I'm still working on it."

He was craving approval. As punishment for stalking me, I withheld.

"What's the story between you and the congressman's aide, the lovely Ms. Colford?" I asked, watching him squirm.

"I should have known it was only a matter of time before you started poking around in *my* direction. We had a thing; it ended. I'm not successful enough for her," he said. "She's dated a guy from the *Washington Post*."

Suddenly he reminded me of the nerdy twelve-year-old who didn't get picked for softball. Not only did I forgive him, now I wanted to help him make points with the little snob.

"That guy probably makes up his stories. Don't worry. By the time this thing is over, you'll be fielding job offers from all over. Just stay on the high road, okay? Lighten up on the 'Mother's Anguish.' The story's good enough without playing to the lowest common denominator."

I told him my idea about looking for someone who'd videotaped their wedding ceremony the day Hugo and Anna were at the marriage license bureau, and he was on it in a flash, scribbling notes and inventing a story line.

"I don't even have to say what it's about," he said, "in case someone is nervous about getting involved."

"Any ideas about your girlfriend's boss?" I asked.

"Win Fifield and Yoly Rivera didn't exactly travel in the same circles, but it's not impossible they knew each other. Pretty girl on her own, maybe on the sidelines at some high-profile parties? They could have met."

It was more likely she knew Guido Chiaramonte, especially with his taste for Hispanic women. But I had yet to find that connection. I debated whether I should tell Jon my theory about the Peacock sisters and their secret garden.

"Do you know much about herbal remedies?"

He perked up. "That reminds me of our other little drama. Margery Stapley."

We agreed there was something fishy about the one-glass-of-wine-and-she's-on-the-floor story.

"I ran out to e-mail my story about Margery collapsing. When I got back to the party, it had already broken up. I stuck around, offering to help clean up, and I got an earful. Did you know Richard isn't Margery's first husband? She was Margery Russell, married her high school sweetie, a guy named Henry Pierce. The honeymoon was barely over when Henry shipped out to Korea. He never came back."

"Richard was a transplant from Boston, an up-and-coming attorney in her father's firm," Jon continued. "It took a while, but Margery finally agreed to marry him. Seems Dad had a hand in it."

More than a hand. Apparently Margery's father had orchestrated the whole thing, including the financial arrangement that kept all Margery's assets in her own name.

"So she's loaded," I said.

"Correct. And she was so *delicate* at the time, her father was worried she might kill herself and her inheritance from her mother, who was a . . ." He shuffled through his notes. "Her mother was a Hutchinson—"

"As in the parkway?" I asked, astonished. "All those tolls must really add up."

"Dad didn't want the dough to go to an outsider in the event that something happened to Margery. Stapley married her in the early seventies; my Deep Throat at SHS wasn't sure when."

Jon had done well. "Did you notice the old guy at the party?" I asked.

"Which one?" he asked, and thought back to the crowd at the party. "The guy in the denim shirt? You think that was Margery's first husband? He didn't really die?"

"Calm down. It's not that weird. It was William Peacock."

"No shit."

"Keep your distance. Gerald and I are going to see him first."

CHAPTER 38

The lobby of the Hotel Criterion was a faux South-western style I placed as early 1980s. Large, dusty foliage plants softened the institutional atmosphere, but it still had the feel of a private hospital or sanatorium.

The place was empty except for a chubby desk clerk sorting mail and William Peacock, sitting near a small table set up with complimentary coffee and tea.

He was wearing the same tweed jacket and denim shirt he had had on the night before. In his face, I could see traces of the heartbreaker the thrift-shop ladies remembered. It was craggy and lined now, probably from too many years in the sun, and certainly from smoking. The ashtray in front of him was already full, and we weren't late.

"William, thank you for seeing me. Well, us." Gerald Fraser introduced me as the new caretaker of the garden, and, for simplicity's sake, I didn't correct him.

"I hope you don't mind if Ms. Holliday joins us. This is just a chat, not a police matter. As you know, I'm retired, and officially there's no case and no charges regarding the body found on your sisters' property. But there have been some strange goings-on lately. We thought you might enlighten us on a few things."

William had no problem talking to Gerald, or with my being there when he did. Once again, Richard Stapley had been my advance man and had been singing my praises about the good job I'd been doing at Halcyon.

"Not at all. Richard's firm usually handled my sisters' affairs, but he's recused himself in light of her bequest to the Historical Society. Brennan, Douglas and Marshall is handling the will. They just needed me to sign a few papers, and I thought I'd come back and take one last look around. I've got no quarrel with any of Dorothy's decisions." He stubbed out his cigarette. "I guess you're the gal that found the body?"

"Yes, sir."

"Which most people in town seem to think belonged to one of my sisters." He patted his pockets looking for his cigarettes. When he found them, he offered the pack to us. We both passed.

"I understand my sisters were very fond of you, Gerald, so I think I can trust you. 'Course, you may already know."

"That Renata wasn't really your sister?" Gerald said gently.

William nodded. "I was just a kid when I found out. I was pretty torn up. I wanted to get as far away from Springfield as I could. My plan was to hitchhike to California—I thought that'd be more adventurous than taking the train. I got stuck, though, in Texas. Spent the early years there, ranching, moving around quite a bit. Eventually, like most folks, I wanted to settle down, get a place of my own.

"I came back once, in 1959, to borrow money from my sisters. They thought I'd fallen off the face of the earth. I'm not a big letter writer," he explained unnecessarily. "You should have seen them fussing over me."

He smiled to himself at the memory. "They wanted me to stay, of course, but I had other plans.

"Anyway, I got a little lucky with the piece of property I bought. We struck oil." He stubbed out his cigarette. "Once that happened, everything else happened so fast, the time just went by. Got a family there. Three sons, eight grandchildren, and"—he paused, counting on his fingers—"twelve great-grandchildren."

He fumbled in his wallet and produced an informal family portrait taken on the sprawling veranda of an enormous house, framed by rambling roses.

I passed the picture to Gerald. "Beautiful family."

"The little gal in the middle is my wife, Lupe. She looks like she could be my daughter, but Lupe and I have been together for over fifty years."

As he put the picture back in his wallet, he asked, "Do you all know about the other stuff? About the garden?" he added.

Gerald looked perplexed.

"I think I do," I said. "Dorothy and Renata were herbalists. They . . . offered herbal remedies to some of the women in the community."

William smiled. "Thank you, Ms. Holliday. They would have appreciated your putting it that way."

"Abortions?" Gerald asked, putting two and two together quickly.

"They were granny healers. Women's problems and contraceptives, primarily. But I couldn't swear there weren't induced miscarriages. My own mother had eight. I don't think they were intentional, but I suppose I'll never know. In any event, she must have figured out what was causing them, 'cause here I am. That's why there was such an age difference between me and my sisters."

I liked that he still kept referring to them as his sisters.

"Dorothy and Renata loved children," he continued. "That may be the only thing they regretted about choosing each other—not being able to have their own. But they also understood most women at the time couldn't make their own choices. My sisters tried to help."

"That's what the unlocked door was for?" I asked.

William nodded again. "Any hour of the night or day, if a gal needed help, Dorothy or Renata would be there for her with teas, oils, or just a shoulder and some good advice.

"I was only here for two days that time I came back. Had to go back to Texas and close on that property. One of those nights, I was in the back, having a smoke, and I hear this little gal whimpering in the garden, crying her eyes out."

"Can you describe her?" Gerald asked.

William shook his head. "It was too dark. And she was hiding behind those little shrubs near the path. Made me promise to stay on the terrace. Poor little thing, she sounded like a kid herself. Wouldn't let me help her or take her inside or anything. I didn't know what the heck to do for her, so I just tossed her a little medal Lupe had given me for the trip and suggested she pray."

CHAPTER 39

We left William Peacock in the hotel lobby. In a few days, he'd be back with Lupe and the grandkids, and Gerald and I would still be knee-deep in more questions than answers.

"So the baby and the mother might not even have been Mexican," I said.

"It'd be quite a coincidence if they were."

"I'm happy about that, for Hugo's sake. It's one less motive the cops will think he had to stab Guido. I'm disappointed, too. I thought we were onto something."

Gerald Fraser checked his watch. "Do you have some time? If you're not in a hurry, I'd like to go to Halcyon. It might inspire us."

We drove to the house in silence, each of us trying to fit William's new information into what we already thought we knew. Gerald made his way to the terrace in the back, where William said he'd heard the woman.

"I'll get you a chair from the cottage," I said.

I brought Gerald a metal bistro chair, and I sat on the brick steps, leaning against one of the stone dogs and looking around at the almost-finished garden.

"What are you thinking?" Gerald asked.

"I'm thinking about what William said. About the roses."

Dorothy's father had been inordinately proud of his rose garden. There was even a hybrid variety he developed, the Lady Sarah. When Dorothy returned from Italy, she had all the roses ripped out of the garden. Some who bothered to think about it thought it was a hatred of their father that made her do it. Others, like Mrs. Cox at the library, believed Dorothy's story that she was allergic. William had told us the truth.

"After Rose's death, she couldn't bear to see another rose wither and die," he'd explained. "The only roses she'd have in the house had to last forever. Her needlepoints, the china, the stained glass window she commissioned.

"That was the real reason for the name change, too," he continued. "It would have been easier to just call her friend Rose, but it would have broken Dorothy's heart to have to say Rose's name over and over again, knowing she was gone."

"Such a beautiful spot to be holding so much sadness," I said.

"Look," Gerald said, "I know you're disappointed about the baby, but there was never any guarantee it was Yoly's, just because of the medal. We may have to rule her out as the mother."

"All that hunting for her and her mother . . . all of Chappell's work . . . for nothing. And if William was back here and gave the mother the necklace sometime in the fifties, we have to rule out Win Fifield as the father. He was my prime suspect." I must have looked as deflated as I felt.

"Don't worry. We're not going to forget about Yoly. Not again. We just seem to have two mysteries here instead of one. And they still may tie in to Guido's stabbing.

"All right," he recapped, "the attorneys contacted William; that's why he came back. Sometime in 1959, when William says he bought his land—"

"You think he may be lying?" I asked.

"People do. It's easy enough to check, though. In 1959, a woman in this town was pregnant and didn't want to be." He threw me a crumb. "The timing fits right in with your candy wrapper research. What do you think happened?" he prompted.

"The woman goes to the Peacock sisters to terminate the pregnancy, but when she gets there, she has a change of heart and coincidentally bumps into William, who gives her the Virgin of Guadalupe medal. Woman has the baby, and unfortunately it dies, probably of natural causes.

"No signs of trauma on the body, and if she went ahead with the pregnancy," I continued, "it's not likely she'd commit infanticide."

"Possible, but not likely. Especially given the careful way it was buried. Let's say the baby predates Yoly; who might the mother be?" Gerald coached.

"Someone who was young, not married . . . or married to a man who wasn't the father . . ."

"Who else . . ."

"Someone involved with an inappropriate or unsuitable . . ." I stopped myself.

Gerald must have seen what I was thinking: he exhaled deeply. "It can't be Hill. Hillary had something called premature ovarian failure—a freakish condition connected with the mumps she had when she was a kid. She went through three years of tests at the Yale Reproductive Center."

With Hillary out, I was running out of suspects.

"If only I'd found Dorothy's journal. Neil MacLeod and I looked for it," I confessed, "one day when Richard was in Hartford at the Wadsworth Atheneum."

"What was he doing there?" Gerald asked.

I shook my head. "Who knows? Something about a painting for an upcoming exhibition." I'd only been half listening when Inez told me.

"The Prendergast?" he asked. "That's the only thing SHS owns that I can imagine the Wadsworth being interested in."

"No idea. I was too busy playing Nancy Drew to listen. I was convinced there was a clue in the damn journal."

"We may have to forget about the journal for now. Use your head," Gerald said.

"Someone pregnant in 1959 who didn't want to be. Someone who'd been raped or was the victim of incest?" I suggested.

I tried to think of all the older women in town. After some time, I said, "How about a grieving war widow? One yearning for the past?"

CHAPTER 40

Hillary was waiting when Gerald and I got to the Paradise parking lot. She did not look pleased. Gerald mouthed "I'll call you" from her car as she tore out and headed east onto the highway, and probably back to her place.

I'd planned to grab a bite at the diner but saw Mike O'Malley through the miniblinds and backtracked to my Jeep instead. The last thing I felt like doing was sparring with O'Malley and then winding up having to apologize, which seemed to be the way most of our encounters went.

I'd go home, take a short run, and eat clean. Digging in the garden the last few days had been a good upper-body workout. I wouldn't be worrying Serena Williams anytime soon, but my arms looked good. There was still an hour or so of daylight, and the run would help me think.

I quickly changed and strapped the heart-rate monitor on, making sure the watch was set for Workout. At the last minute, I grabbed my baseball hat with the reflective tape on it and a nylon anorak. The rain Al Roker had promised hadn't materialized yet, but there was a good chance it would come soon, probably while I was out running in the middle of nowhere.

For the first two miles, everything hurt. Then I settled into a rhythm. My heart rate was good, and if I'd been running with anyone, I would have been able to keep up a conversation.

I got to the intersection of Huckleberry and Glendale. If I turned left, it was another six miles back to the house; if I turned right, I could cut through the UConn parking lot and be home in twenty minutes. Just then it started to drizzle, and that made the decision for me. I pulled on the anorak, tied the drawstring hood tight around my hat, and took the shortcut home. The cloud cover made it dark sooner than I'd expected. I was sorry I hadn't brought a small flashlight with me, but hopefully the reflective tape on my hat would keep me from getting killed by oncoming traffic.

As I jogged through the deserted parking lot, I noticed a vehicle at the entrance to the recycling center. The center was padlocked after 3, so I couldn't imagine who'd be there. I tiptoed across the street, past the cemetery, and onto the fringes of the Sunnyview property, where I knelt behind a staggered hedge of Japanese barberry to find out.

I saw a nursery pickup—open in the back, with two or three power lawn mowers and rakes and other garden implements strapped to the raised wooden sides. A brown tarp was tied down, covering something in the back of the truck, and the bottom of the tarp obscured my view of the license plate.

I heard the sounds of shuffling feet, then the clang of metal against metal—a chain dragging across the chain-link fence, but I still hadn't seen anybody. I crouched down a little lower. The gate squeaked open. The rain was coming down pretty good by then. The prickly barberry was scratching my legs and I was getting paranoid about ticks, but I flattened myself as much as I could behind the hedge. Someone must have heard me, because I saw a flashlight switch on and point in my direction. I remembered the bit of reflective tape on my baseball hat and tore it off and stuck it in my pocket. Then I held my breath and waited.

The light moved back to the recycling center and disappeared. After a while, I crab walked closer to the road for a better view of the truck. It was dark green. Big deal; most nursery trucks were. The scratches on my legs were stinging now. Great, I was probably sitting in a patch of poison ivy, and for what? To watch somebody dumping a refrigerator or pilfering compost? I was just about to stand when I heard cursing and angry muttering. I hunkered down just as the door slammed and the truck screeched out of there. A second vehicle followed, swerving close to the shoulder where I was hiding. I fell backward, hitting my head on a tree stump. The next thing I saw was a man standing over me whacking his palm with the long object he held in his other hand.

CHAPTER 41

"You wanna come outta there?"

Soaked to the skin, legs covered with raised red welts, leaves and twigs stuck to my hat and anorak, I must have presented a ridiculous picture to Sunnyview's security guard.

With his flashlight, he lit my way out of the brambles, and we got to the entrance of the nursing home just as the patrol car did. Officers Guzman and Smythe tried unsuccessfully to hide their amusement.

"I thought you were going to wait for us, Uncle Rudy," Guzman said, kissing the security guard.

"We could use a little excitement around here," he said. "I knew it was nothing I couldn't handle."

The cops walked toward me as I sat on the steps of the porch, rubbing the back of my head and drying myself with a towel someone had tossed me. I was bigger news than the bingo game going on inside, so I was garnering quite an audience. All the residents who were ambulatory and not hearing-impaired drifted out to see what was up.

"Are you okay?" Officer Smythe asked.

"I'm all right."

"I know there's a very simple explanation for why we're here. Isn't there?" He was almost laughing.

"There is. At least, there was a while ago."

I checked my watch and groaned. It read 54. Somehow I knew my heart rate wasn't going to be helpful, so I pressed a button on the side of the watch and switched from Workout mode back to Time. It was 10:15. I'd been out there much longer than I realized. I must have passed out when I hit my head.

"I'm not sure what time it was when I saw the truck, but it was just after the rain started."

"And what truck was that?"

I described the truck but had no information on the vehicle that knocked me into the woods.

"The center closes at three, but a few local businesses have the keys," Rudy said. "They get special permission from the town, 'cause they drop off a lot of stuff and they're too busy during regular hours." He seemed disappointed I hadn't been observing aliens or waiting for the mother ship to pick me up.

The cops were satisfied with this explanation, but they, too, looked like they were waiting for another, more outlandish story from me. When, exactly, had I turned into the town loony?

"I didn't hear any bottles or cans," I said lamely.

"Maybe it was catalogs, dear," one of the Sunnyview residents volunteered. "We get so many of them."

"What if somebody was dumping something they didn't want anyone to see?" I said, convincing no one. Not even myself.

"We'll make sure the lock's not broken, but if they had the key, there's nothing illegal about accidentally leaving a gate open," Smythe said.

Guzman was kinder. "What exactly do you think you saw?"

I was uncharacteristically speechless.

"Is there anything else you can tell us about the truck?"

I was grateful she didn't just blow me off, and I described the truck as best as I could.

"It's not much to go on. No name on the truck, no plate numbers, probably green, but not sure . . . tarp in the back." She reread the list of my useless observations.

I was a lousy witness. I tried to recall anything else, any small detail. I closed my eyes to get a mental picture. In the background, I heard one of the codgers whisper, "What is she doing? Is she going to sleep? Luann Barnhart did that at dinner the other night."

"The mud flaps had pictures of women on them. You know, hot pants, legs in the air." I'd just described every other truck in America. I knew how it sounded. I'd staked out a conscientious nursery worker who grumbled about working late. What did I expect them to do, put out an all points bulletin?

"I can find out who's got keys to the recycling center, but unless we can prove it was someone not on that list, you're the only one here who's actually done anything illegal. Technically," she said, "you were trespassing on Sunnyview property."

"No, she wasn't. She's my guest." Inez from the thrift shop stepped out of the crowd, happy to be part of the drama. Just as Inez was bailing me out, a black Lexus pulled up, and Hillary Gibson and Gerald Fraser joined the circus on the nursing home's porch.

The cops were relieved to be let off the hook, and my entertainment value was fading, so the crowd broke up. I could hold my own against bingo but would lose every time against ice cream sundaes, which was the next course in Sunnyview's dining room.

"Take care of yourself, dear," Inez said. "She's one of my best customers," she said to the others, ushering them back into the building. She'd probably dine on the story for weeks.

"Are you following us?" Gerald asked, once everyone else had gone.

"Of course not. Just a little extracurricular activity that went nowhere."

"You look like you're freezing," Hillary said, looking me over. She took off her large woolen shawl and wrapped it around me. "I'm taking you home."

CHAPTER 42

Hillary's car was not like my Jeep—no plastic water bottles littering the floor, no stray CDs in the wrong jewel cases, no coffee splashes on the gearbox. I held myself in tightly so as not to sully her vehicle.

"Are you warm enough?" she asked.

I nodded, but it came out like a shiver, so she turned up the heat on my side.

She drove aggressively for an older woman, with none of the nose-peering-over-the-steering-wheel, hands-frozen-at-10:10 timidity of most of her generation. We got to my place fast.

"Thanks for the lift." I peeled off her shawl, folded it, and placed it on the passenger seat.

"You're welcome." She seemed in no great hurry to leave.

"Would you like to come in for a drink or something before you head home?"

"I'd like that."

She parked the car and followed me in.

"What a charming house."

"It's getting there. I'm too much of a pack rat. Sometimes I look around and think, *What* is *all this stuff?*"

"They're things you enjoy. That's very different from acquisition merely for the sake of acquisition."

I guessed she was thinking of her former husband. I put the water on for tea and excused myself to change into dry clothes.

When I got back Hillary was checking out my bookshelf, leafing through the copy of *Culpeper's Herbal* I'd borrowed from Dorothy Peacock. She saw me and replaced the book on the shelf.

"Quite a collection you've got," she said, still scanning the shelves but tactfully not confronting me about the pilfered book.

"I'm always on the lookout." I walked past her into the kitchen, where I set our tea on an old painted tray and brought it into the living room.

"Not very elegant, I'm afraid, but it should chase the chill away."

"It's perfect, thank you. The Peacock sisters had an extensive gardening library."

"Yes, I know. I spent a few hours there. Ms. Gibson, I didn't steal that book, I just borrowed it."

"I didn't think you had. I've borrowed a book or two from them myself."

"There may be a few that are quite valuable—I've told Richard," I said.

"Oh, I don't think there's much you can tell Dick Stapley about that house. He even worked there one summer. The bluestone wall with the pear trees? Richard built that himself."

"Margery mentioned it. It certainly has held up, I'll give him that," I said. "Maybe he thinks it gives him something in common with Winston Churchill; although I'm pretty sure Churchill used brick."

"If it does, it's the only thing they've got in common," she said. "You've inadvertently brought back a lot of memories to some of the people in this town. Some good—" She wavered.

"Some bad?" I interrupted. I kicked myself for not letting her finish.

"I was going to say 'uncomfortable.'"

This time I was patient.

"You said you've spent some time in the Peacocks' library. Were you looking for anything in particular?" she asked.

"Should I be?"

"No wonder Gerald likes you. You're alike," she said with a sly smile. She looked me straight in the eye as she spoke. "I didn't believe for a minute that one of the sisters was the mother, but I didn't want their names dragged through the mud. Then Gerald went off again on his Yoly Rivera obsession and you encouraged him."

Oh, shit. I felt a lecture coming on.

"Please don't misunderstand me. Gerald has always been pigheaded. No one could make him do anything he didn't want to do. But now that it seems the baby has nothing to do with Yoly, why not drop it?"

She was right. Given everything I knew—or thought I knew—about the Peacocks, they'd probably want to protect the mother, even if it meant tongues would wag about them. After all, gossip couldn't hurt them now.

Hillary got to the point. "Gerald says the two of you are planning to talk to Margery. I've tried to talk him out of it. I know I don't have the right to ask," she continued, "but I wish you wouldn't." She chose her words carefully. "Margery's fragile; she's had a hard time."

"You mean losing her first husband?"

She nodded. "Margery was a ghost those first years. I remember seeing her at Halcyon when I was a child and thinking, *Who is that terribly tragic and romantic figure?* Pale, painfully thin—almost invisible. Renata told me we must always be kind to Margery, because the world had not been."

Margery Russell's father had been a tyrant. She'd married against his wishes, and when her husband was killed in the war, the father practically celebrated. Richard Stapley ingratiated himself with Margery's father, and after only a year, he and Margery were married. Some doubted she was even consulted. All that dovetailed with what Jon Chappell had told me.

"People make mistakes," Hillary said. "There's no need to spend the rest of one's life paying for them."

"Ms. Gibson, I appreciate your loyalty to your friends. We may never know how that baby came to be buried in the garden, but I've got a bigger problem. I'm loyal, too, and my friend is in jail for a crime he didn't commit. I'm convinced either the baby or Yoly Rivera or both motivated someone to stab Guido Chiaramonte. And I'm going to find out who did it."

"I suppose I knew you'd say that. Just like Gerald." She got up to leave. "I hope you find the person and find out what happened to that girl. I just hope you'll be sensitive and give some thought to the living, too. And don't judge people too harshly if you find out some other things in the process."

She put down her teacup, and I walked her to the door.

"God knows, I'm no fan of Guido Chiaramonte's," she said, "but if there is some connection between him and Yoly Rivera, this could get dangerous for you. And for Gerald. Please be careful. I've just found him again, and I don't want to lose him a second time."

As soon as she was gone, I called Lucy.

"She knows Margery's the mother," I said, "and doesn't want the old girl pushed off the deep end. *Or* . . .

Margery knows Hillary's the mother and will spill her guts as soon as anyone asks her."

"What about the fertility issues?" Lucy said.

"Maybe she did have mumps as a teenager. How do *I* know the mumps can really make you sterile? Maybe she's just flat-out lying to me *and* to Gerald."

"She was helpful at the beginning," Lucy said.

"When she thought it was the answer to the big unsolved case from her sweetie's career."

"Sounds like you've narrowed it down to two candidates. What does your accordion player think?"

"O'Malley?" I asked. "Who knows? He's pissed at me because I didn't tell him that was Hugo's car at the nursery."

"Too bad. He could be useful," she said. I had a feeling she was referring to his other possible talents.

"How's the lovely Anna holding up?"

"She's amazing. Baking goodies for Hugo and the guards. He's been moved to Stamford; they have a larger facility there."

"And Felix?" she asked.

"I got a voice mail message, but it was vague, and he didn't leave a number."

"At least he called. I'm free this weekend. Still need help?"

"Sure."

CHAPTER 43

Mike O'Malley once told me Springfield had everything the big city had, just less of it. I wasn't so sure Springfield didn't have more than its share.

After talking to Lucy, I poured myself a drink and made a fire. It wasn't that cold, but there was a chill in my bones I couldn't shake. I wanted to blame it on my snooze in the ditch, but as I settled in with my wine and a yellow legal pad in front of me, I knew that wasn't it.

I made three columns—Yoly Rivera, Guido Chiaramonte, and Baby. Then I sat and stared at the blank page, filling in the things I knew, or thought I knew, about each of them. I scribbled down thirty different scenarios, but no amount of English would make all the cherries line up.

I was putting a few more logs on the fire when I heard the fax machine chugging in my office; I went to investigate. Printed on Springfield police department letterhead was a typed note from Sergeant Guzman.

Dear Ms. Holliday,
    Six companies/entities are authorized to enter

and use the facilities of the Springfield Recycling
Center during off-hours. They are:

    UConn at Springfield Extension Services
    Harleysville Raceway
    Aardvark Refuse
    Morning Glory Cemetery
    Fairmont Lawn Funeral Home
    Springfield Historical Society

Yours truly,
Sgt. Rosaria Guzman
Springfield Police Department

The raceway I could understand. The town couldn't
be cruel enough to make someone open the gates for a
dump truck of steaming horse manure and then force
him to spend the entire day babysitting it. The sanita-
tion company probably had a contract with the town—
Gerald could find out. Presumably, the funeral home
and the cemetery were dumping faded floral arrange-
ments and nothing more sinister. That left the university—shredded term papers, probably. But why should
SHS need to dump anything after hours?

I gambled that Gerald Fraser would be one of the few
Sunnyview residents still awake at the ungodly hour of
11 P.M.

The switchboard operator kept me on hold for twelve
minutes before returning to tell me, "He's gone."

"You mean he's out?"

"No, ma'am, he's gone."

Stay calm, I told myself. *If your voice betrays the
fact that you think she's an idiot, she'll be even less
helpful, if that were possible.*

"Gone where, dear?" I said, through clenched teeth.

"Well, usually they go across the street."

The fax from Sergeant Guzman made me ask the next stupid question. "To the recycling center?"

"No," she said solemnly. "Morning Glory. The cemetery."

"But Mr. Fraser didn't, did he? He went somewhere else." This conversation was going to be work.

"The main office is closed. I really don't know anything. You can call back tomorrow, during regular hours," she added.

And relive this? No, thanks. I thought fast, *What the hell was her name?*

"What about Genevieve? The attendant? Is Genevieve there?"

"Genevieve Barkley?"

"Yes," I said, exhausted. It was a small facility; how many Genevieves could they have?

"Why didn't you say? I'll get her."

After another ten minutes, Genevieve came to the phone. Mr. Fraser was indeed gone. Genevieve had helped him pack up two suitcases and three boxes of his belongings.

"Just about everything he had," she said. "He left most of his books to our library here. He gave me his stereo and a very generous gift as well."

Fraser's forwarding address was on file in the office, which was, as the excruciating switchboard operator had told me, locked. His belongings were to be shipped the next morning and I could practically hear Genevieve crane her neck to read the address on the shipping label.

"It's definitely New York, but that's all I can see. The lights are off and the box isn't facing the door. I can call you with it in the morning, if you like. We start at six."

"That would be great, Genevieve. Thanks so much." I gave her my cell number. "I was just a little worried."

"Don't you worry none about Mr. Gerald. He looked very happy when he left here. If that lady takes as good care of him as she does of that car, he's got no problem."

CHAPTER 44

"I'm sorry for calling so early."

"We've been up for hours; Gerald's anxious to speak with you, too." Hillary was cool but passed Gerald the phone.

"Hey, kiddo. So you tracked me down. I told Hill we'd get busted, but she just couldn't keep her hands off me."

I apologized again. "I've been doing some thinking."

"Always dangerous. Did you talk to Margery?"

"No. Yesterday flew. Did you reach William?"

"Yup. He had no problem leaving a DNA sample. I picked up a testing kit from Sergeant Guzman; she showed me how to do it. Piece of cake." He lowered his voice a bit. "Are you going to see her? Want some company?"

"You bet."

We agreed to meet at 9 A.M. in the Paradise parking lot.

"Looking good," I said, hopping out of the Jeep.

"Hillary thinks I need more exercise, so she dropped me off two blocks from here. She's resurrecting her workout room and hot tub, too. Somewhere her ex-husband must be laughing his fat ass off; sounds like she gave him a lot of grief for that stuff back in the eighties."

I offered him a hand getting in, but he didn't need it; under Hillary's care, he'd be snowboarding by this winter.

"When I called, Margery started to give me Richard's schedule, but I told her we were coming to see her."

"She all right with that?" he asked.

"I think she knows why we're coming. She just told me to come early so we could talk privately."

The Stapley home looked like a smaller version of the Historical Society's building. Lots of lawn exactly an inch and a half tall, with a putting green in the front and thick, unnecessary pillars designed to impress. I'd learned my lesson with Hillary and decided, on the way over, to take it slow and let Margery do most of the talking.

There was frailty, but also something resolute in Margery Stapley's diminutive frame as she answered the door. She led us to a parlor just off the center hall, with a fireplace and a conversational grouping of chairs. Over the fireplace hung a lovely painting of a garden. Gerald admired it and stepped a bit closer. "Is that a Childe Hassam?" he asked.

"Yes," Margery answered. "Father gave it to me for my twenty-first birthday. Richard had it reframed for me recently, but I'm not sure the new frame is an improvement. Please sit down. And help yourself. My housekeeper put this out for us." She motioned to a small cart with coffee and cookies.

"My wrists aren't what they used to be, and using the computer doesn't help."

She massaged her wrists as she began. "I used to be quite strong. I played tennis with my first husband,

Henry. He was so much taller, we must have made an odd-looking couple on the court. But we were a good team. He had the power and I had the touch. He died, you know."

"Yes, ma'am. I'm sorry."

"I was quite young. All my friends were busy with their own husbands, their families. Father wasn't much help either. We'd never been close," she explained. "I was unhappy for a long time, the kind of unhappiness that's so profound it's as if you'll never be happy again. Do you know what I mean?"

I nodded mechanically, but Gerald seemed to share a deeper understanding.

"One night I forced myself to go to one of the free concerts in the Peacock band shell. Just to get out of the house. It was a lovely night, this time of year. They were playing a program of standards from before the war."

She looked down, momentarily lost in the patterns of her rug, and then told us how one night she met a boy there.

"He was visiting Springfield for the summer. After the concert, we walked down to the pier, just talking. I felt as if the floodgates had opened. We talked all night and laughed like I hadn't for years. We stayed up to watch the sun rise. I saw him only once after that night. He came to the house I'd shared so briefly with Henry. I was so naive. Another woman would have known she was pregnant much sooner.

"I didn't know what to do," she went on bravely. "I'd heard rumors. About the Peacocks. I heard they could help girls who were . . . in need of help. I planned to go very late one night when I was sure I wouldn't be seen. When I arrived, a strange man was there on the terrace. I was terrified. I hid in the bushes, sobbing, waiting for him to leave, but he just stayed on the terrace, smoking one cigarette after another. It was agonizing. The longer I waited, the more confused I got, and the louder my sobs became. Finally the man heard and called to me. He asked if I wanted him to get Dorothy, but I was too frightened and upset to even reveal myself. When I wouldn't come out of the bushes, he softly said, *'Vaya con Dios'* and tossed me a small medal."

"William Peacock?"

She nodded. "I didn't know it was William until much later, when I was asked to find him for the Historical Society. I told everyone I couldn't find him, but that was a lie."

She took a deep breath and continued. "I decided to have my baby, then give it up for adoption. I was so alone. Henry was gone, and Father was always working. I rarely saw him.

"I saw so few people in those days. It wasn't difficult to conceal my condition. And Dorothy Peacock was a godsend. She acted as midwife; she delivered my beautiful baby boy, Henry, Jr. I thought of him as Henry's, you see."

It would have been hard to keep him and impossible to give him up, but Margery never got to make that choice. Henry, Jr. died of fever before he was three weeks old.

"When I saw William at the party, it all came crashing back," she said.

The next voice we heard was Richard's. He was standing in the open doorway. "You people have no right to be here."

"It's all right, Richard. All these years of keeping it bottled up inside. I'm relieved to finally tell someone. I'm tired though. Will you tell them the rest?"

He sat on the sofa next to his wife, the strain evident

on his face. "Margie's father thought she needed looking after; I'm just glad he gave me the job.

"When Henry, Jr., was taken, the Peacock sisters agreed to handle things. They treated the body with some herbal concoction and kept him in a makeshift chapel in the Peacocks' basement, where Margie could visit him. It was no one's intention, but he wound up staying there for forty-odd years."

"Wearing the medal that William had given Margery," I added. They both nodded.

"Any idea where that damn candy wrapper came from?" I was glad that Gerald asked, because even if it proved nothing, I was still dying to know.

"Renata couldn't do without her English chocolates," Margery said. "She imported them for years before they were available here."

"Once Dorothy died, I knew the insurance inspectors would go through the house with a fine-tooth comb," Richard said, so I moved the baby's body, just temporarily, to the white garden, until Margery could decide on a permanent burial site.

"To be honest, Ms. Holliday, one of the reasons I gave you the job was because I didn't think you'd be quite so thorough. And so fast. I thought I'd bought myself some time."

My ego was bruised. So it wasn't my expertise and salesmanship that had gotten me the job.

At Margery's gentle prodding, Richard continued, "I'm afraid I'm the one who locked you in the greenhouse that night; I'd been searching for something. Margery remembered a journal that Dorothy kept of her . . . clients. I wanted to find it before anyone else did, in case there was anything in it that might embarrass Margery. When I saw you come back, I panicked.

I just wanted to get away without you seeing me. I certainly didn't mean to harm you."

"Did you send me any e-mails?" I asked.

"No, dear," Margery said, raising her hand like a schoolgirl. "That was me; Richard is hopeless on the computer."

The former cop broke the silence. "None of this absolutely needs to come out," Gerald said kindly. "What you've done may not even be a crime. And it has nothing to do with the attack on Guido Chiaramonte."

"You mean the *murder* of Guido Chiaramonte."

We all turned toward the front door. Standing in the doorway was Mike O'Malley.

"Guido Chiaramonte died about an hour ago at Our Lady of Perpetual Help Hospital."

CHAPTER 45

Three hours later, Gerald and I were released, with stinging slaps on the wrists and strict instructions to stay away from Guido's nursery and the Stapleys, who were still in the police station being questioned. No one was sure what charges, if any, would be brought against them regarding the baby's body; it was completely uncharted territory in Springfield's history.

Hillary Gibson had been looking at paint chips when she got the call to pick her honey up from the slammer, and the way she glared at me told me I should keep my *boca cerrada*. I felt like the bad kid your parents didn't want you to hang out with.

Alone on the steps of the police station, I wished someone was coming to pick me up. To take me home, pour me a drink, rub my shoulders, and tell me everything was going to be all right.

The whole way home, the Bruce Springsteen lyrics kept going through my head, "One Step Up, Two Steps Back." We'd learned who the baby's mother was, and how it died, but that was only part of the puzzle. Now that Guido was dead, anything he might have known about Yoly Rivera's disappearance died with him. Was he responsible for Yoly's death; was that why he was killed? Or did he know someone else was?

That's what I was grappling with when I eased into my driveway and saw someone waiting for me. I rolled down the window. "What are you doing here?"

"That's a gracious welcome. Is that what they teach you in the suburban matron's handbook? You invited me, remember?"

"Today's Friday?"

"Last time I checked," Lucy said.

I helped her in with her bags. "How did you get here?"

"I availed myself of that quaint cab service you've got at the train station. Had to share with three Dashing Dans. Good way to meet men, I guess, if you like the harried, married type. I waited fifteen minutes, then called your cell. Helps to check messages every once in a while."

"Don't be mean to me, I've had a horrible day."

"Worse than it's been?" she asked suspiciously.

"Just as bad. Guido Chiaramonte?"

"Sure. The guy who looked like John Gotti." She stopped on the stairs. "What about him? He got . . . whacked?"

"For God's sake, it's not TV. The man's dead. And Hugo's about to be charged with murder. I'll give you chapter and verse when we get upstairs, but please tell me there's food in one of these bags. They weigh a ton."

"Better. Booze."

I opened a bottle of Grey Goose and brought her up to speed.

"So, you find a body and think that the mother is a missing girl from thirty years ago, but it turns out to be someone else. Now a local man is murdered and you think *he* had something to do with one or both of those other things," she recounted.

"Something like that."

"Nice friendly place you've got here. Whatever happened to town meetings at the old firehouse to resolve local disputes?"

"It *is* a nice town. It's like the garden, though: everything looks beautiful from a distance. It's only when you look closely that you see the snakes."

"That sounds like something on a needlepoint pillow, like 'Old Gardeners Never Die, They Just Spade Away.'"

"That reminds me. There's something I keep meaning to look up. Some quotes."

"If they're from the movies, I'm your girl. Otherwise, don't think I can help you."

I poured us each another martini, then went inside to get my copy of *Bartlett's Quotations*. "Why would Richard Stapley risk his reputation by burying a body in a soon-to-be public garden?" I asked when I returned.

"He told you. He's a wonderful husband," Lucy said. "He wanted to spare his beloved wife the agony of being exposed as a whore and unwed mother. Or worse."

"After all this time? Who'd care? She could have made up some story or said she was pregnant when her husband died. Who's still around to say otherwise?" I leafed through the *Bartlett's*.

"Look," Lucy said, "the happy townsfolk were skewering the Peacocks when they thought the baby belonged to one of them. And those girls are dead. They'd probably crucify a living person. Those poor women probably lived in fear for years, worrying someone would find out about the baby. I'd risk it. That sound?" Lucy said.

"What sound?"

"It's your cell. Feel free to delete the half-dozen snippy messages from me," she yelled.

I couldn't find my backpack and couldn't find the phone once I did. It had stopped ringing by the time I found it buried among the other squarish black things in my bag. The message light flashed eight. I skipped over the messages to missed calls. The last one was a Springfield number I didn't recognize. I called it.

Felix Ontivares kept it brief. Did I want to meet him and Celinda Rivera for breakfast the next morning?

CHAPTER 46

The next morning, Lucy and I drove downtown to the same hotel where I'd met William Peacock.

"Charming. Is this where the locals come for a nooner if they don't have a greenhouse?" Lucy smirked. "You still haven't told me the whole story. I need details."

"Grow up."

I was relieved that my first meeting with Felix since the greenhouse episode would be in a group and not one on one. They were waiting for us in the hotel's coffee shop. I'd forgotten how good-looking Felix was, and unconsciously pressed down my shoulders and sucked in my stomach, Pilates style. He stood up as we approached, nodding to Lucy and giving me a brotherly peck on the cheek.

"How in the world did you find her?" I asked.

"The power of television. In Mexico, everyone watches the soaps. I simply had a friend of mine say a few words after one of the episodes. We were inundated with phone calls."

That was because Celinda had kept her daughter's memory alive, plastering hand-lettered signs—¿ *Usted conoce esta muchacha?*—everywhere she went and pestering officials on both sides of the border for so long they ceased to hear her. A neighbor brought her the news that now someone else was looking for Yoly.

Celinda Rivera spoke almost no English, so there was a lot of smiling and gesticulating with little actual dialogue. She was not quite five feet tall; pleasantly round; with gray-streaked hair coiled into a bun at the base of her neck. Despite the mild weather, she wore four or five layers of brightly colored clothing. And if the clothing was cheery, it was in sharp contrast to her face, which was dark caramel, deeply lined, and ineffably sad. She reminded me of the Argentinean women going to the Plaza de Mayo to show they hadn't stopped looking for *their* lost relatives.

"You'll be happy to know that Mrs. Rivera says there is no connection between her family and the family of Hugo Jurado. The families lived many miles apart in Mexico, in different states. And Yoly has been missing since long before Hugo arrived in Springfield," Felix said, "so they couldn't have met here."

I tried to sound happy. "That's wonderful. There is some bad news though. I don't know if you've heard; Guido Chiaramonte is dead."

They didn't know. Felix had repeatedly tried to reach me and Jon Chappell yesterday but was only able to leave messages.

"I haven't seen a paper today."

"It's bad for Hugo, but it was just a theory of mine that Guido knew about Yoly's disappearance, a possible motive for his murder." It was the first time I'd spoken the word out loud, and instantly regretted using it in Celinda's presence.

Felix explained the situation to her, but the familiar word spoke volumes.

"Jon and Felix have brought this case back into the public eye. Sometimes that's all that's needed."

As I fumbled for other, more comforting words, Lucy bent over to whisper to me. "I appreciate the thought, but, uh, Felix *owns* that network. That was how he got Yoly mentioned on the air. Have you really been out of the business that long? They live for this stuff," Lucy continued. One of her many ex-boyfriends had slid seamlessly into my old TV job, and was churning out true-life tragedy on a weekly basis. Lucy thought she could interest him in Yoly's story.

"And these guys work fast. They have a basic template and just plug in this week's gory details," she said thoughtlessly. She started to apologize, but Felix cut her off.

"It's not necessary. Mrs. Rivera couldn't understand you. She knows only that you want to help."

Half the story would be Felix's successful search for the mother, and the other half, our search for the daughter. It'd make a good feature. I didn't want to get Celinda's hopes up, but it was worth a try.

While Lucy made some calls, Celinda brought out a stack of blue airmail envelopes, tied with a brown and gold nylon shoelace. She took out Yoly's last letter and handed it to me.

She watched me struggle with the Spanish, and started to speak. Recite, really. As many times as she'd read that last letter, she knew it by heart, like a prayer.

"Yoly was happy," Felix said, in his rough translation. "She'd met a man. An older man she said had been good to her. He'd even taken her on a trip to Newport, Rhode Island. He said it reminded him of his home, the boats and the water. He wasn't from here, originally."

For the first time, a little smile crossed Celinda's face, and words passed between her and Felix.

"Yoly joked that they had something in common," Felix said. "He had an accent, too."

Celinda said something else to him.

"It wasn't in the letter, but Celinda believes Yoly was *embarazada*—pregnant." Another heartbreaking smile and more words.

Maybe that was the connection. Could Yoly have gone to the Peacocks for help? "What made her think that?" I asked.

"Yoly said she'd need a new rebozo soon."

"A shawl?" Lucy asked, phone to chest, obviously on hold.

"It's also used to carry a baby," I said, appreciating the shorthand between mother and daughter.

"She thinks Yoly didn't want to tell her until she and the man were married, but there was a difficulty. That's why she didn't give the man's name."

"Already married?"

"Perhaps. Perhaps an immigration issue," Felix suggested. He was thinking of Guido.

"Senora Rivera, where was Yoly working the last time you heard from her? Could she have met this man at work?" I asked in halting Spanish.

"She was a cleaning lady, at a big house near the water," Felix translated. "Live-in."

"Right in Springfield?"

"We think so. Most of her letters have a Springfield postmark."

Obsessed with where Yoly's letters had come from, I'd neglected to ask the obvious.

"Senora Rivera, when you wrote to Yoly, where did you send your letters?"

When Yoly worked as a nanny for the crew leader, letters were sent to her at that family's home. Once she switched jobs, her mail went to a post office box in

Springfield. At the request of her new employers, mail should not be sent to their address. Celinda showed me the one letter that was returned to her as undeliverable—2381 Hawthorne Lane. One bus stop away from the Peacocks. And the Fifields.

CHAPTER 47

The house on Hawthorne Lane had been torn down years ago, replaced by a newer, bigger, no doubt uglier model. The original residents were long gone, and judging by the FOR SALE sign and uninhabited look, the current owners had already packed their bags. I did the next best thing.

"You're not really here about the landscaping, are you?" Dina Fifield had seen through me five minutes into my visit.

"No, ma'am. Not entirely."

"Please don't 'ma'am' me. Not unless you're from the South, which I suspect you aren't."

When I called Mrs. Fifield, she agreed to see me right away. It was only after I hung up that I realized she thought I was moving in on the gardening business recently vacated by Guido Chiaramonte. The guy hadn't been dead for forty-eight hours. Now I knew where Win got his ambition; these people wasted no time.

"Win does it all the time, of course. Ma'ams people. As I said, unless you're from the South, *or* running for office, it's unacceptable. After the age of forty, women hate it. You'll hate it in about four or five years, won't you, dear?" she said, with one glance, assessing my age, weight, and economic status.

And I'll hate you in about four or five minutes, I thought. Dina Fifield had to be sixty-five but looked forty-five. Very slim, spray-tanned, and highlighted by masters, she was dressed in a form-fitting tennis dress that would have done any of the current crop of tennis nymphets proud. Gossips claimed the Nalgene water bottle she was never seen without was filled with gin; if they were right, it didn't seem to be doing her any harm.

"So, at the risk of being rude, if you're not here about the garden, why are you here?"

"I'd be delighted to discuss your landscaping needs," I lied, "but you're right—there is something else I was hoping to speak with you about. Have you read any of the articles in the *Springfield Bulletin* about a missing girl named Yoly Rivera? She was last seen—"

"Yes, yes, I know . . . 'Where is my daughter?' So you're the one who lit a fire under Jon Chappell. Andrew Chappell's boy. Cute kid, but a classic underachiever."

I kept talking. "Yoly Rivera worked as a cleaning lady in this neighborhood about thirty years ago. I thought you might remember her."

"Are you serious? I don't remember *my* cleaning lady from thirty days ago. They come and go. They make a little money and go back home to live like queens."

I'd thought the same thing myself, but cringed at hearing it from Dina Fifield. "Not this one. She wrote her family that she met a rich man who was going to take care of her."

"What was she supposed to write? 'I'm in a low-paying, boring job; my boyfriend slaps me around; and I cry myself to sleep every night?' Look, I get a name, a phone number, and a few references. That's it. I'm grateful if they show up and don't steal anything. I don't adopt them.

"Now let me ask you something," she said. "Why are *you* asking these questions and not the police?"

"I guess they've got their hands full with Guido's murder."

She softened the tiniest bit. "Yes, it's terrible. Guido was the best I've ever had," she said nostalgically. "Gardener, that is. I don't know what I'll do. It's so hard to find a good man."

Thank god I didn't really want this heartless bitch as a client.

"He worked here for over thirty years. He used to say it would take another twenty years to get the garden the way he wanted it. Of course, he was a terrible flirt."

The way she said it made me think Guido didn't always strike out.

"He just rang my doorbell one day, not unlike you. I'd seen him around town, of course. How could you miss him? I know what you're thinking. But thirty years ago he was quite dashing. Thick, dark hair; chiseled body; smooth as Carrara marble. Probably from lifting so much of it. Men around here don't lift anything heavier than a golf club, if they can pay someone else to do it. When you meet a man like that, that's the way he always looks to you—no matter how fat or banged-up he gets." The old softie sipped from her Nalgene bottle and led me through the French doors to her garden.

"We can walk around the property, and if you're seriously interested, we'll make a real appointment." She pointedly checked the time. "I have thirty-five minutes until my court time, so you have fifteen. Shall we?"

No wonder Guido said he needed another twenty years. A large square, it was bordered on all sides by mature trees and squared-off English yews. Between the yews and the enormous, high-maintenance lawn, useful for touch football photo ops, Guido probably guaranteed himself a weekly maintenance gig for life. And then there was the fountain.

That first summer, Guido sold Mrs. Fifield on the idea of an Italian marble fountain. Eager to see Guido with his shirt off, Dina agreed. That's how I came to be standing eyeball to marble penis with an oversized Roman god who, from a certain angle, looked like Guido and appeared to be ejaculating twenty feet into the air. No doubt one of his little jokes.

"What do you think?" she asked.

"It's remarkable," I said, failing to come up with any other word for the twenty-by-twenty-foot marble excrescence in front of me. Roman gods and sea monsters cavorted incongruously with wood nymphs, satyrs, and assorted animals. Four angels with long trumpets stood in each corner, and the entire fountain was surrounded by a collection of statues that seemed to be haphazardly assembled for a fire sale. Despite the occasional lapses into good taste, the end result was more Pizza Napoli than Piazza Navona.

"Guido designed it. I hated it, too, in the beginning," she said, admiring it as if for the first time. "There are twenty-seven separate statues. Guido just kept piling them on all that summer." She laughed.

He probably got a nice kickback from the marble supplier, I thought. "When was the fountain installed?" I asked politely, steering myself away from any conversation that might require me to comment on its beauty.

"Oh dear, it was so long ago." She took another swig from the water bottle, to refresh her memory.

"Let's see, it was the summer my late husband was away so much. In Washington, D.C., of all places . . . in the summer. He was an attorney, and something was going on. The Peacocks were having work done in their garden, and the street was a terrible mess—dust and trucks everywhere . . . it was chaos. Anyway, Guido and I decided we might as well do it. Put the fountain in, that is," she said coyly.

"Was that when Congressman Fifield got interested in politics?"

"Win? He's not even that interested now, other than getting reelected. He couldn't have been less interested back then. That was the year he graduated from prep school. He spent the whole summer chasing ass in Maine, at our summer house. Oh dear, I've shocked you."

"What year was that?" I said, ignoring her crude remark.

"Who remembers? They grow up so fast. Ask that mousy little thing who works for him. She's probably got all his old report cards filed."

Another stolen glance at her watch told me I'd exceeded my fifteen minutes.

"I can drop off some garden books if you like, to give you some ideas," I said, finishing up.

"Would you? I'd adore that. Just leave them with the housekeeper if I'm not in. Any fresh ideas for the garden would be wonderful. There are just so many times you can redecorate the houses."

The lady of the manor dismissed me and I headed next door. Walking slowly, I stole a last glance back at the fountain and found myself thinking I should go for the job. It would be a service to the community to destroy such an atrocious thing.

CHAPTER 48

I walked back through the hemlocks, no smarter than I was before talking with Dina Fifield.

Halcyon's official opening was a few weeks away, but I had a hard time staying focused. Hurtful, decades-old secrets were in danger of coming out; Anna was distraught, confined to her bed, lighting candles and praying; and, most important, Hugo was still in jail, now facing even more serious charges. And I'd done nothing but stir things up needlessly.

Thinking of Hugo reminded me of his last, curious words before O'Malley led him away. I headed for the espaliered trees blanketing Richard Stapley's stone wall. I'd forgotten them in the days since Hugo's arrest.

Espaliered trees were fashionable in small Italianate gardens in the twenties and thirties. I was grateful Hugo had taken an interest, since I had no experience with either fruit trees or espaliers. The pear trees had already blossomed, and wouldn't need pruning until after the growing season, but Hugo said they needed some attention, so I went to check them out.

Over the course of many seasons, the trees had been pruned and trained to grow horizontally over the handsome stone wall using an intricate grid of wires and bamboo canes forced between the chinks in the stones. I resecured some of drooping branches, but nothing else seemed amiss, until I noticed a deep pile of mulch, sloppily shoved up against the bottom of the wall at the far end. I bent down to spread it around. As I did, I un-covered the top of a hand-hewn cornerstone. I dug far-ther, with only my gloved hands, and saw the date, as Hugo must have before shoving the mulch there to cover it: A.D. 1974, the same year Yoly Rivera vanished.

I pulled off my gloves and phoned Lucy and Felix, but I couldn't reach them. I tried Gerald Fraser, but his line was busy. When the phone rang, I assumed it was one of them calling me back, but it was O'Malley.

"I thought you'd like to know, we released Hugo Ju-rado early this morning. We found our two witnesses, a Mr. and Mrs. Galicia. They confirmed Hugo's where-abouts the morning Guido was killed. They shot plenty of video in the waiting room of the marriage bureau before tying the knot. You were right," he added grudg-ingly.

In the background of the Galicias' wedding pictures, only occasionally obscured by themselves, were Hugo and Anna, canoodling. And as if their testimony wasn't enough, there was an exonerating time code in the lower-right-hand corner of the frame.

"The Galicias went home to Guatemala for their hon-eymoon," Mike continued. "They didn't know we were looking for anyone until they returned yesterday."

I felt an adrenaline rush of success. "What about the fingerprints and the car?" I asked, pushing my luck.

"Felix's lawyer friend grilled the woman who saw Hugo's car, and she finally admitted she couldn't be sure of the time. As far as the fingerprints, the lawyer's in-vestigator lifted them from a number of other items at Chiaramonte's. Hugo did work there for a time, so the fact that his prints were on the weapon, too, was inconclusive. We had to let him go."

At least for now. That was left unsaid and hanging in the air when O'Malley hung up. I reached Anna's daughter and she told me that Felix and Anna were already downtown picking up Hugo. The phone rang again.

"Hey, it's about time you called me back," Gerald Fraser said. He'd left me a message I must have accidentally erased with all the snotty ones from Lucy.

"What was it?" I asked.

"Probably just another false lead," he said. "I'll let you know if anything pans out. What's your big news?"

I told him about the witnesses and Hugo's release.

"That's terrific," he said. "You're a pretty good little detective once you get going."

"I knew it wasn't Hugo," I said, pleased with myself. " 'Take a look at the espaliers'? Does that sound like a man being dragged off to the gallows?" I told him about the date on the wall and the fountain. "That's the reason I called you, even before I heard from O'Malley."

"What do you think it means, kiddo?"

"Dina's fountain was installed the same year as the stone wall at Halcyon, 1974. That's a lot of digging in a one-block radius that we know our missing person frequented. What if Guido killed Yoly and buried her body in the fountain? That was the one thing he personally attended to at the Fifield home, other than the lady of the house. He designed the fountain, oversaw its construction, and had plenty of access day and night, thanks to Mrs. Fifield."

"It's a good guess, and you may even be right, but there is one small problem. You've got zero proof."

Gerald was right, of course. No one in his right mind was going to tear apart the family compound of a local politician on my gut feeling.

"I'll just have to check out that fountain myself," I said.

"How, pray tell?"

Dina's own words told me how. "There are just so many times you can redecorate the houses," I repeated.

The second time I rang the Fifields' doorbell that day, I was armed with half a dozen garden books fringed with pink Post-its, my sketch pad, and a digital camera. Dina was still at her club, but I managed to talk my way past the housekeeper and into the garden.

The blank slate of her garden cried out for paths and separate garden rooms. Within thirty minutes, I'd sketched out a raised dining (or more likely drinking) pavilion close to the water; a cozy serenity garden nestled in the trees; and a cheery gazebo garden, right near the house for newspapers and morning coffee. All would be connected by a circular path. And each area would feature statuary harvested from Guido's marble monstrosity. I was shooting the fountain from every conceivable angle when Dina returned.

"I may have misjudged you," she said. "I like a go-getter."

I showed her my rough sketches, and she declared me a *genius,* a word I had a feeling came as easily to her as the word *moron.* She didn't ask what it would cost, and I hadn't a clue, but money would not be an issue for her.

"You won't really destroy the fountain, will you? I have such fond memories attached to it."

"Of course not, Mrs. Fifield. The plan is simply to remove some of the statues and repurpose them elsewhere in the garden."

And to see what, if anything, was underneath.

CHAPTER 49

"Just hold off on the sledgehammer until we shoot video," Lucy said, thinking ahead.

"I'm not razing it. Besides, I've got over a hundred stills."

"This isn't public television—I need video. I can't just zoom in and zoom out on the same damn pictures for twenty-seven minutes."

Characteristically, Lucy had become obsessed with the Yoly project and had all but moved in with me. In no time she'd written a script, shot a ton of additional footage, and interviewed everyone remotely connected to Yoly, including, with Felix acting as translator, Celinda Rivera, who was still in the United States, visiting cousins in New York.

Jon Chappell's help was invaluable. Lucy had dangled a coexecutive producer credit as the carrot to keep him engaged, but he needed little incentive—being in the same room with Lucy seemed to be payment enough for him.

"If there were Kennedys involved, even distant ones, I could be looking at a Peabody Award," she'd said early on.

"Well, don't start writing your speech now," I'd said.

"Not only aren't there Kennedys, we may not even have a Fifield." I replayed my visit with Dina.

"Something *going on* in Washington?" Lucy said. "In the summer . . . in the early seventies? She ever hear of Watergate? It must be dark, living your whole life with your head up your butt."

Evidently, the summer Yoly disappeared, both Mr. Fifields were out of state, otherwise engaged, and could prove it. Which left the amazingly well-preserved—some would say pickled—Mrs. Fifield with only her lusty Mediterranean gardener for company. She made do.

"That rascal," Lucy said. "I guess even a broken clock is right twice a day. But if Guido Chiaramonte was boffing the very rich, very worldly Dina Fifield, would he waste his time with poor, simple Yoly Rivera?"

"In a heartbeat," I said. "Dina might have made him feel like a Roman god in the sack, but once they were vertical she probably fell right back into character and reminded him that she was slumming with him. With Yoly, *he'd* be the worldly, upper-class partner."

By the time I had a realistic estimate and a signed contract with Dina, Felix and Hugo had assembled a workforce and we were ready to start as soon as the ink was dry. Not surprisingly, our first task was dismantling the fountain.

The marble pool and some of the statues would remain intact. The trumpeting angels would lead Dina to her gazebo; the cherubs would frolic in her serenity garden; the massive Roman god would preside over her waterfront pavilion. The rest I'd figure out along the way.

The smaller statues weighed close to three hundred pounds each and required three men to lift them off the brass rods anchoring them to the fountain's base. We hired a piano mover to raise Neptune and deposit him on his new perch facing the water on a quickly built platform of gravel and Pennsylvania bluestone. That alone took half a day, and anyone watching might well have wondered why I was more interested in a hole in the ground than a thousand-pound marble statue hanging precariously by a cable. Once Neptune was enthroned, I sent the men home.

Lucy was there to record the event, if, in fact, there was one; and Felix and the newly sprung Hugo provided the muscle.

In the center of the now empty marble pool was a concrete ring housing the fountain's pump and tubing. Four cinder blocks surrounded the pump.

We moved the cinder blocks and external pump. Underneath the pump was a thick square of black slate. It took Felix and Hugo and two heavy crowbars to flip over the slate. Black landscape fabric was wrapped around a lumpy, unidentifiable object, but poking through the weed mat was something that looked eerily familiar. A bone. A bone I was convinced belonged to Yoly Rivera.

CHAPTER 50

"There's such a fine line between cheesy and clever." Babe Chinnery held up that morning's edition of the *Springfield Bulletin*. "GARDENER DIGS UP TRUTH IN 30-YEAR-OLD MYSTERY." I curtsied and slid onto a stool at the counter to a smattering of applause from my fellow diners at the Paradise.

"Breakfast is on the house," Babe said, pouring me some coffee. "If I had a liquor license I'd buy you a drink."

The previous week had been a blur. The bones found underneath Dina Fifield's fountain were conclusively identified as Yoly's remains by matching a sample of her DNA with Celinda Rivera's. Guido Chiaramonte had apparently stashed her body under Neptune and, over the years, in the course of checking on Dina Fifield's plumbing, kept an eye on Yoly.

Jon Chappell's editor had unleashed his inner Rupert and given him carte blanche on Yoly's story. To Jon's credit he kept the tone reasonably respectful.

Guido's killer was still at large, but as long as Hugo was in the clear, I was leaving that problem to the professionals. The closemouthed day laborer community wasn't providing many answers, and Mike O'Malley feared the killer had already left the country and would never be found. Like Yoly, Guido would wind up on a yellowing flyer on someone's bulletin board.

It wasn't my problem; I'd solved my two mysteries and was happy to be back digging in the dirt. As people had predicted, I was inundated with job offers once the story broke.

"Where've you been? Busy giving interviews?" Babe asked.

"I've been working my little tail off," I said, picking at the crisp, parsleyed potatoes next to my omelet. "Halcyon opens to the public next week, we just finished Dina Fifield's hardscaping so the landscaping starts soon, and I am booked solid until the end of this season. And I've got a meeting set up with a small golf course in Westport that could be big."

"*Muy bien.* Any word from the beautiful muchacho?"

Felix Ontivares had accompanied Celinda Rivera and her daughter's remains back to Mexico. Mexican news online ran the story for three days, complete with pictures of Felix and Yoly's surviving family members, including her mother and beautiful nineteen-year-old niece, a budding Tejano star.

"Ships passing in the night," I told Babe. "He had his arm around the niece in that picture, and if he's anything like his father, he likes them young. I'm a big girl. At least I'm not still mooning about the ex."

"True. I always say the best way to get *over* someone is to get *under* someone."

"Lucy said the same thing. Was that something you got in a fortune cookie?"

"Just a saying. Neil's the quote guy. I don't think it's Shakespeare, but I'll ask him."

"While you're at it, ask him about these, too." On a clean napkin I scribbled down some of the lines I'd seen on the Peacocks' needlepoints. "I've been meaning to look them up but keep getting sidetracked."

The Springfield Historical Society had agreed to let Hugo and Anna have a small ceremony on Halcyon's brick terrace the day after the opening, in appreciation of all the work Hugo had done there. Anna was thrilled; she'd been lobbying me since they set the date.

"I've got a few final touches for the garden. Then on Saturday night, I'm going to bring in an arbor and cover it with vines and flowers as a surprise."

"Cool. You know Pete's baking their cake."

"Don't tell him I said this, but his cooking's getting better."

"Be nice. He's been practicing for weeks, even took a cake-decorating class in Wilton. Here, try a piece of today's test cake. I've gained three pounds being his guinea pig."

It was charmingly decorated with a cluster of wisteria made entirely of sugar. Impressive, but it was a little early for buttercream, so I asked her to pack up the huge slab she'd cut for me and promised to try it later.

I considered swinging by SHS to pick up the bonus check Richard finally agreed to, but there was time. Besides, next week I'd have a new assistant to handle collections, the future Mrs. Hugo Jurado.

CHAPTER 51

The stone planters on Halcyon's brick terrace were overflowing with coleus, sweet potato vines, and dwarf fountain grass. Smaller, lightweight containers held masses of colorful zinnias and licorice plants spilling over the edges. I dropped my backpack and lunch in a shaded spot on the brick steps and got to work.

I wriggled one of the heavy stone dogs out of the way to make room for the rectangular buffet table SHS was delivering tomorrow. I rolled the other stone dog out of its regular spot to accommodate a small lectern where Richard would say a few words at the opening on Saturday, and a priest would marry the happy couple on Sunday. All the other planters were repositioned to flank the arbor under which Hugo and Anna would be married and to make room for the folding chairs for the wedding guests.

The work left me sweaty and a little winded, so I took a break on the steps for some water and a sugar rush from the buttercream icing on Pete's test cake. It was a home run—quite possibly the best thing I'd ever tasted.

Only a few months before I'd sat on these same steps, my life a shambles. Now I had more work than I could handle and I'd solved two mysteries; and two good friends were getting married. Life was good. I treated myself to another swipe of icing, surveying my work.

In all the time I'd been at Halcyon, I hadn't paid much attention to the maze, which was a ten-foot-high privet hedge of five interlocking circles. It needed only the annual crew cut, which Hugo had given it early in the season, and the occasional nip and tuck, which I decided to give it now. I placed a napkin on top of the cake to keep the ants away, and left it and the water on the steps for later.

My long-handled loppers were in the toolshed; I found them and walked past the white garden to the maze, where I trimmed a few wayward branches and yanked out errant strands of Virginia creeper and wire-like, mile-a-minute vine. The maze wouldn't be open for the ceremony this weekend, so if all I got to do was a little cosmetic pruning on the outside, that would be enough.

I was almost finished when my phone beeped with the Caribbean music that let me know I had a text message. It was from Neil MacLeod: *Needlepoint quotes in Peacock house are from Song of Solomon, pretty amazing under the circumstances. Neil*

Under the circumstances? What did that mean? I put down the loppers, crossed the terrace, and entered the Peacock house through the unlocked door that had welcomed so many other women. In the mudroom, the two needlepoints I'd seen on my first visit were still there. *I am a rose of Sharon, a lily of the valley,* and *Like a lily among thorns is my darling among the maidens,* each bordered by rambling roses, now grimy with age. I went upstairs to the library to check on the others Neil and I had seen. On the paneled wall were two more.

What shall we do for our sister? Okay, I get it. *Come to my garden, my sister.* That wasn't much help. I scanned Dorothy's library for a copy of the Bible, kicking up a puff of dust when I set the heavy, leather-bound book on the table. I flipped through the pages until I located the Song of Solomon. *Come to my garden, my sister, my spouse; a spring shut up, a fountain sealed.*

I dialed quickly. No answer. I waited for the beep to leave my message. "Gerald, it's Paula. Look, I'm at Halcyon. There's something strange here. The Peacocks had a series of needlepoints with lines from the Song of Solomon. One's missing, and it's about 'a fountain sealed.' What if the empty shelf isn't missing books? What if it's missing another framed needlepoint that was resting on the shelf? A needlepoint with a message someone didn't want seen? I'll call you back in ten minutes, but meet me here as soon as you can, okay?" I hung up.

I hurried outside to escape the suddenly claustrophobic atmosphere in the library. I went back to the maze to wait for Gerald. I checked my phone. Still no calls or messages. I picked up my loppers and kept working, more out of nervousness than anything else.

Deep inside the maze, farther than I had ever been, something dark green, like a lawn and leaf bag, caught my eye. "Jeez, I asked those guys not to leave garbage around," I said out loud. As I got closer, I saw it wasn't a trash bag. It was an oversized army surplus poncho draped over a twelve-speed bicycle with a bent rim.

"They won't be able to blame Chiaramonte for this, but I'm sure I'll think of something."

I froze. Stepping out from behind a wall of privet was Richard Stapley. "You killed Yoly?" I said, stepping back. "Why?"

"I had to," he said calmly. "Boring as she is, I could

hardly give up an heiress for a penniless piece of fluff.
When Yoly told me she was pregnant, I had no recourse.
She interfered with my plans and had to be dealt with.
Just like Guido.

"That son of a bitch was sneaking out of Dina Fifield's bedroom when he accidentally saw Yoly and me
in the Peacocks' garden. He's been holding it over my
head ever since. It took some time, but I dealt with him."

I took another step back, bumping into the privet.

"And now you're interfering with my plans."

Stapley lunged at me, grabbing my shoulders. I pulled
free and cracked him on the side of the head with my
loppers. I heard a squishing sound, and Richard's silver hair turned pink as blood poured from the gash on
his temple. I bayoneted him with the loppers and tore
ass out of the unfamiliar maze, bouncing from side to
side as I ran. He caught me by the sleeve as we exited
near the stone wall, and he slammed me against it. He
swung me around to the left, and it was just the windup
I needed to land a powerful left hook to his kidneys.

He crumpled over. "Bitch," he spat.

I ran a few yards, hurdling over the first row of boxwoods, then I felt my legs give out from under me as he
knocked me off my feet. I rolled over to my left and
instinctively covered my right cheek so the punch he
landed wasn't as bad as it might have been. I grabbed
a handful of crushed oyster shells and threw them in
Richard's eyes. It bought me just enough time to scram-
ble to my feet and run to the steps of the terrace with
Richard close behind.

"Dammit!" he yelled. I heard his big frame crash to
the ground. He'd stepped on the wedge of wedding cake
and slid on the thick buttercream, smacking his knees
on the bricks.

I made the mistake of turning to look, and he grabbed

my ankles, bringing me down again, my chin hitting the pavers. I tasted blood and let out a scream but kept kicking with all my strength at his hands, his chest, finally connecting with his face. His head snapped back and hit the long nose on one of the stone dogs I'd repositioned not an hour before. I crawled away on all fours, reflexively kicking, even as I moved farther away from him.

I climbed to my feet and ran to the edge of the terrace, still shaking. My mouth was filled with blood, and tears were streaming down my face. I watched Richard's motionless body for a few minutes. Blood was splattered everywhere—some his, some mine. I turned away, unable to look anymore. If I'd been wearing my heart-rate monitor, it would have been off the charts. I fumbled in my pants pocket for my cell and dialed 911, bloodying the phone.

Something moved behind me. I switched the phone to my right hand, twisted my torso, and landed a hard right—square in the face of Mike O'Malley.

CHAPTER 52

O'Malley and I sat opposite each other in the emergency room at the Springfield Hospital, holding ice packs to our faces. He massaged his jaw. "Not a bad punch."

"You're supposed to pivot that back foot and twist your hips," I said, my cheek full of cotton wadding. "Ellen's boxing class at the sports club."

A doctor approached us. "Mr. Stapley is in stable condition. It looked worse, because of all the blood," she said. "I told the other officers no questions, but he seems to be rambling on his own." Mike leaped up and jogged down the hall to Richard's room.

"How are you feeling?" She gently turned my face to the side to inspect my stitches. "You'll have a respectable shiner but no scars on the chin. I'm a good seamstress. He got the worst of the deal. Good for you."

The emergency room's swinging doors flew open.

"Would it be heartless of me to ask you for an exclusive?" Jon Chappell called, rushing toward me.

"I'm fine, thank you for asking," I said. "Go ahead, ask your questions. The public has a right to know."

He got out his pad and tape recorder. "Shoot."

"Richard Stapley killed Yoly Rivera."

Jon let out a long, low whistle.

"He killed Guido, too."

"*He* was the rich man with the accent that Yoly wrote to her mother about?" Jon asked.

"Yup."

When O'Malley returned, he helped me flesh out the story. "One night in the summer of 1974, after an athletic evening at Dina Fifield's, Guido was peeing in the hemlocks that separated the two properties and saw Stapley. Stapley claimed he was working on the stone wall, but Guido spotted Yoly's shoulder bag hanging on the nose of one of the stone dogs. Then he saw her feet, poking out from behind the stone wall."

"Richard told me Yoly was pregnant," I said, "just like her mother suspected."

Mike nodded. "He's claiming he panicked and Yoly's death was an accident."

"Yoly accidentally fell and hit her head on a heavy rectangular object . . . six times?" Jon asked, citing the autopsy report. "If that's true, why not just go to the cops?"

"A good citizen; just the thing we in law enforcement like to see. Guido wasn't. He helped him hide the body."

"Did Richard tell you how they met?" I asked, refolding my melting ice pack.

"Yoly was hired by the Fifields' regular housekeeper," Mike said, "to help at Win's graduation party. Dina Fifield probably didn't even know she was there, but Stapley certainly did."

Chappell was writing furiously.

"Care to continue, Ms. Holliday?"

"Richard thought he'd get away with murdering a poor Mexican no one knew and no one would miss.

Guido must have convinced him a marble fountain was a better hiding place than a stacked stone wall. They buried her, and Guido has been blackmailing Richard ever since—not about Margery's baby, about Yoly's murder."

"I told you he was a bastard," Jon said.

"Once Richard became a pillar of the community, Guido began to really squeeze him," Mike said.

"Maybe that sewer deal was part of it, the one that tripled the value of Guido's property," Jon added.

"But that was two years ago," I said, "and only pays off when you sell. What if Guido wanted his money now?"

Mike continued, "Richard was desperate. He'd run out of his own money, and although Margery's was tantalizingly close, he couldn't touch it. Guido promised Richard he'd leave the country after he got one last payoff, but Stapley was broke."

"What about his art collection?" Jon asked. "I heard he had a Childe Hassam."

"Not him, *her*," I said. "Margery says she doesn't like the new frame, but I bet it's the painting she doesn't like, ten to one it's a fake. I bet Richard sold the original on that trip to Hartford." Things were coming together.

"So, Stapley tells Guido to be patient, he needs time to raise the money. Two or three weeks tops, then they can meet at their regular drop-off spot," Mike adds. "The recycling center. Another of Guido's little jokes.

"In the meantime, you and Neil accidentally tell Guido about the journal. Now he claims to have two things on Richard and gets even greedier. At the meeting they argue, Guido demanding more money and storming off until Richard promises to deliver. Now Richard knows that Guido will never leave him alone. There'll always be *one last payoff*. He knows there's only one way out."

"Guido interfered with his plans," I explained. "Richard parked the black Lincoln conspicuously in front of Halcyon so that I or anyone passing would assume he was there. Then he called the nursery, probably from a pay phone, to make sure the afternoon help had arrived and Guido would be alone in the trailer. That was Tanya's hang-up, right?" I asked Mike.

"Keep going, you're doing pretty good."

"Richard bicycled to the nursery, stabbed Guido, then rode back to Halcyon, stashing his bike and poncho in the maze. Somewhere along the way, maybe in the deep gravel at the nursery, he bent one of the rims, but that didn't matter. He'd be driving back in the car."

"The tracks at Guido's nursery we initially thought were made by a wheelbarrow were made by a specialized bike," Mike said. "Same make and model as Richard's.

"Why didn't he go back for the bike sooner?"

"He probably tried, but someone was always there. He told Margery it was in the shop anyway; and, given his track record, he probably thought he could leave it stashed in the garden for years and no one would notice. Sorry, Mike."

"What about the weapon?" Jon asked.

"Richard unwittingly returned one of Guido's own tools," Mike said. "He took the *coa* from Halcyon's greenhouse and peeled off the orange tape Paula had used to identify the tools, assuming correctly that the handle would be covered with other people's fingerprints. Hugo's just happened to be a set we were able to identify. What Richard didn't count on was our criminalist's finding microscopic traces of cashmere stuck to the adhesive residue on the handle. Not too many garden workers wear cashmere gloves. All circumstantial until you forced his hand and he tried to kill you."

"And, not to be too grisly," I added, "anyone who knew how to use a *coa* wouldn't have missed Guido's heart. The curved blade enters much lower than you'd think unless you've used it enough times to get the hang of it."

"So, Sergeant O'Malley, how did you happen to be at Halcyon at just the right time?" Jon asked.

"Fraser called me." Mike turned to me. "You might eliminate the middleman next time. He learned a painting from the Hassam series was sold to a private collector in Hartford three weeks ago by a man claiming to be Benjamin Russell, who happens to have died in 1984. We'd been watching Richard anyway since the day we brought all of you in for questioning. Your alibi for him wasn't exactly airtight. That's the reason I went to the Stapley home in the first place.

"When we found Hugo's prints we had to hold him, and it let Richard think he was in the clear. But you pushed his hand; he got careless. As Paula has so tactfully pointed out, given the police department's history, and his, he probably thought we'd take another thirty years to figure it out," Mike said.

"Any thoughts on the famous missing journal?" Jon asked. "Or is that Springfield's newest mystery?"

"That's what Stapley was looking for the night he sideswiped you at the recycling center."

"That was him?" I was shocked, but it didn't take me long to fill in the blank. "When he didn't find the journal in Guido's office, he waited until he thought it was safe, then borrowed one of Guido's own trucks to search for it in their usual hiding place."

"A plus. *¿Quién sabe?*" Mike said. "Maybe the journal never even existed."

"And the candy?" Jon asked.

"Purely an accident. Must have fallen out of Renata's pocket without her even knowing."

"All right, I've got enough here to keep me busy for a month." He checked his watch. "If I write this up in the next hour, it can make tomorrow's paper."

O'Malley and I watched him fly down the hall.

"*¿Quién sabe?*" Mike said. "Is that what you really think about the journal?"

"No. Now that the press is gone, I'll tell you. I think Hillary Gibson took it that very first day at Halcyon, tucked it under her shawl the whole time she was talking to me. I don't know what's in it, and I don't need to know. It's none of my business."

"And gardening is a dirty business," he said.

"You know, that's a much better name for my company—Dirty Business."

EPILOGUE

DNA evidence proved the baby Yoly was carrying was **Richard Stapley's.** He was convicted of the murder of Guido Chiaramonte, and is awaiting trial for the 1974 murder of Yoly Rivera. While in custody his eBay auction for *The Temple of Flora* ended with no bids since he wasn't able to answer the 235 questions from members regarding its authenticity. A total of 197 members left negative feedback.

After divorcing Richard, **Margery Stapley** sold her house and embarked on a round-the-world trip for single seniors, on which she met a wealthy Italian clothing manufacturer. Margery and Enrico were married in a fifth-century church in Lugano, Switzerland. No charges were ever filed against her, and the *Bulletin* never retracted its original report that the baby I'd found "almost certainly belonged to one of the Peacock sisters."

On the strength of the Rivera articles, **Jon Chappell** received a job offer from the *National Enquirer*, but declined, in favor of more serious journalistic pursuits at the *New York Post*.

Babe Chinnery and **Neil MacLeod** opened a small herb and tea kiosk in the parking lot of the Paradise Diner. Honeybush tea is now on the menu at both places.

Gerald Fraser and **Hillary Gibson** are living together. She's arranging for an exhibit of his sculpture in a tony Bedford gallery. He's hand-carving a new sign for her home's entrance but no one's seen the name yet.

Felix Ontivares returned and was my date for Hugo and Anna's wedding. His involvement in the Rivera case further burnished the family name at home and he is currently entering local politics in Mexico.

Win Fifield's aide released a statement that the congressman "hadn't rested a day since the disappearance of that poor girl" and "his mother was proud to be instrumental in the resolution of this long, local tragedy." Win's approval rating shot up ten points, due to support from Springfield's Hispanic community, which he had largely ignored in the past.

Lucy Cavanaugh didn't get nominated for a Peabody, but she did make a deal with a cable network for a thirteen-part series tentatively titled *Sin in Suburbia,* which she is actively researching in Main Line Pennsylvania.

Anna Peña and **Hugo Jurado** were married, not on Halcyon's terrace, which was still surrounded by crime scene tape, but on Dina Fifield's new dining pavilion, under a borrowed arbor, facing the sea. Pete's buttercream cake was a huge hit.

Mike O'Malley and I are now sparring partners at the local gym. He is still smoke-free and has lost twelve pounds due

to his new modified Zone diet, which I am advising him on.
He has yet to play the accordion for me.

And the white garden at Halcyon is in full bloom, currently
with masses of gypsophila, baby's breath.

Keep reading for a sneak peek at Rosemary Harris's next
Dirty Business mystery

THE BIG DIRT NAP

Available soon in hardcover from Minotaur Books

CHAPTER 1

Maybe I'd have had a drink with the guy if I had known
the next time I saw him he'd be sprawled out in a Dump-
ster enclosure, with a greasy newspaper tented over his
face. Then again, maybe not.

Nick Vigoriti had unsuccessfully hit on me as I sipped
club soda at the bar. There were two or three likelier
candidates in skimpier outfits who weren't working on a
laptop, but he zeroed in on me.

I knew him, sort of. Earlier in the day, Vigoriti had
been on line behind me checking into the Titans Hotel
in Connecticut's wine country. We'd spent what seemed
like twenty minutes listening to a statuesque redhead
spitting out demands and fidgeting almost as much as
the white Maltese she carried in her plastic designer bag.

"That is not friendly."

The pimply kid behind the reception desk nodded
furiously. That, combined with the oversized jacket
that hopefully fit his night-shift counterpart better, gave
him the appearance of a life-size bobble-head doll.

"April does not need a sitter. I only came to this estab-
lishment because it's supposed to be pet-friendly. I could
have gotten comped at Hunting Ridge." She towered

over the poor kid, the pile of hair on her head giving her
an extra four inches, as if she needed it.

Vigoriti and I exchanged brief "whaddya gonna do"
glances, until the dog's owner finished tormenting the
desk clerk, then teetered off accompanied by a full lug-
gage cart and the only bellman in sight.

When it was my turn, I set my backpack on the
counter, leaned over, and told the clerk my name.

"I don't see you," he said, scrolling down the computer screen. He forced himself to say the words, anticipating another pain-in-the-neck customer. Beads of
sweat popped up on his forehead like condensation on a
glass. I felt for the guy; he was getting a crash course in
Difficult Guests 101 on what I was guessing was his
first week on the job. "I'm sorry," he said, his voice
cracking. "Did you make the reservation online, by any
chance?"

Great. I'd sat through rush-hour traffic on the highway and now there was no room at the inn. "It has to be
there," I said, trying not to betray my real feelings. "Will
you please look again?"

He continued to scan the screen; then it occurred
to me that my friend Lucy had made the reservation.
Maybe it was under her name or her company's.

"Can you check under KCPS-TV? Or Cavanaugh.
Check *Cavanaugh*," I repeated, louder, in that stupid
way people do when they're talking to foreigners, as if
saying something louder is going to make it easier to
understand.

"Okay, okay, I got it. Here it is. 'Two adults, two dou-
bles, no pets,'" he read off the screen. Relief washed
over the kid's face; he didn't need another guest with
problems. This job was already an interruption of his real
life—which was probably football, getting good grades,

and procuring the perfect fake ID, not standing in a gold-braided uniform two sizes too big and catching verbal abuse. I didn't blame him; I was in a service business myself and sometimes it wore thin.

I gave him my credit card for the "incidentals" and watched as he mindlessly swiped it and handed it back without even checking my name or the photo on the front.

"I'll just need one key. My friend will be joining me later." I plucked the paper folder from the counter and slid one plastic key back to him.

"Thank you, Ms. Cavanaugh."

I started to correct him, then thought, *What's the point?*

"You're welcome." I snatched my bag from the counter and turned to leave. Asking him where the elevators were would only have extended the experience, so I went off in the same direction as the woman with the dog. I was hardly going to get lost in a suburban Connecticut hotel.

On the way, smack in the middle of the lobby, was an octagonal enclosure about twenty feet wide. Inside it, in a huge terra-cotta pot, was the reason I was there. Well, one of them anyway. Inside the glass enclosure was a corpse flower. I moved in for a closer look, setting my things down briefly on one of the laminated benches that circled the glass gazebo.

The pot itself was about four feet in diameter, and shooting straight up from the center was a light green veined shaft tinged with purplish pink. I hadn't seen one in a few years and there was no getting around it—with that color and that shape . . .

"Pretty sexy if you ask me," Vigoriti had said, over my shoulder.

"I didn't ask you," I said, firmly enough to let him know I wasn't about to engage in a junior-high-school-level conversation regarding a certain part of the male anatomy. Not with a stranger anyway.

I picked up my bags, headed back toward the bank of elevators, around the corner from reception, and made a beeline for the first white triangle pointing up. Once inside, I pushed the button for my floor and crumpled, exhausted, against the side of the car. Just as the doors were closing, a hand slapped them apart.

The hand was an unlikely combination of manicured and rough, as if a boxer had buffed his nails. A black leather strap was twisted around the thick wrist and the large tanned hand held, of all things, a man bag, almost lost in its owner's large palm. The shirtsleeve was rolled up, thin gray stripes on black silk. Expensive, but not top of the line. And it half covered the muscular forearm of Nick Vigoriti.

"Hello, again." He smiled, pushed the doors open, and settled politely into the opposite corner of the car. I could tell he was looking at me, but I pretended not to notice.

Vigoriti gave off the very appealing scent of whiskey, sweat, and, if I remembered correctly from two boyfriends ago, a dash of Armani—ordinarily a winning trifecta and one I'd succumbed to in the past. But I was tired from the long drive and wasn't feeling particularly friendly. Besides, this was an all-girls weekend. Lucy and I each had work to do, but it was really about two old friends catching up. I flashed him the fake one-second, toothless smile you use to acknowledge someone's existence, then fixed my gaze straight ahead at the diamond pattern on the wall of the elevator until six pings told me I'd reached my floor. Vigoriti got out, too.

For an instant, my antenna went up, but he turned left before I'd committed to either direction. Happily, my room was on the right and I rushed down the hall, shifting my bags to one side and trying to remember which pocket I'd stuck the room key in.

I fished the plastic card out of its sheath and slipped it into the lock. Nothing. I tried it stripe up, stripe down, toward me, and away from me. Five minutes later, after repeated wipes against my sweatshirt, the uncooperative sliver of plastic still refused to admit me to my room. I sank my forehead against the door and let out a low groan like a wounded animal.

"They're a pain, aren't they?" Vigoriti said, standing over my shoulder.

I hadn't heard him approach, and was so startled I bumped my head looking up. Assessing the damage with one hand, I gave him the key with the other. "I'm not proud. You try."

He dipped the key once and the light flashed green.

"How did you do that?"

"Magnetism. You have to have a magnetic personality."

He had spared me a return match with the sweet but dopey desk clerk, so I resisted the urge to snort at his lame come-on.

"I'm kidding," he said. "Sometimes technology just likes to . . . *mess* with you." He held on to the key a few seconds longer than necessary, slapping it against his palm. Then he blew on it—as if to blow imaginary cooties away—and handed it back to me.

I picked up my bags, held the door open just a crack with my hip, and waited for him to leave. "Thanks," I said, hoping he'd take the hint.

He shrugged and strode down the hall to the elevators. Trailing him, in the air with his pheromones, was the word he almost said, but didn't. *Fuggedaboudit.*

*   *   *

I wouldn't have been at Titans at all if Lucy Cavanaugh hadn't lured me there at the last minute with the offer of a free room, a spa weekend, and the promise of a corpse flower just about to bloom. Any one of those might have done the trick, but all three were irresistible. And I needed to believe I still did things spontaneously.

I'd gotten freebies all the time in my old television job, but they were few and far between since I'd started Dirty Business a couple of years back. Dirty Business was going through the terrible twos—sometimes wonderful and sometimes not. This was one of the *not* periods—before the season started, when I was planning my year but some of my clients still had holiday wreaths on their front doors. I had jumped at the chance for a few days of rest and relaxation on someone else's dime. Once I knew we were going to Titans, I managed to squeeze a few bucks and a byline out of my local paper to let me write a piece on the rare corpse flower on display at the hotel. If nothing else it would get my name out in front of potential clients.

Lucy was venturing outside of New York City to chase down a story for *Sin in Suburbia,* a cable series I'd inadvertently helped her start a year ago. The series had seemed like a good idea at the time and the network had ordered more episodes, but it hadn't initially registered with Lucy that she'd actually have to spend time in the suburbs, and that was tough duty for a woman who got vertigo anytime she went further north.

If we hadn't planned to meet at the bar I'd have been in bed with room service and the remote, and I'd have saved my picture taking until the morning. As it was, I swapped my sneakers for short cowboy boots and my T-shirt for a plain white shirt, which I tucked into my jeans. With a not-too-out-of-style dark blazer and a little bronzer I convinced myself I looked professional, French—simple and elegant.

Not that Titans had anything remotely like a dress code—the few people I had seen when I checked in could have been going to a kids' soccer game. But I spent most of my days in gardening gear—pants tucked into socks to avoid ticks, baggy long-sleeved tops to avoid scratches, and when necessary a white mesh bug suit that covered me from head to toe and made me look like something out of a 1950s horror movie about the aftereffects of the hydrogen bomb. I welcomed any occasion to clean up my act.

An hour later, after taking more than two dozen pictures of the corpse flower, I was at the bar nursing my third club soda, feeling bloated and losing patience. There was a grand piano in the bar but judging by the amount of dust on it I didn't think I was in for any live music. I tried to ignore the third Muzak go-round of that weepy song from *Titanic* and passed the time by filling in the details for the corpse flower story. I Googled the hotel's history and checked out the clientele. No one was paying any attention to the plant. The seven-foot object in the glass box might have been a priceless sculpture or a giant turd for all anyone at Titans seemed to care. I scoured the room for someone to interview but the pickings were slim: a few Asian guys, a skinny blonde reading a romance novel, and a twitchy guy who looked like he desperately needed a drink. Then I saw *him* again.

Vigoriti entered the raised bar area and surveyed the place as if he owned it. He unwrapped a candy and popped it in his mouth, tossing the wrapper at a nearby ashtray and missing. I hoped he wouldn't notice me or would have the good sense to realize I wasn't interested, but my limited experience with him already told me what to expect. Uninvited, he slid onto the bar stool right next to me.

"You going gambling? If you're calculating the odds on that computer I can tell you they always favor the house," he said, his breath first-date minty. He must have been joking with that line.

This time I took a better look at him. He was handsome in a banged-up, been-around-the-block way. Built like a quarterback, or at least what they look like with all the padding—big shoulders, small hips. And he had great hair. Long, but intellectual long, not aging-record-business-skinny-ponytail *what are you thinking?* long. Then there was that intoxicating scent. There was no denying it, Nick Vigoriti smelled like trouble, or at the very least, an adventure. And I hadn't had one lately.

"No kidding," I said, snapping out of his thrall. "And is that your finding after years of careful research?" I flipped the computer screen halfway down.

"I just got back from Vegas," he said. "Thought I'd save you some dough."

"I'm waiting for a friend," I said, hoping to head him off *before* the pass.

"Could be I'm that friend."

He was losing points rapidly. Good looks got you so far with me, but a guy needed to have some gray matter. "Do you get many takers with these lines?" I asked.

"Depends. On how young they are, how smart they are," he said, smiling and eyeing the other women at the bar. He turned back to me. "Now, those girls are girls. I'm looking for a woman, about thirty to thirty-five, long dark hair, athletic build," he said, giving a pretty good description of me.

I held up my hands to stop him. "I'm going to give you the benefit of the doubt. This may not even be where you're going, but I'm not looking for a good time. Not that kind of good time. I'm waiting for a friend. A real one, not one who's in town for the widget convention. And *she's* late. Other than her, the only reason I'm here is the titan arum," I said, attempting to scare him off with a little Latin. "The corpse flower." I motioned in its direction.

"Corpse flower? Is that what they call that stinkweed in the glass box?"

He pointed to the plant we'd been looking at earlier, the titan arum, the largest unbranched inflorescence in the world. In simple terms, the biggest flower that isn't on a tree. Spectacular and rare, but unsettling, since the corpse flower looks like a giant phallus, and smells, well, like rotting meat; hence the name, and the need for an enclosure. I was guessing some dumb schmuck who didn't know any better thought the titan arum would be a clever promotion for Titans. I was also guessing same dumb schmuck was currently looking for another job.

"I heard the Mishkins had to fork over five grand for that box," he said, "to keep the stench away from the paying customers. And they're probably going to trash it once the damn thing blooms and it's shipped back to the jungle."

"I doubt they'll do that. Smarter to donate it and get the tax deduction. The University of Wisconsin has a few corpse flowers. I'm sure UConn would love to have it; theirs bloomed a few years ago." He eyed me as if I'd just spoken in tongues or cracked the human genome. Okay, he wasn't into plants . . . or big words. But the longer I looked at him, the less I cared. Brains weren't everything, and anyway, we were just talking.

If I stuck to club soda and we stayed in safe territory conversationwise, he could stay. Besides, I'd enjoy the look on Lucy's face when she rushed in breathlessly with stories and apologies and saw me sitting with a sexy beast like Nick Vigoriti. She and the rest of my friends had been after me to start dating again ever since I left New York City, and this little encounter might shut them up for a while. He might even contribute something interesting about the hotel that I could use for the article. Who knew?

"Who are the Mishkins?" I asked, surreptitiously keying that info into the laptop.

"Bernie Mishkin and his sister," he said, watching me use the computer. "Are you writing this down now?"

"Yeah. Is that a problem?"

Vigoriti shrugged. "Same difference. The Mishkins own the place," he said, waving the sad-eyed bartender over. "They and their numerous partners."

The bartender had a heart-shaped face and lank hair that hung in a skinny braid halfway down her back.

"What're you having, Nicky?" she asked, in an accent I couldn't initially place, then decided was Russian. She wiped nonexistent spills from the bar and slipped a coaster in front of him, grazing his fingers.

"Dirty martini," he said, pulling back his hand. "You?" he asked me.

Every stupid thing I'd done in my adult life had come after a few drinks, and I could imagine getting very stupid with Nick Vigoriti, so I stuck with club soda.

"Can you introduce me to them?" I asked. "The Mishkins?"

"You think that's a good idea?"

"Why not?" I said. "I may have a lucrative proposition for them."

"They're always interested in money." He laughed. "I haven't talked to Bernie for a while, but that may change. His wife died a few months back. I haven't seen much of him since then. . . . I was really friendlier with her."

Why was I not surprised? What woman wouldn't want

to be friends with a handsome stud who hung on your every word and made you feel as if you were the only woman in the room worth talking to?

The bartender brought our drinks. Nick's had six green olives on two plastic toothpicks. The bartender moved off to another customer but not before giving me a look that suggested she wouldn't mind seeing my head on a sharpened stick.

"What did *I* do?"

"Oksana's a good kid," he said, swallowing hard and nodding in her direction.

"Adorable."

"I used to work here," Vigoriti continued. "Before Mishkin brought in the Malaysians, the Ukranians, let's see . . ." He rattled off a laundry list of ethnic groups, then took a long pull on his drink. "Who is it now, Oksana?" he called out to the bartender.

"Chinese, I think," she said, over her shoulder, already fixing him a second drink.

"Their board meetings must look like a Benetton ad," I muttered.

"Most of them cut bait."

"It doesn't look like business is too bad; there are people here," I said.

"We could go somewhere private to discuss this," he said, signaling Oksana that he was ready for round two. He polished off his drink and slid all the olives into his mouth in a surprisingly suggestive move that made me rethink how friendly I wanted to appear.

"You know, I was just trying to be polite. Always dangerous at a bar. I'm sorry if I misled you, but I really am waiting for someone, and it isn't you." As if on cue, my phone beeped with a text message. Lucy was running late. Typical. She'd gotten a late start to begin with and one of the cheap Chinese New York-to-Boston shuttle buses had collided with a construction-materials truck. Gravel was spread all over I-95. The result was the same as if a load of ball bearings had spilled out on the highway; cars were drifting side to side as if they were in a Japanese video game. Lucy was stuck on the road, near Stamford, and wrote that she'd call when she got closer.

Locals were trickling into the bar for after-dinner drinks, working guys with puffy baseball caps. And businessmen who might have heard about the mess on 95 and preferred to sit here instead of in traffic. I debated the pros and cons of staying at the bar with Nick and possibly moving on to the harder stuff but decided against it. Life was complicated enough.

I chugged my drink and shut down the computer. "I'm gonna cut bait, to use your expression. I have to go. I was serious about meeting the Mishkins, though. I may have a buyer." I whipped out my business card and handed it to Nick as I got up to leave. He looked puzzled and studied the card for longer than it took to read the six or eight words on it. Was it possible the guy couldn't read? "For the greenhouse," I said, "the glass enclosure?"

A smile crept over Nick's handsome face.

"What's so funny?"

"My mistake," he said, flicking the card with his index finger. "Not the kind of dirt I thought you dug up."